Perils in Yorkshire

The British Book Tour Mysteries | Book 3

Emma Dakin

CAMEL
PRESS

Seattle, WA

A Camel Press book published by Epicenter Press

Epicenter Press
6524 NE 181st St. Suite 2
Kenmore, WA 98028.

For more information go to:
www.Camelpress.com
www.Coffeetownpress.com
www.Epicenterpress.com

Author website: www.emmadakinauthor.com

Cover art by Teresa Hanson
Design by Rudy Ramos

Perils in Yorkshire
Copyright © 2021 by Marion Crook

ISBN: 9781603813877 (trade paper)
ISBN: 9781603813884 (ebook)

Printed in the United States of America

DEDICATION

To Jill Brandon who reads every word, makes good use of her correcting pencil and who, as a "London gal", keeps the manuscript authentic. Her enthusiasm is boundless and her criticism appreciated. I include here the group who went on a Blue Roads Tour with Jill and I and who were willing to go out of their way to include a visit to Ralph's Cross. You made research a lot of fun.

ACKNOWLEDGEMENTS

First, my thanks to Jennifer McCord of Camel Press who takes my work and makes it shine. I truly appreciate her. My thanks to my B & B hostess in York who took time from her busy life as a graduate chemist at the Nestle Rowntree Factory to instruct me on the intricacies of chocolate making. My thanks also to the docent at the York Minster whose hilarious account of the Minster still didn't diminish my awe of that magnificent building. I appreciated the dignified clerk in the hat shop in the Shambles area where Amanda and Sheilagh bought their husbands a Harris tweed cap. My son was the recipient of my purchase. And thanks to the restaurateurs who encouraged me to graze my way through York on their fabulous wares. It was a gourmet experience. Special thanks to Jan de Gras, writer and editor and a "Yorkshire lass", who checked the parts of the book that contained the Yorkshire idiom and put me right.

CHAPTER ONE

I watched the chocolate pour from the spout of a complicated metal tower into the vat below. The bitter-sweet, artisan product promised luxury, elegance, even romance. It was all in our imaginations, but we were entranced nonetheless. My tourists gazed in fascination, focusing on the rich, brown aromatic stream. Automatically, I counted heads. One missing. Phillip Saunders. Again.

That man was as elusive as a bat in the dark. I thought he would be captivated by our tour of the Shambles Chocolate factory in the center of York. He'd told me he was a chemist and interested in the chemistry of chocolate making. Where was he? My tour was The British Mystery Book Tours. I took tourists to the sites of mystery novels. This excursion to the chocolate factory was added as a relaxing way to start the tour. The only literary reference I could find was *Charlie and the Chocolate Factory*.

I tapped Geraldine on the shoulder and whispered. "I'm going to look for Phillip."

She rolled her eyes. "Good luck. A little ADD, that one." She turned back to the white-coated young woman who was explaining the importance of temperature to her audience.

'ADD' Attention Deficit Disorder. Geraldine had been a teacher. She was used to assessing people. Still, I didn't trust a snap diagnosis. There may be many reasons for Phillip's constant movement. Even if he was ADD, that's a normal human condition, giving energy to talented people. He might be anxious, bored, upset by something in his life. There were myriad motivations for his behavior besides ADD. What I understood from her comment was Phillip annoyed her. Not a good start to the tour. Phillip had been late for breakfast and kept us waiting about five minutes at the beginning of the tour because he had wandered onto the street to "get a feel for the place". I wouldn't have any problem with that if he would just tell me when he was leaving and when he'd be back. I run on a schedule, after all. Besides, why sign up for a tour, if you didn't stay with the tour? I could feel a rising anger and suppressed it. I couldn't react every time a tourist caused me trouble or I'd be a constant jangle of nerves. I had years of experience dealing with irritating tourists. I'd handle this one.

I was across the room and heading for the stairs when a uniformed young man touched my sleeve. "Madam, you must stay with your tour. I'm sorry. You can't wander on your own." He was tall, thin, with fair hair cut so close to his head he appeared bald. He had broad shoulders and muscled arms, and a patch on his sleeve that declared his status—security guard.

"I understand." It was time for calm, smooth words, the oil on the water, the balm for the senses. I glanced at his badge 'Jason' and showed him my business card. "I'm Claire Barclay. I run British Mystery Book Tours, and I've lost one of my tourists. Did you see a man of about forty-five?" I described his height and weight with my hands. "Short, a little rotund, bright black eyes? He slipped away from the tour."

Jason frowned. "He's not allowed to do that." He pulled out his mobile phone—he might have already had it in his hand as it was instantly available—and hit a speed dial. "Tourist wandering. Male." Then he clicked it off.

"I don't think he'll do himself any harm," I said. "He's totally sane but independent." I couldn't be sure of that, although Phillip appeared normal enough.

Jason raised his eyebrows. "Oh, brilliant." That sounded sarcastic. "I haven't got a maniac wandering around then, do I, luv?"

"No." At least, I didn't think so.

He sent me a searching look as if he could determine my veracity by mind-reading. "Can't have him at large. He might wander into our kitchens, nick recipes or sabotage production." He straightened, stood tall and peered down on me.

Obviously, he took his job seriously. He was protecting the factory as a responsible, dedicated employee. I sighed. He looked intense and young enough to be in school. I concentrated on how I could keep Phillip from being arrested.

"People do that?" I stalled.

He nodded grimly. "They try. They send their chemists here to see what they can learn or wiggle out of the employees. They offer bribes. We make the best chocolate in the world, you know. First class."

I could debate that with him. Their chocolate was excellent but so was the chocolate from Belgium. Then his choice of enemy hit me. Chemists. Phillip was a chemist.

Jason strode toward a far door, his black trainers squeaking a fast rhythm on the tile floor. I'm five-nine with long legs, but I had trouble keeping up. I tucked in behind him as he thumped down the stairs. We emerged two floors below. He pushed open a swinging door and we were in a kitchen.

There was Phillip backed against a wall with three tall broad-shouldered men in professional whites confronting him. One of them had a cleaver in his hand.

"Phillip!" I didn't quite yell, just projected a loud demand in the hopes of stopping any mayhem the chefs might be contemplating. "What are you doing here? This is out of bounds."

The man with the cleaver didn't take his eyes off Phillip. The other two glared at me.

"Sorry," I said. "So sorry." I had to get Phillip out of there. If they knew he was a chemist, they would call the police. They might even damage him first. Better they think he was slightly deranged.

I jettisoned the "totally sane" image I'd given Jason and cast Phillip in the role of the slightly odd.

"Phillip. Now you come with me. You stay with the group. You know you promised you would."

I spoke soothingly and hoped Phillip would have enough sense of self-preservation to play along. "Come along smartly, now Phillip. It's time to join the tour."

"Okay," he said. "Sorry. So sorry." He smiled with the assurance of a five-year-old that charm generated forgiveness.

I took him by the arm and led him away, followed by the menacing stares of the chocolatiers. They weren't about to forgive him. I escorted Phillip, backed by Jason who almost ran us up the stairs and into the lobby.

I shoved Phillip into a chair, more gently than I wanted to, took a few steps away and turned to face Jason. "Thanks, Jason. I'm going to remain with him and see that he stays put. Can you tell my tour I'll meet them here when they're finished?"

"Right you are. I'll do that." He sent one more suspicious look at Phillip and took a picture of him on his mobile. Phillip moved just as he took it, so I don't know how clear it would be. "Don't come back here," he spoke directly to Phillip. "You're banned."

Jason would be capable of apprehending Phillip if he tried to return. He had youth and muscle on his side.

"Oh, certainly, certainly," Phillip said and lifted his shoulders in a shrug.

Jason narrowed his eyes. "You understand me, mate?"

Phillip shrugged again, his hands palms up as if to say, "As you like."

I pointed to the coffee shop tucked into one side of the lobby. "Order something for yourself and for me," I directed Phillip and followed Jason as he headed back to the elevator. I planned to thank him again.

Geraldine Smith, one of the ladies from Tucson, half-walked and half-trotted toward me.

"Norma's missing."

Oh, no. Not another one. Norma was the one who looked like the fairy godmother in Disney's Cinderella—rosy cheeks, curly grey hair but with more intelligence than I'd ever credited to the fairy godmother.

"Jason," I called.

He stopped and came back to join us.

"Where did you see her last," I asked Geraldine. Why were my tourists slipping away?

"She wanted to go to the rest room. I have to tell you; she probably just turned the wrong way when she left it. She's always doing that."

"Which loo?" Jason asked.

Geraldine pointed.

Jason moved quickly, heading for the hall, with Geraldine and me trailing behind him. I hoped Phillip remain in the lobby area. I promised I'd watch him. However, I couldn't be two places at once. I felt as though I was trying to herd a clutch of wayward goslings who were drifting away from me. I had to know where they were at all times.

Jason stopped at the cloakroom door, scrutinized both ways and headed toward a corridor.

"What's her surname?" Jason asked.

"Channing," Geraldine said.

Jason called, "Mrs. Channing."

A head of grey curls popped out from around a corner. "You found me. Thank you."

"Yes, Madam. If you would just join your group."

"I'd love to. What's your name?" She bustled toward us.

"Jason," he said as he strode toward the lobby. Norma kept pace beside him.

"Well, Jason. Many thanks. I thought I might get stuck in the corridors like a lab rat, running from hall to hall never finding an exit." She passed him a folded bill.

He raised his eyebrows but tucked it into his shirt pocket. "You're welcome, madam. Just stay with your group."

"Take one of us with you to the rest room next time," Geraldine said.

"I'll do that," Norma said, responding the worry in Geraldine's voice.

I sent Norma and Geraldine to join Phillip. Jason and I stood for a moment at the elevator, watching the group of three to be sure they stayed put.

I touched his sleeve. "Thanks for finding Norma and thanks for not calling the police on Phillip."

"We're sweet. He was in the kitchens, though. That was bad enough. If he'd wandered into the research and development area, I'd have held him and called the police."

What a mess that would have been. "I can be grateful for small mercies."

He smiled a little. "I'll send his picture around to the staff. We'll make sure he doesn't get in here again."

"I won't bring him," I said.

"Good. He's French?" Jason asked me as he stepped into the elevator.

"No. British, I think. He has a British passport."

"He has a French accent."

That was true. Were the French more likely to steal chocolate secrets? Was that accurate? Or was that prejudice? I'd no idea of the state of corporate espionage in York. It might be reasonable to be on the alert for spies.

York was the center of the chocolate industry for Britain. At one time, it had four factories. The most famous was Rowntree owned by Quakers who had a firm belief in the value of workers and the moral imperative to treat them well. They provided their workers with medical benefits, recreational facilities, housing and pensions. The factory flourished. The owners of the other factories, including Terry's, had Quaker religious connections as well, and because of that, the chocolate industry had a reputation for honest dealing. The public relied on the principled Quaker owners not to add wax to the chocolate or coloring poison to the candy. There were only two large chocolate factories left in York—the one that had been started by Roundtree, presently owned by Nestle, and this one, the Shambles Chocolate Factory. There were other smaller chocolatiers, but these two produced huge volumes of chocolate for export. Jason could be proud of The Shambles Chocolate Factory. It was world renown.

My plan was, after this tour, to shepherd the group through the sites of York before heading into the surrounding countryside tomorrow. The itinerary was supposed to be relaxing. I hoped it was for the others in the group. At the moment, it was stressful for me. I could feel my stomach knot and my shoulders tense. I took a deep breath. This was the first day. I couldn't get wound up by my tourists on the first day of the tour.

I rejoined Phillip and tried to enjoy the excellent hot chocolate he'd ordered. Norma and Geraldine were standing in line to order mocha coffee. The ladies were willing to be cooperative. I wasn't sure about Phillip. I had to try to get him to conform, or, at least, to stay out of forbidden areas, and I wasn't certain he'd cooperate.

"What were you trying to do, Phillip? Were you trying to steal recipes? "

He looked affronted. "Of course not. I was simply curious. You know they have these huge machines that bring the chocolate from one place to another. It's fascinating."

He sounded like a child who wasn't apologetic for straying into the kitchen. He should be contrite. He knew he wasn't supposed to wander into private areas. He *couldn't* be that naive.

"Look, Philip. You came close to being detained by the police. Jason would have called them and handed you over. I can't protect you from being arrested if you slip off and enter restricted areas."

He waved his arms. "Those boys over-reacted. They should give us a tour of the kitchens. We need to *see* the kitchens if we want to understand the chocolate making." His black eyes flashed. He almost bounced in his chair with energy. He was going to be a problem to supervise.

I wasn't convinced that his foray into the kitchens had been innocent.

"You're lucky they didn't know you're a chemist or the chef might have used that cleaver."

He sat perfectly still for a moment. "I'll be careful," he said.

'I'll be careful' wasn't the same as "I won't wander". Before I could ask him to be more specific, the other members of the tour—two married couples and another woman from Tucson, Arizona—fluttered in from the tour of the chocolate factory. They chatted about what they'd seen and most ordered the hot chocolate. It was a blustery March day, and the hot drink was welcome. I noticed Allan White ordered coffee. He seemed a bit withdrawn, as if he'd rather be back in Bristol. Both he and his wife were in their sixties. Sheilagh was intrepid, curious and extroverted, while Allan looked as if his mind was elsewhere and he wished his body was with it.

I'd picked up the three American women yesterday after their long flight from Phoenix to New York and then, on Virgin Atlantic, to Manchester. The arrival time was about seven in the morning. I'd arranged for a VIP suite at the airport where they could have a bite to eat, freshen up, change clothes and sleep a little if they wished. That way, I didn't have to be at the airport until ten. It was the most comfortable flight I could find for them, but it took over twelve hours. They had been tired and slept in my van most of the hour-and-a-half drive to York.

It was a normal tour for me except I'd left my dog Gulliver with my sister and her family in Guildford. On my last tour, Gulliver had traveled with us. This tour had too many people to include a dog.

"The kids will be glad to have Gulliver," my sister, Deirdre, had said as she headed out the door for her law office. Her practice was in Guilford, not far from the kids' schools. "It might pull Kala out of her funk."

I'd studied her. "What's the matter with Kala?"

Deirdre rolled her eyes. "I don't know. Ten-years-old going on fourteen, I suppose."

I didn't agree that Kala acted older than her age. She was just right, I'd have thought. Curious, usually happy. She and her mother quarreled sometimes, but I hadn't seen anything I'd describe as a 'funk'. However, I hadn't seen her for a month.

"Is she home?"

"Still in her room." Deirdre had called up the stairs. "Get down here, Kala. You'll be late for school."

I'd caught a glimpse of Kala as I pulled away from the curb. She was climbing into Deirdre's car, and she did look subdued. She glanced my way but didn't wave. That wasn't like her. I had a sudden worry that she was unhappy and then dismissed it. Deirdre and Michael were attentive parents. They'd get to the bottom of whatever problem she faced. I could listen to her worries later. My dog, Gulliver, might help her. He would be a warm body to hug.

I was going to miss him, but there were too many people on this tour to complicate it with Gulliver. Even with this big vehicle, there was no room in the back for all the luggage and his crate. My sister had given me the dog only a few months. I'd become used to him traveling with me, and there was an empty place where a panting, enthusiastic travel should sit. *Enough, Claire. He will be fine.*

Mr. and Mrs. White from Bristol were at the guest house when I drove from the airport with my American tourists as were Mr. Corbett and his wife, Amanda Atkinson, from London.

I established the three ladies and the two couples quickly in the small guest hotel. Phillip Saunders arrived from London just as I was presenting my credit card to the proprietor.

It had been difficult to get six rooms in one place in the heart of York, even in March. I hadn't used this guest house before. I was impressed with the cleanliness, the existence of parking spot for the van, wi fi and the proximity of the Minster which was only a five-minute walk.

Everyone had retired to their rooms and stayed there until evening. We'd met for dinner at the Go Down Restaurant where I'd introduced them to each other, handed out itineraries, and hoped such a disparate group could manage to get along. All were over sixty which was usual on my tours—except Phillip who must have been in his late forties. The American women were over seventy and obviously friends. Geraldine was about five-two, had a clear complexion with only a few laugh lines around her brown eyes and some silver streaks in her brown hair. How had she managed to keep that complexion into her seventies when she'd been an upper form teacher? Her friend, Evelyn, was about my height perhaps a little taller. She favored L.L. Bean clothes and gave the impression of athleticism, someone who could run marathons. Their other friend, Norma, appeared to be someone who enjoyed the moment. She was plump with smooth, pink cheeks, curly, grey hair and the beaming benevolence of the kindergarten teacher she had been. I thought I'd like those women once I knew them better. I'd spoken a little with Amanda, a legal assistant and the wife of Grady Corbett, who sat beside me. She'd been pleasant. She was thin, but ate without fussily separating food into likes and dislikes the way I've seen others do. I'd managed a conversation with Amanda on one side of me and Sheilagh on the other. I watched the group throughout the dinner and saw that, for the most part, they were inclusive. Phillip was sociable and interested in others. Allan was the exception. He'd been quiet, almost morose. However, his wife, Sheilagh, had been garrulous enough for two. She'd told me all about her coming retirement from her nursing career. I thought she was worried about retiring. She was attractive with almost white hair cut in a cap around her head and large brown eyes. I expect she'd inspired many confidences in her nursing career with those eyes. She would have heard thousands of stories from her patients. It must hard to give up a productive career simply because one turned sixty-five. I wasn't going to give up my life as a tour guide when I turned sixty-five, a long time from now. Even with a hefty bank balance, I'd want to work. Sheilagh might be the same. I thought the laws had changed and working past sixty-five was now a choice. Perhaps, the choice was worrisome.

Today was the official first day of the two-week tour of York, the Yorkshire Dales and Moors. Over the next two weeks, I planned to expose my group to the settings of the books by Reginal Hill, Peter Robinson and Frances Brody, although I wasn't planning on taking them to Leeds where Brody's character Kate Shackleton was based. I'd take them to Nicholas Rhea country where the *Constable Around the Park* and others in the series are set. His works aren't considered mysteries by some, but they are engaging, and some of the tourists would have read them. His D.I. Montague Pluke series fit the mystery genre more aptly and might appeal to the British. I wasn't sure if the American's knew about them. They might like to learn. We were going to the Yorkshire Moors, the setting for Wuthering Heights. Emily Bronte could provide some fodder for discussion. Usually, the tourists have pre-read mysteries set in the area and added information and tidbits of knowledge to the experience. I always learned something from them.

There had been no argument about allocating the rooms last night. The couples had their rooms, Phillip had his, and the American women were used to traveling together.

"Norma has to have her own room," Evelyn said. "She snores."

That wasn't unusual. Most of my tourists over sixty snored.

"I mean *really* snores. You'd think a train was shuffling cars in your room if you share with her. Elephants in rut make less noise. Steam engines with faulty gears make less noise."

"Enough, Evelyn," Norma said. "She gets the point."

Evelyn stopped describing Norma's affliction and gave me directions. "Geraldine and I will have the twin. We'll all sleep better."

So, I arranged it that way.

In the morning, we'd toured the Jorvik, the Viking museum. York was settled by Vikings when Ivar the Boneless conquered the resident Angle Saxons in 866. I didn't know much about him, but I loved his name. He had a brother called Sigurd Snake-in-the Eye, another fabulous name. That Viking heritage is strong in Yorkshire today in the language, the place names and in the Scandinavian physique of some of the people.

We sat in a small train as it took viewers through the museum while a guide gave information on the various exhibits. Interspersed among some of the animated mannequins were real people. It was a game to try and distinguish which characters were human and which were dolls. It was often hard to do.

"It makes you think," Evelyn said. "Some people are nothing but rigid dolls."

"Mentally frozen, you mean," Geraldine queried from the seat behind her.

I caught the eye of the mannequin as we passed—and she winked. Was she real?

We had finished our afternoon at the Shambles Chocolate factory situated appropriately in the Shambles district, the medieval heart of the city where narrow, winding streets and Tudor-style buildings jostled modern construction—modern in the 1960s that is. The group had enjoyed themselves and up to that point had been no trouble. Now, with all tourists restored to my care, I tried to relax. Norma had not stayed lost for long. Phillip had been hauled back to the tour without involving the police. I hoped he'd settle.

They finished their hot chocolate and coffee and wandered into the gift shop. I bought a chocolate football for my nephew Josh and a chocolate cricket bat for my niece Kala who was just learning the game. I stood in line behind Grady Corbett and his wife Amanda Atkinson.

"Those are beautiful, Grady," she said.

I peered over her shoulder at Grady`s choice, a box of assorted, elegant chocolates.

"I thought the kids would find it acceptable," he said.

"Chocolate is always acceptable. I buy them the chocolate oranges every Christmas, and they love them," Amanda said.

I remembered those. My mother who had been poor when I was growing up always managed to have a Rowntree chocolate orange in our Christmas stocking.

"I'm not sure they will appreciate the quality," Amanda continued, "but they will devour them. You order from this factory to distribute around England, don't you? Didn't I see some samples in your office?"

Grady lowered his voice. "Not Rowntree Oranges from here, but other chocolates, but I don't expect wholesale price here in the gift shop, so don't mention it, all right?"

"Oh, of course I won't. Anyway, we're on holiday. I shouldn't mention business."

He smiled at her. "That's right. No business."

"And you'll stay off your mobi?"

"I'll try to," he said.

She leaned over and rested her cheek on his shoulder for a moment. "I'm glad you agreed to this tour. I know it's more my interest than yours. Nevertheless, it's a treat to get away, just the two of us."

They moved up to the cash register, and I held back.

It sounded as though Amanda had little time with Grady. He was probably a businessman beset by details. She sounded a bit needy. Oops. That was judgmental. Their relationship was none of my business. Honestly? I was curious.

Amanda had told me she had two children by her first marriage who were with their father while she was away. Nice that Grady thought of them and bought chocolates. In my observation, second marriages were often better than first because you learned what you wanted, what you couldn't deal with and what didn't matter the first time. *My* first relationship—ten years long—was a disaster. Of course, that didn't necessarily mean my second one with Mark Evans was going to be rosy.

The rest of the group found something to buy, and it wasn't long before we had collectively dropped quite a chunk of money in that gift shop.

Usually, I get hop-on-hop-off bus tickets for the group and send them on a tour of the city, but this March afternoon was cold. There was a brisk wind picking up the papers on the cobbled streets and fluttering them through the air. So, after everyone was satisfied with their purchases, we climbed into the rented van. This Mercedes Sprinter seats nine plus the driver while my van seats only seven. It was a little longer than I was used to but not hard to drive.

I activated my microphone and began the tour of York. At least in the van, Phillip couldn't wander off. Allan fell asleep before I'd gone a block. He'd only come from Bristol, so jet lag couldn't be a problem for him. Was he disinterested? Physically frail? Plain weary? The others didn't seem to be sleepy and were interested in my description of the city and some historical facts.

I told them a little about the War of the Roses and the dissolution of the monasteries. The American's were only politely interested and the British already knew that history. I moved on to talk about the setting of Julian Cole's mystery *Felicity's Gate*.

"'Gate' is Yorkshire for 'street', isn't it?" Geraldine asked.

"It is. Do you know some Yorkshire?"

"My grandparents were from Thirsk, so a few sayings filtered down through American English."

"You might feel right at home here," I said. Language carries the culture. If a person knows the language, or even some of the idioms, they feel more comfortable in the culture.

"I might."

"I didn't know you had Yorkshire ancestors," Evelyn said. "I've known you since you first started teaching, that has to be over fifty years, and I didn't know that."

"Ah," Geraldine said. "I'm a woman of mystery."

Evelyn snorted.

"Does anyone else have Yorkshire antecedents?" I asked the group. No one did.

"Do they have their own language," Norma leaned forward, her eyes bright and inquisitive.

"They do," Sheilagh answered for me. "At least it's English, but I find it very hard to understand. Some of the old Yorkshiremen have many words that are only used here in Yorkshire, so you have to guess what they mean. And they have a broad way of speaking, of running their vowels into each other."

She'd given a good, if brief, summary of the language. I didn't understand the old people myself, but I was interested in linguistics, I used to teach English to executives in different cities in Europe and North America and found languages fascinating. Yorkshire speakers were certainly unique. Usually, they spoke understandable English to foreigners, that is, people from outside Yorkshire. They slipped into broad Yorkshire when they didn't want you to understand them—even the young people did that.

"Would you find that incomprehensible speech more in the countryside than the city?" Phillip asked.

"You would," I responded. "City folk, like city folk everywhere, become more like the dominant language, in this case Midlands English."

I parked as close as I could to the rampart walls that surround the center of York and allowed my group to scuttle out of the bus and up the ramp to the top of the walls. It wasn't possible to move completely around the city on the walls. They could walk two sides of the square, descend, travel through the city and then ascend to complete the square. Still, it was March, and a cold wind sliced through scarves, hats and coats.

"A half-hour?" I suggested.

"I'm going to walk all the way around the walls using the paths through the city when I have to," Phillip said. "Where should I meet you for dinner?"

I put on my tour guide pleasant face. "About seven, at The House of the Trembling Madness on Stonegate. Can you find your way to it?"

"Most assuredly," he said. "Is that truly the name of the restaurant?"

"It is."

I handed him a business card from the restaurant. York isn't that big a city. He should be able to find it. If not, I had his number on my phone. I gave him my business card as well with mobile number on it.

"Call if you have trouble." I wanted to add "and stay away from the chocolate factory" but decided he wouldn't appreciate the reminder.

"*Merci*," he said and was off.

The rest of the group spread out along the walls. The American ladies found a shelter where they were protected from the wind. If they wanted to suffer the wind, they could look over the countryside. If they wanted the shelter of the walls, they could look into the Museum Gardens below. On this late March day, a few early daffodils heralded the beautiful display that would arrive in about three weeks. The variegated green of the trees and shrubs were lovely, and the birds singing from the bushes magical. I heard the faint peep of a ruby crowned kinglet and the determined, robust aria of a chaffinch. I left the Tucson women searching for the source of the songs and kept one eye on the Whites and the Corbetts who were braving the wind and peering out onto the Vale of York that stretched far north. In spite of the wind, they appeared to be enjoying the view. They might be appreciating the ancient nature of the setting. The walls gave a strong sense of the history of this medieval city. They had been here a long time and, if the planners and voters decreed, they would remain guarding the city for infinity.

I found a corner behind which I could hide from the wind and phone Mark.

I let it ring and then left a message. "Established in York with group of eight. Nice people with the exception of Phillip Saunders. I know he's going to cause me trouble. Hope your conference is going well."

Detective Inspector Mark Evans had been in Manchester with fellow police officers for the past week, studying how to deal with the rising problem of drug overdoses and the importation, distribution and manufacturing of the whole business. He was likely in a session and had turned his phone off. He wasn't, strictly speaking, responsible for policing drugs, but he was responsible for homicide investigations and they often occurred in the drug world. His superintendent thought he should attend the conference and liaise with officers from the drug law enforcement community. He dutifully had been attending sessions and having a beer in the pub in the evenings with officers from the National Crime Agency. Policing in England is complicated with different local designated groups of officers and national specialized groups.

Mark and I tried to stay in touch. Keeping a relationship going when one or the other was often out of town was a challenge. I've enjoyed it. There had been a few harrowing moments when I'd stumbled into danger, more from my contacts than from his, but we tried to keep our professions separate. He was a good man. In spite of the twisted villains he dealt with, he remained a good man, and I was beginning to trust that he was a reliable one, even if I didn't see him on a regular schedule. His job was demanding. A detective inspector runs into physical danger and personal threats quite often. I, on the other hand, only stumble into that kind of thing on rare occasions.

CHAPTER TWO

We gathered after breakfast the next day for our tour of York, starting in the Shambles, the heart of the medieval city. The sun had struggled through the clouds to give us snatches of warmth. Protected from the wind by the two and three-storey buildings lining the narrow streets, we were fairly comfortable. My group bunched around me like ducklings with their mum and listened to my dissertation on this neighborhood.

"The whole district nearby is called the 'Shambles'. I'm now taking you down the *street* called 'Shambles'. It was established so long ago it's in the Doomsday Book."

"That was 1086?" Evelyn stated with confidence.

"It was. Originally, it was recorded as a street of butchers. They hung their meat from iron hooks that you can see if you look up." I pointed out the hooks and the metal rods.

"There were slaughterhouses behind the shops and meat hung around the windows. Notice the low windows. They used to have wide shelves where butchers placed their meat to sell it. Those shelves were called shammels, and from that we get 'The Shambles.'"

"The sidewalks are flagstone," Geraldine said. "They must be ancient."

"They are," I agreed. "They are raised a little from the cobblestone center of the street so the butchers could throw their offal and waste onto the cobblestones and wash it away while keeping the sidewalks clear."

"Phew," Evelyn said. "It must have stunk."

Cameras and phones appeared in every hand, and I had a guide's satisfaction of hearing clicks and pings as the group recorded their tour.

"The timber-framed buildings almost lean toward each other above us," Grady said.

"That was deliberate," I told him. "They wanted to protect the meat below from the sunlight. They built those upper storeys to overhang the wattle and daub walls below and the market shelves where the meat lay."

"It must have smelled something awful," Geraldine repeated Evelyn's remark. They were probably right. The smell would have been overwhelming to us but perhaps not to the people of those days. The Hampshire countryside where I lived smelled like manure in the spring when the farmers spread it on the fields. We accepted it.

"There don't seem to be any butcher shops around now," Amanda observed.

"No, they disappeared. Health regulation would make this street unacceptable for a slaughterhouse now."

"I see mostly tourist shops: souvenirs, cafés and a bakery," Grady scanned the surroundings, "a woolen shop, a coffee lounge, a chocolate retail shop, a sweet shop. Quite a variety—and all except the woolen shop look to be independent operations."

He was right. Many independent shops make the area more attractive than a street of chain stores. You're never sure what an independent shop might contain.

"That's what probably gives it a homey, old-fashioned feel," Norma said.

"Yes, it is homely," Sheilagh agreed. "You could almost imagine yourself in the twelfth century." She patted Allan's arm and he smiled at her. Good. They were enjoying themselves.

I was distracted for a moment by the difference in their

language. "Homely" to Sheilagh meant the same thing as "homey" to Norma. Yet "homely" in America meant ugly. Not at all what it means in British English. I didn't point out the difference. They understood one another.

"Oh, look," Geraldine called out. "There's a gorgeous dog."

I saw the dog and my heart flipped. He looked exactly like Gulliver, except Gulliver was smaller and younger.

"It's a King Charles spaniel," Evelyn said.

The woman leading her dog on a leash didn't even glance our way. She was probably used to admiration of her dog.

We stopped to watch the prancing prince accompany his owner to the end of the block and nip behind her into a snickleway, one of those tiny, pedestrian alleyways that wind between tall buildings to create short cuts to the next street.

"It wasn't a King Charles," Geraldine said. "It was a Cavalier Spaniel."

"Don't be ridiculous," Evelyn said.

Geraldine turned her head slowly and stared at Evelyn. She said nothing, just held her gaze for a moment and looked away.

"Now, see here, Geraldine," Evelyn began. Evelyn stood even taller as if she was preparing for a fight. She had both hands free as she had her belongings in a small rucksack on her back. She wore trainers, jeans and a loose top with a blue, quilted jacket. For all her seventy-five years, she was athletic and almost formidable.

I interrupted the imminent quarrel. "We are expected for lunch in a few moments. Could you all follow me, please." I rushed along the street and my group trotted behind me to the Gusto Restaurant on Little Stonegate at the edge of the Shambles.

We settled, Geraldine on the opposite side of the table from Evelyn, and ordered. I contributed two bottles of white wine and had the waiter pour everyone a drink. "When trouble brews, mellow the group." If that isn't a motto for tour guides, it ought to be.

"I know my dogs," Evelyn began. She was determined to resurrect her quarrel with Geraldine.

Amanda interrupted, pleasantly. "Would you like to see a picture of my dog?"

"I would," Evelyn said, distracted from her argument.

Thank you, Amanda. I mentally praised the peacemaker. I watched Amanda's hands as she searched in her bag for her wallet. They were thin, with almost translucent skin, but graceful. She fished out a picture of two little children hugging a tall brown dog.

"Lovely," Evelyn approved.

"She's a boxer," Amanda said "and very gentle with the children."

Sheilagh pushed a picture of her dog over to Evelyn. "That's Mini. She's a Yorkshire, a miniature Yorkie."

Evelyn chucked. "What a sweetie."

"She's good dog," Allan pronounced.

I was tempted, truly tempted, and it was too strong an urge to resist. I dug into my rucksack, pulled out my mobile and clicked up Gulliver's latest photo. I passed it to Evelyn.

She smiled as she glanced down, and then her smile froze. She looked up and stared at me.

"What is it?"

"A Cavalier King Charles Spaniel."

"No!"

"I'm afraid so."

Geraldine grabbed the mobile from Evelyn and stared at it. Then she met Evelyn's eyes and burst out laughing.

"Your King Charles Spaniel and my Cavalier Spaniel are the same dog."

Evelyn held her face straight for a moment and then joined in the laugh.

"And here we were squabbling over the same thing."

"That'll teach us," Geraldine said ruefully.

Whew. Quarrel averted. I hoped they wouldn't argue often. I poured more wine.

"Your children are lovely," Geraldine said to Amanda. "However, I expect it's relaxing to be away from them."

Amanda smiled. "It is. Grady and I have only been married a few months, and we haven't had much time alone."

"Getting away to improve your own relationship. Good idea," Geraldine advised. "Evelyn, you should pay attention to Amanda and give that poor guy Max a chance. If you don't want to marry him then just go away with him for a while. You could golf ..."

Evelyn interrupted her. "*If* you don't mind." Her voice was indignant. I didn't blame her. That was more personal information than Evelyn was comfortable hearing.

"We all have loved ones we have left behind for this holiday," Norma said. "I'm sure they'll enjoy some time away from us."

Phillip had been explaining the nature of chocolate to the men at the far end of the table. Now he spoke to the whole group.

"It's pretty fascinating. You have to get the particles of chocolate reduced to below 20 microns. At that level, your tongue can't feel them."

"Above that, would they feel like grit?" Allan asked.

"Assuredly," Phillip said. "Then they pour the mixture into a machine that stirs the cocoa powder, the cocoa butter and sugar and grinds it with rollers until it's smooth."

"And?" Geraldine asked.

"And then they temper it. Heat it and cool it to exact temperatures to make the butter crystals shine."

"I thought it was complicated," Allan said. Clearly, he was interested. "They have a lot of chemical compounds in those natural ingredients, don't they?"

"About 600, and they are volatile."

I tuned Phillip out. I'd been on the chocolate tour so many times I knew that information. I excused myself and headed to the cloak room, passing Grady in the hall. He was talking on his mobile, and I overhead his instructions.

"Just get a new truck. Rent it. That's all you need to do and transfer the product."

You'd think he would have left someone in charge who could have managed that transaction. Possibly, he was a micro-manager who couldn't delegate. He might have started another business and had to shepherd it in the first few months. I could understand why Amanda wanted him to leave his mobile alone. Business details could be never-ending.

We left the Gusto Restaurant and walked the short distance to the Minster. It was a spectacular sight. Twin towers rose high above us with ornate, almost lacey, small spires rising from the towers. Each tower had six of these delicate spires, making the church more glorious than imposing—but still grand. The central tower, the Lantern Tower, was even bigger, acting as a background for the front two towers.

Allan stopped beside me and stared. "God, it's amazing."

It was truly magnificent.

"Henry VIII left it standing because it wasn't a monastery," I said.

"Lucky us."

I agreed. "His men smashed the faces off all the statues of the Virgin Mary because Henry considered Catholics idolatrous to worship her. Other than that, he left it. It's been subject to abuse and neglect since then, but, somehow, it gets renovated and continues to inspire us."

"Is it just because I haven't been many places that I'm awed by this?" Allan asked.

"No." I shook my head. "I've seen many churches and I'm awed by this one." Some churches made me think of an authoritative god, who was watching humanity to punish transgressions. This church made me think of a celebratory god who reveled in beauty and glory.

He continued to stare at the Minster. "I grew up on a farm in Cornwall, and I've been a shipping clerk in Bristol all my life, sending containers all over the world, receiving containers from everywhere. It's odd, but I haven't been farther than London. Sheilagh wants to travel. Maybe I will if I can see sights like this."

I smiled at him. "Is that what you want to do in retirement?"

"It's what Sheilagh wants to do. I want to find a farm and raise chickens and ducks, maybe a sheep or two. Yes, definitely a sheep or two. Haven't been able to do that since I was a nipper. If I could just get out of all the pressure...."

The others caught up to us then, and we entered the Minster together.

We were lucky to find a docent free to give us a tour, and I turned my group over to him. He was amusing and a little irreverent, showing us the jokes carved into the pulpit and timbers by cheeky carvers in the fourteenth century. He talked about the famous Rose Window built in 1515 to commemorate the union of the Royal Houses of York and Lancaster and then took us below the floor where, in 1972, the workers discovered the remains of a Roman headquarters. The Romans called York 'Eboracum' and considered it an important part of their British empire. Constantine was here in York when he received news of his father's death and assumed the title of Emperor of Rome.

"Tom Harper," Geraldine whispered to me.

"Tom Harper? Oh, *Secrets of the Dead.* That book was wonderful."

"Yes, I liked it. He moved between the present day and Constantine's time. I don't usually like those time-flashback books, but I liked his."

"Claire." Norma clutched my sleeve. "Can you believe that there's been a Christian religious structure of some kind on this site since the fourth century? Truly. Isn't that amazing? There must be ghosts here, centuries of them. Can you see it in the dark of the night? Ghosts arguing old political positions, old love affairs, old ambitions. It would be fascinating."

I laughed. I could almost see those ghosts, some in seventeenth century elaborate dresses and some in homespun.

"I thought Williamsburg, Virginia, was old, and they didn't get there until the seventeenth century."

"Somebody was in Virginia before that," I pointed out.

"Oh, true. Probably in the fourth century, too. We just don't have records of them."

I wondered what the Indigenous people of North America could have told us if they had kept written records. They did draw their stories and pass them down orally, but those stories were hard for present day scholars to interpret. Here, the language written in the fourth century was fairly easily read.

"It's impressive, Norma. I agree."

After the tour, I trailed my group past Constantine's statue at the rear of the Minster and then on to the Dutch House on Ogleforth. This house was built in the seventeenth century, much later than the Minster, and designed by an apprentice architect as the first entirely brick house in the city. I imagine it was considered ostentatious then. Today it is a private B & B, so we can't tour it.

Sheilagh almost squealed. "Barbara Whitehead, *Death in the Dutch House*. This is exciting."

I offered to take the group to The York Cemetery. It wasn't far but we would need to drive. Julian Cole set *Felicity's Gate* there.

"No," Phillip said. "I'm going to wander. This is a fascinating city. I'll see you all at dinner." And with that he disappeared down the nearest snickleway.

We were standing in the center of the York with its winding streets, narrow alleys, Tudor-timbered buildings leaning toward each other. It did look intriguing.

"He 'wanders' into conversation with strangers," Evelyn said without bothering to lower her voice. "I've seen him chatting away on street corners. Oh, well. He might prefer them to us."

Uh. Oh. She was miffed.

"What would you like to do, Evelyn?"

She immediate dropped the subject of Phillip and concentrated on her own needs.

"Shop for some of their woolen scarves. They look attractive."

"And the rest of you?" I asked.

The Corbetts and Whites decided to shop for souvenirs.

"We might get some Chocolate Oranges," Amanda said. "The chocolate bought here seems smoother and more delicious than the ones I buy in the store. But first, I want to buy Grady one of those tweed caps the farmers wear. I saw some in a window on Petergate."

Sheilagh glanced at Allan. "You would look good in a farmer's cap, Allan. I'll get you one." They waved at us and left.

While they were devoted mystery fans, the remaining two ladies didn't want to drive out to York Cemetery. They wanted to return to the Shambles Chocolate Factory to buy some more chocolate.

As we approached the chocolate factory, Geraldine said," Isn't that Phillip going in? He didn't say he was going to return to the factory."

I caught a quick glimpse of Phillip's back as he disappeared into the building.

"He isn't supposed to go there. They'll call the police." I sprinted and left the ladies behind me as I raced for the doorway.

I was slowed by a clutch of tourists milling, around and handing out entry tickets. When I finally managed to pass them, I saw a door swinging shut. I had no way of knowing if Phillip had gone there, but it was my best option. I pushed through it without setting off any alarms or having any employees chase after me. I was in the stairway. Up or down? I decided on down. That's where the kitchen and research and development sites were. I didn't trust Phillip to be a benign visitor.

I raced down the stairs, one hand on the bannister, my shoes clicking on the hard linoleum, the sharp sound echoing off the walls. I rounded the corner on the landing and stumbled over a man lying across my path. I clutched the bannister, righted myself and stared. Not Phillip. Too tall, too thin. I stood for a moment, frozen in place. Then I squatted beside him. Jason. He was exceptionally still. I put my hand in front of his mouth. No movement of air. I put my fingers on his carotid artery. No pulse. A red stain on his white shirt made it clear this was not a natural death. I watched in horror as the stain spread. Was he alive? I pulled out my mobile and hit 999.

"E.O.C. Police, ambulance or fire?" the dispatcher asked.

"Police and ambulance."

"Address, please."

"The "Shambles Chocolate Factory. Inside the stairwell."

"York?"

"Yes, York. There is a man in the stairwell of the Shambles Chocolate Factory. He looks dead, but the blood is spreading." I could hear hysteria in my voice. I tried to control my breathing and stay calm. "Should I do CPR?" I did not want to do CPR. *Please tell me it's too late.*

"Yes, madam. Do that. Someone will be with you as quickly as possible. Please stay on the line."

The Emergency Operations Centre dispatcher could give instructions calmly, because he wasn't here. He didn't have to do CPR. I felt a flush of resentment and was ashamed of myself. *Just do it, Claire.*

"I'm on my mobi. I'll have to put it down to do CPR. I can talk to you, but I won't be able to hear you."

"Hit 'speaker.'"

"Oh, of course." I did that and put the phone down.

I turned Jason completely on his back, He was heavy, but I didn't have to turn him far. Just a push on the shoulder and he was flat. I tilted his head back and blew into his mouth. I hoped Jason did not have any disgusting diseases. *Forget it, Claire and concentrate.*

"Your name, Madam." The steady voice floated around me.

I took a breath and gulped out "Claire Barclay, British Mystery Book Tours." I blew in again. This was not going to work. Jason's body felt inert, as if it was wooden.

"Should I do chest compressions?" I asked the disembodied voice on the phone.

"Yes, five breaths and then two chest compressions."

I don't know why I felt compelled to follow instructions— perhaps because the man's voice sounded definite. Surely, he was thinking more clearly than I was at this moment. I kept breathing for Jason. I don't think I was making any difference. There was no flutter of life, no twitch, no gasp. Nothing.

"Are you in harm's way, madam?"

I scanned the area quickly. "No."

I hadn't thought of that. Was this attack on Jason a random act of a mad man who was hovering around the crime scene? I looked again. There was no one.

I heard the door open above me and then heavy clunking footsteps on the stairs. I saw dark trousers and shiny shoes on the step. I stared up at a police constable. Good. Not a maniac with a knife.

"Can you take over?" I asked quickly.

"Yes, madam. Don't leave." He was young, but he knew better than I did how to deal with sudden death. He was welcome to the whole mess.

"I'll stay."

I rocked back on my heels and watched the constable blowing

into Jason. His breaths were stronger than mine. I hoped he would make a difference.

"Can you do the chest compressions, madam?" he said between breaths.

"Yes, of course." I positioned myself above Jason, put one palm over my other and pushed hard. I kept it up. It wasn't more than five minutes before the ambulance paramedics arrived.

I picked up my phone. "Can I hang up now?"

"Yes, madam. Thank you for your help."

"Thank you for your instructions." I truly was grateful he'd been talking to me. I supposed I'd felt more part of a team, and not alone. I clicked off.

The paramedics took over and the police constable regained his helmet, pulled out his note book and shepherded me down a few steps, where we were out of the way. I sat on a stair. The constable sat on the step below me.

A medic leaned down and said. "We've got him on positive pressure, but it doesn't look good."

"Where are you taking him?" The constable waited for an answer. "York."

I presume he meant The York Hospital.

"What's his name?" the constable asked me. I expected the hospital would need his name.

"Just Jason is all I know. He works here."

The medic threw a wallet to the constable. He caught it, opened it and scanned a card.

"Jason Taylor," the constable told the medic. By then, a worried looking official from the factory was hovering.

"Thanks," the medic said. "We're off."

"Go with the ambulance," the constable instructed the factory official. "And give the hospital your employee's information."

In minutes, only the constable and I were left sitting on the steps. The muted hum of voices from the lobby sounded far away.

No doors slammed. No one clattered down the stairs. We seemed isolated. The constable opened his notebook, a regulation pen and paper notebook and began to write.

"Your name?" He went through all my information.

"Why were you on the steps?"

I had been thinking about what I would say when asked that question. I didn't want to throw Phillip to the police. On the other hand, if Phillip had been responsible for this, I wasn't going to protect him. I equivocated.

"I thought I saw one of my tour members go into this stairwell. It's out of bounds for the public, and I wanted to haul him back before he walked into trouble." That was true, even if it wasn't the complete truth. I didn't tell the constable that Phillip had been banned from the factory.

"Foreigner, was he?"

"He speaks English with a French accent." That didn't make him a foreigner. I wasn't going to point that out.

"What's his name?"

I reluctantly gave him Phillip's full name and the address of our B & B.

"I will be around this evening. Could you be home? And this Phillip?"

I gave the Constable—Poole was his name—my mobile number.

"Please, let me know the time you're coming. I'm responsible for eight other people, and I'm busy."

"Yes, madam." I definitely was tired of that impersonal "madam".

"Claire," I said. "Since we've been trying to save a life together, I feel I know you a little."

He smiled. "Charlie," he said.

We sat there for a moment.

"Do you think he'll live?" I asked.

"No, Claire, I don't."

I didn't think so either. "What happened?"

"Stab wound."

"Oh." That would be quick. Phillip might have had time to do that.

"Murder," I said and shivered.

"Murder," he agreed.

Could Phillip be capable of murder? I'd no idea.

"Do you get much of that?" I asked Charlie to keep my mind off Phillip.

"Very little. I don't think we'll get this sorted locally. The chief inspector may call in the Major Crimes Investigations Team."

Why would they do that? Was Jason more than a security guard? Major Crimes. Mark. He was an officer, a detective inspector, in the C. I. D. seconded to this new homicide unit, but he was from Hampshire. They would likely have their own officer for this area. I sighed. "Thanks for coming so quickly. I have to get back to my ladies. I left them in the lobby, shopping."

Charlie stared at my hands. "You might want to wash."

I had blood on my hands. "Oh, crikey. I got it when I did chest compressions." I glanced at his hands. He had a little blood as well.

I tried a half-smile. "Both of us should clean up. I'll see you tonight." I left him on the stairs. Still writing.

I washed in the ladies' cloakroom and then tried to call Mark. As before, there was no answer. This time I left a demanding message.

"You MUST call me. I fell over a body, and I tried to do CPR, and I was a dunce at it, and the police want to talk to me."

That ought to fetch a response.

CHAPTER THREE

I met my group in the lobby near the café. They'd seen the police and paramedics depart with Jason's body on a gurney. While my tourists appeared festive with their parcels and bags—chocolate oranges peeking over the top of Amanda's bag and pale-yellow truffles boxes with their gold bows stacked up in Evelyn's—their faces were serious.

"It's been harrowing," I admitted. Mentally, I added: *disturbing, traumatic and worrisome.* I swallowed. "Care to join me in a drink at the Old White Swan?"

They nodded and followed me outside, around the corner, through the Old White Swan courtyard and into the bar.

We settled on either side of a long wooden table. The ambiance of timeless stability oozed from the brick walls, the wooden floors and the glinting copper hood over the fireplace.

Geraldine looked at me sharply. "You could use a drink?"

"Yes, I could. I definitely could."

Geraldine signaled the waiter.

"What?" she asked.

"Scotch."

Her eyebrows rose. She ordered a single malt scotch from the now hovering waiter. Everyone ordered and the waiter returned with a tray-full of drinks. Grady put his elbows on the table and held my gaze. "What happened?"

"Jason," I said. "Jason is dead."

"Who is Jason?" Grady persisted. His quiet question created calm. I relaxed a little. Grady was a tall man, probably about six foot, with pale skin and sandy hair sprinkled with grey. His glasses fitted closely to his face. He exuded the image of a self-assured business man who dealt in facts. I felt comfortable with him. He was a man used to solving problems. There was a part of me that skittered into thoughts of blood, the incredibly profound absence of life and my own helplessness. I wanted to acknowledge my anxieties, cry, even wail. Grady's voice steadied me.

I answered. "A security guard at the factory. A nice boy." I gulped some scotch. I truly didn't know if he was a "nice boy". Death conferred sanctity. "He was stabbed. He's dead."

Norma was stricken. "That young man who helped me?"

Geraldine turned a little white and gulped her wine.

Sheilagh patted my hand. "I suppose you found him."

"I did.

"And did CPR?"

"Yes," I said abruptly. I remembered she was a nurse. She would know exactly what I'd experienced.

"She might need another scotch," Sheilagh said to Geraldine.

"No. No, thanks." Another scotch and I'd be asleep. "This will be fine."

They stared at me solemnly. I was their tour guide. I had to give them a pleasant holiday. My experiences shouldn't be theirs. I took another sip of scotch.

"Sorry," I said again.

Norma patted my other hand. "You take your time now, you hear? We'll remain right here with you until you're calm." I felt my shoulders relax a little.

"I thought England was safe," Evelyn said.

I didn't answer her. She must know that no place was completely safe.

"Did you know this Jason?" Grady asked me.

"No. No. I'd met him earlier because he insisted I keep Phillip with the tour. Geraldine and Norma met him. I didn't know him—really know him."

Geraldine and Norma nodded. I realized the others wanted some kind of explanation.

"I thought I saw Phillip going into the factory." I studied the area. "Where *is* he?"

"Doing his own thing as usual," Evelyn said.

I felt my lips tighten. I would not lose my temper. I'd talk to him later. "I was looking for him when I stumbled over Jason," I told the group.

I didn't want to give a description of Jason. I took a deep breath and tried to smile. "I'm okay. Thank you all for taking care of me. I'll be fine. I'll get the bill."

Amanda protested, but I was firm. "No really, you've all been kind." At this rate, my profits were going to go into alcohol, although I appreciated the scotch. I took a deep breath and pushed myself to be a tour guide and not a shattered witness to sudden death. It wasn't easy, but I took several deep breaths and gained some control.

"I'd like you all to continue on the itinerary. This afternoon you were going to wander around the shops, perhaps the Castle Museum or the art galleries. You might even want to take a cruise on the Foss, although it might be a little chilly for that."

"Those offerings sound interesting," Sheilagh said. "What time is dinner and where?"

I smiled at her, appreciating her support of my attempt to get this tour back on track.

"We should meet about six-thirty at the Café Concerto. It's close to most sites. The police will come to the hotel about eight tonight to interview me and anyone else who might have seen anything. So, a six-thirty dinner would give us time to relax before they arrived. I have some maps here."

I passed out maps of the city upon which I'd marked our hotel and the restaurant.

"What is the name of the street outside the door here?" Geraldine asked.

"Goodramgate. It's supposed to be haunted."

Evelyn raised her eyebrows. "By whom or by what?"

"Considering the neighborhood," Norma said, "it should be a herd of cows seeking revenge." I supposed she imagined resentful cattle haunting the old slaughterhouse area.

I smiled. "No, not cows. A man rolling a barrel down the street."

Evelyn snorted.

"Watch out for it, Evelyn," Norma teased. "You never know who is going to bowl you over."

"I'll keep my eyes peeled," Evelyn said with obvious cynicism. "Where are you going to go, Norma?"

"I'm going back to the Minster. It's sublime. I have never seen such an edifice. Glorious." She threw out her arms. Her several bracelets jangled, emphasizing her exuberance. She made me feel much better for no reason at all. I suppose because she enjoyed the moment so much.

Evelyn sat back a little. Geraldine leaned forward.

"You love that architecture?" she asked Norma.

"*And* the atmosphere. So holy. So peaceful. During the day in any case. I can imagine the holy men and women chatting about their daily lives and making charitable comments on the tourists."

"Really?" Geraldine's tone was disbelieving. The two friends couldn't have been more different in personality. Norma was the epitome of a fabulous kindergarten teacher: creative, exuberant, intuitive and tolerant. Geraldine reminded me she was science teacher, looking for facts. I'm sure she'd want Norma to *prove* the Minster had an ethereal vibe.

"It feels like that. I know it has a history and probably, given the number of wars there were in the past, a bloody history, but it suits me."

"It's certainly beautiful," I agreed.

"I love the art gallery as well," Norma said. "The whole city is a work of art with its curving streets and beautiful buildings. My husband would love all this. He's a potter and would be entranced with the sights."

"Come back with him next time," Geraldine suggested.

"Well, you know Tony. He doesn't leave Tucson. I'll take pictures."

"I like the names of the streets," Sheilagh said. "Many of them end with 'gate' which I take it means 'street' in Old Norse."

"Yes, that's right. There are a lot of Norse names around here," I said.

Allan White finally asked a question. "Some of the streets like Daveygate are named after long ago people. Who was Davy?"

I knew that one. "His name was David and he lived in 1135. He provided the food for the larder of King Stephen, and he was called a lardier. He must have been an important man, procuring all the supplies for royalty which probably meant managing herds of cattle, crops and fishing. There is a plaque on the street."

"I'll look for it," Allan promised.

"1135," Evelyn said. "Imagine that."

They had successfully calmed my jittering nerves with their questions and interest in the city. That might have been deliberate. In any case, it had been kind.

"Thanks for the drink," Grady said and helped Amanda gathered her parcels. "We'll return to the hotel to deposit our loot." He smiled at Amanda. "Then possibly take in the Castle Museum and some art galleries."

Amanda almost glowed; she looked that happy. She hadn't known Jason. She didn't have an emotional reaction to his death. Why should she? I was glad she was contented with the tour.

There was a moment of silence after the Whites and Corbetts left. The remaining three ladies moved their chairs closer to me and leaned forward.

"So," Evelyn said. "*where* is Phillip?" They acted as though they were my confederates.

"We saw him enter the factory," Geraldine said. "Where did he go?"

"We're witnesses," Evelyn insisted. "The police are going to want to talk to us."

They were like hens pecking away, determined to get every last morsel of information out of me.

"I appreciate you not telling the others about all my concerns around Phillip," I temporized.

"We know what happens to witnesses who talk too much." Evelyn mimed cutting her throat.

I was shaken for a moment. It was too close to what I'd seen this afternoon.

"We'll save our story for the police," she assured me.

I concentrated on their questions. "I really don't know much," I said slowly. "I certainly don't know anything about Phillip." He was a chemist, but I didn't know where he worked or what kind of chemistry he was interested in.

They were disappointed in me, but resigned. They gathered their parcels and left.

"See you tonight," Geraldine called to me from the doorway.

I waved.

I stayed in the Old White Swan savoring my scotch for a few minutes. I found Phillip's number in my contact list and texted him. "Where are you? Worker at the Shambles Chocolate Factory was killed this afternoon. Police will be at the hotel tonight at 8 p.m. Be there or they will look for you. Dinner at the Concerto Café at 6:30 p.m."

There was no answer.

I was just sipping the last of the scotch when I heard a ping on my mobile. Mark. He was responding to my message telling him I had fallen over a body.

I read, "You what? Can't talk right now. Will call tonight? Are you okay?"

I answered. "Sort of." What did he mean by 'okay'? I wasn't bright-eyed and chipper, but I wasn't paralyzed with fear.

I typed more. "The police are coming to interview me about 8 tonight."

No answer. And no answer from Phillip. I walked back toward the hotel. If Gulliver had been with me, I'd gone for a long walk. We would have stopped for every bird he noticed and for the pats he'd receive from admirers. Alone, I lacked the energy. I noticed very few dogs as I walked through the streets. I wondered about the people of York. It was the first British city I'd been in where the dogs weren't obvious and ubiquitous. I wondered if there was a prejudice against them here. The idea distracted me from my worries about Phillip for a few moments.

It was as if thoughts of Gulliver conjured up Deirdre—Gulliver was staying with her—as my phone buzzed. Deirdre wasn't calling to listen to my problems. She had concerns of her own.

"Kala was beaten up at school today."

I stopped walking. My stomach cramped, and I sank onto a park bench. "How is she?"

"She's okay. Bruised. Going to have a colorful black eye. Nothing broken."

"What happened?" I croaked.

"I don't know," Deirdre almost wailed. "She won't talk to me. She says it's none of my business. She says she doesn't want me to talk to the headmistress, although I know the headmistress is going to phone because one of the teachers saw Kala and will report the incident."

"Why doesn't she want you to help her?"

"She says I'll make it worse. I'll threaten legal action and the girls will get at her again. I don't know what to do. I want to respect her wishes, but she's only ten, and she can't know that this is serious. These girls shouldn't be able to get away with something like this."

I didn't know what to say. I could understand Kala wanting her mother to stay away from the school because Deirdre could be verbally aggressive. Perhaps she had to be in this case.

"What does Michael say?"

Deirdre's voice was a little calmer. "Michael says to send her up to his brother's place in York. John and Fiona will look after her, and she will be some distance from those girls."

That sounded like a good plan, a way to keep Kala safe. "How long would she be here?"

"A week we thought. And, in spite of what she wants, I *will* go talk to the headmistress."

I thought about that for a moment. "I wouldn't do anything Kala didn't approve of, Deirdre. If you do talk to the headmistress when Kala specifically asked you not to, she won't tell you anything the next time she is in trouble."

There was silence while Deirdre considered that advice. "Is that what the Americans call "between a rock and hard place"?"

"Perhaps. You could think about how those girls could get help. They don't sound normal."

She snorted. "That's beyond me." Deirdre was used to controlling most things in her life. This was complicated. "Could you see Kala while she's in York."

"I have a full tour here, but give me John and Fiona's number and I'll try."

I typed the number into the contact list on my phone.

"Michael will drive her up tomorrow, but he can't stay."

Both Michael and Deirdre had jammed appointment books. Nevertheless, they'd make time for Kala. I was glad Michael was driving her. He's an empathetic father and would be a soothing influence. He wouldn't badger her and would give her space to relax.

What kind of school did Kala go to where girls beat up other girls? It sounded like something from a bad film. Would she be in danger here? Not likely. Her aunt and uncle would look after her. I could help a little. I'd try to spend some time with her while she was in York. I was preoccupied with my own concerns about my tour: a murder which I desperately hoped had nothing to do with my tour; Phillip who was turning out to be a problem; Evelyn who was prickly and I didn't know what kind of argument she could start; and Norma who wandered off and became lost. I couldn't fire anyone from my tour. They'd already paid for it. It was up to me to try and give them as pleasant a time as possible, even Phillip.

My guests had dispersed to explore York and would return this evening, I slipped into my room at the hotel. I planned to have a quick nap but was too restless to relax. I responded instantly to the ring of the phone when Evelyn called at 4:30.

"Norma's lost." The bald statement hung in the air.

"What do you mean lost? When did you last see her?" Lost? How could she be lost? There were three of them. How could they lose one?

Evelyn explained. "Either Geraldine or I usually stay with Norma because she has a terrible sense of direction. We didn't realize she wasn't with either of us until just a short while ago."

"Lost?" I said again, looking for more of an explanation.

"Missing. Not with either of us," Evelyn elaborated.

"How worried should I be? Does she usually find her way back?" I lifted my rucksack as I talked and shrugged into it.

"Pretty worried. She doesn't find her way back. We have to find her. Can you meet us in the lobby?"

I shoved my feet into my trainers, frantically thinking of all the missing person reports I associated with York. Claudia Edwards, Rory Johnston-Hatfield … names slipped through my mind, all persons who had never been found. I constructed a police description as I was running down the stairs: about five-feet-four, a little plump, grey hair worn away from her face in upswept curls, brown eyes, glasses for reading, energetic walker, inquisitive, sociable.

I hoped I wouldn't have to notify the police.

Evelyn and Geraldine were waiting for me near the door. Grady and Amanda were helping themselves to a cup of tea from the table where the hotel provided refreshments. They turned to stare at me as I joined the ladies.

"Trouble?" Grady asked.

"Norma's missing," I said.

Amanda put down her cup. "Can we help?"

"Yes," Grady seconded her, "can we help?"

"Please," I said.

They joined us near the door.

Evelyn and Geraldine wore their outdoor jackets, small rucksacks and carried their mobiles. They were ready to search.

"First of all, Evelyn, you said Norma has no sense of direction."

"None," Evelyn said. "If she gets off by herself, she's the devil to find."

"She's done it before?" I had witnessed her confusion in The Shambles Chocolate Factory, even though she hadn't been far away.

Geraldine explained. "We usually keep track of her. She doesn't do it on purpose. She always thinks she knows her way around and York is pretty easy to navigate, but. . . ." She frowned.

"We're worried," Evelyn said, "and a little angry. She should be tethered like a goat."

Was this serious? I had to assume they knew Norma well and had reason to worry.

"Right then. Who saw her last, where and when?"

"She was with me, when I went into a bookstore," Geraldine said. "I thought she was browsing through the art books, and I got carried away in the science section. When I paid for my books and went to look for her, she'd disappeared."

Evelyn said, "She probably just stepped out to look at something and couldn't find the bookstore again."

"Likely," Geraldine agreed." I checked around for a few blocks and couldn't find her. I texted Evelyn and we met here."

"Did you try to text Norma?" I asked the obvious.

"I did, but she isn't answering. Her cell phone is likely sitting by her bed or out of charge."

That was a huge handicap to this search.

"Should we call the police and report her?" Amanda asked.

"Not yet," I said. "She might turn up for dinner. Geraldine, would she ask people for directions?"

"Oh, she'd ask," Geraldine said, "but she wouldn't follow those directions."

"She really is hopeless," Evelyn said, "but, to be fair, just in that one area. Otherwise, she's competent enough."

I chewed my lower lip. This could get serious.

"I have a few friends here," Grady said. "I'll put the word out to look for her."

I agreed. "Good idea."

"Description?" he asked, his fingers poised over his mobile.

"She's about five foot…" I rattled off the description I'd composed earlier.

He typed that into his phone.

Where would Norma go, or at least, where would she try to go? "Geraldine," I said. "What would interest Norma in York?"

"The art galleries," she said promptly.

I checked my watch. "They close soon. Which ones would she be most interested in?"

"What's the choice?"

I called up the art galleries on my mobile and described the Braithwaite gallery to them.

"Not that one," Evelyn said.

I described the York Art Gallery and the Anthony Shaw collection.

"Anthony Shaw. That has to be the one," she said. "It has a children's exhibit."

I had to believe Evelyn's definitive answers were as reliable as they sounded. We couldn't cover every art gallery or fine arts store in York.

"Geraldine, you and I will go there. Evelyn, you and Amanda take the York Fine Arts." I gave them the address.

"Grady, I have your mobile number programmed into my phone. So, could you stay here and let us know if any of your contacts find her or she arrives back here?"

"Certainly," he said. "Glad to." He smiled at me as if encouraging me to do my best. I was glad to have someone competent as our central contact.

We separated. I had Evelyn's number in my phone as well, so I could contact her if needs be.

It was bright daylight. Darkness wouldn't come for a couple of hours. We had some time to search. If we didn't find her by seven, I would call the police. Missing Persons would put her description up on an online site so everyone in the country could look for her. I didn't want to do that prematurely. If she was only a little late returning to the hotel, she would be disconcerted to find herself the object of attention from the whole nation—if she wasn't furious at me.

I couldn't help but remember the serial killer the public was sure was stalking women in York. But only young woman, I reminded myself. Older women were more likely to be mugged for their pension cheques than killed. At least, that was my understanding. It wasn't particularly comforting.

We headed out of the medieval section of the city. The Art Gallery was just outside the walls.

"Would she have gone through the gates here?" I asked Geraldine.

"She might not have noticed them. Someone would have said, "Just go straight down this road and it's right there," and she would have gone and then asked someone else in a block or two."

I ignored the gate in the city walls and almost ran across the wide courtyard, past the fountain and up the stairs.

We arrived at the door to find a "Closed" sign. We looked at each other. I saw a uniformed security officer near the door and gestured to him.

He came to the door and opened it an inch. "We are closed, madam."

"I realize that," I said, "and I don't want in. I need information. We have lost one of our party, an older woman about five foot four and ..." I repeated my description.

He smiled. His teeth were bright white in his brown face.

"One moment, madam. I believe we have your lost article." He closed the door.

I sank against the stone wall, weak with relief.

Geraldine closed her eyes. "Thank God," she said.

"Amen," I answered.

We waited what seemed a half-hour but was probably only five minutes. I didn't want to text Grady or Evelyn until I had seen Norma. The gallery might have misplaced her. But in a few minutes, Norma emerged from an office near the lobby, chatting to someone behind her and smiling. Our genial security guard escorted her to the front door.

"How nice of you to come for me," Norma said. She turned to the guard. "Thank you, Maurice. If you are ever in Tucson, you come and see me, now."

He smiled. "Indeed. I certainly will do that—if I'm ever in Tucson."

Norma beamed as she joined us on the steps. "I had the most amazing time. You wouldn't believe the children's art in this gallery. And the way they've integrated children into deciding on the

exhibits. It's revolutionary. Truly. It will captivate children artists
or just those who like art. I'll have to get on the board of the gallery
at home and make some changes."

She chattered all the way back to the hotel.

I let her go ahead with Geraldine while I texted Grady and Evelyn.
Geraldine herded Norma to her room. I stayed behind to
thank Grady.

"No problem at all," he said. "I simply stayed in one place and
answered calls."

"I appreciate it," I said. "It was good to have a reliable hub to
coordinate the search."

"I'm glad we didn't have to involve the police."

I shuddered. The implications of having Norma the subject of
a police hunt, with the consequential publicity for her and for my
tour was huge and complicated. I'm glad the police are there for
people who are truly missing, but I didn't want all that officialdom
involved in getting Norma back unless it was absolutely necessary.
The stress lay in trying to decide if she was truly missing. I'd hate to
have that wrong. On the face of it, Norma hadn't been missing. She
knew where she was, and she hadn't even been late for dinner. But
her friends didn't trust her to find her way back, and I had to give
credence to their experience.

"Again, thanks," I said to him.

He smiled, waved, and escorted Amanda to their room.

While I trusted Evelyn and Geraldine to look after Norma, I was
going to have to watch her as well. Now, I had two unpredictable
guests: Phillip and Norma, and possibly Evelyn, although she had
been helpful in the search.

Phillip arrived for dinner at the Café Concerto on Petergate at
six-thirty. At least, he had read the messages I sent him. He was
there before me and, when I arrived, was deep into a conversation
on the chemistry of chocolate with Grady.

Phillip was short and round with dark hair that had drifted back, exposing a long forehead. His bright, almost black eyes snapped with humor and intelligence. He looked like a happy monkey, eager to entertain himself.

"I had a tour of a chocolate factory," he said to Grady, "not the Shambles Chocolate Factory, another one, and they gave detailed explanations of the chocolate-making process. It was much better than the Shambles."

Phillip had been lucky to get into another factory. I guessed Jason hadn't passed his picture on to the competition. I wondered what he had been doing at the Shambles Chocolate Factory. I swear it was his back I saw.

"They control the temperature, you know. That makes all the difference in the taste," he told Grady.

Grady nodded as if interested. I expected he knew this already. He distributed quality chocolate, after all.

The meal was excellent and the company was making an effort to be civil. The Tucson ladies said nothing about Norma's escapade to the art gallery. Since Norma had not considered herself lost or missing, she also said nothing. I was mum and Grady and Amanda were also circumspect. No one mentioned Jason. I returned to the hotel a little after 7:30 and called Deirdre.

She was less intense about Kala but frustrated because Kala refused to allow her to help. It wasn't only her mothering that Kala was rejecting. It was her mother's legal expertise as well.

"I could get those girls either into court or into a restorative justice program and Kala refuses to allow it."

I calmed her as best as I could. Finally, I was able to tell her about my problem. Her experience as a barrister gave her a lot of knowledge of police procedure.

"What? A murder?" She sounded incredulous. She dealt with murderers in her work. I don't know why she was so surprised.

She was younger than me, but I took advice from her on legal matters. "What I should tell the police?"

"Pretty much everything you know."

I thought about Phillip. I supposed I would tell the police about him. If he had anything to do with Jason's death, I wanted him off the streets and away from my tour. If he didn't, he could explain himself to the police.

Deirdre sent a video of Gulliver to my phone. In spite of her worry about Kala, she'd thought about how I'd miss Gulliver. She was right, I did miss him. He would be enjoying his stay with Deirdre, Michael, Josh and Kala as well as their two genial Labradors. The video made me cry. Gulliver was my emotional stabilizer. I just felt better when he was with me. I sniffed and changed the subject.

"How's Kala?" I asked

"Not talking—about the fight Michael's driving her to York tomorrow to his brother's place."

That was a good plan. It would get her away from school and relieve Deirdre of doing anything in the immediate future.

Constable Poole and his boss arrived promptly at eight. The proprietor sent them to a corner of the breakfast room which, at this time of night, was private. Charlie was in uniform. His boss was in plain clothes.

Geraldine, Norma and Evelyn were waiting in the lobby ready to the interviewed. I had a sudden thought of knitting. Oh, Charles Dickens, the women and the guillotine. My guests weren't *that* macabre. But they were intensely interested, as if I had conjured a tourist experience for them. They hadn't known Jason well. They couldn't be expected to feel any sense of mourning. It was the drama of the event that enticed them, I suspected. They were mystery fans, and here was a mystery. I wondered what kind of a witness Norma would be. Even if she had stared straight at Phillip in the chocolate factory, she'd likely been thinking of something else and not noticed him. I left them to their interviews.

I took a call from the hotel manager about nine asking me to attend the police. If they had conducted three separate interviews in a half hour, they weren't going to spend much time with me. They might have interviewed all three together. I walked into the breakfast room. A tall man stood by the table.

"Inspector Harry Fawthrop," he said. I paid more attention to rank now that I was with Mark. An inspector in Yorkshire was the same rank as a Detective Inspector, Mark's rank. Fawthrop would have more authority than Mark because Yorkshire was his district and Mark was only visiting. Nonetheless, Mark had a national jurisdiction.

"Claire Barclay," I responded.

"Please sit."

I did, and he did.

"What did you see and what do you know?"

That was succinct. He was a tall thin man, with a beak of a nose, blue eyes and heavy black eyebrows. He was unsmiling and gazed directly at me, but I had the impression he wasn't interested in what I had to say and was thinking of something else.

I told him I thought I'd seen Phillip going into the factory and had run after him. Fawthrop probably had heard that from the ladies. I told him I'd gone down the stairs because I'd seen the door swinging shut. I hadn't seen Phillip go through the door because some tourists had delayed me in the lobby.

Inspector Fawthrop glanced over at Charlie. "Did you get that?"

Charlie nodded, his omnipresent notebook on the table in front of him and his pen at the ready.

I continued. "Then I stumbled over Jason."

"Jason? You knew him?"

How did I answer that? I shook my head. "I recognized him. I didn't know him. I'd met him earlier in the day when he had warned Phillip away from the factory."

"What's that?" Inspector Fawthrop now gave me his complete attention. "Tell me about that."

So, I did. Charlie dutifully recorded everything I said. Eventually, I stopped. We waited while Charlie finished writing. Constables have to write everything in their daily notebook. Inspectors can use tablets. Charlie promised to bring all the prepared statements to the hotel in the morning for signatures.

Fawthrop didn't keep me long, and I was back in my room about nine-thirty. I entered my expenses onto the spread sheet in my computer and aimlessly tidied the room. I was waiting for a call from Mark. It wasn't Mark who called me about ten. It was the manager of the guest house.

"There are two men in the lobby arguing loudly. One is Mr. Saunders."

Damn. Phillip was in all kinds of trouble.

"The other is a Mr. Mark Evans who says he is your guest. Should I call the police?"

I sighed. Phillip was a problem for me. "No. Mark Evans *is* the police. Send them up to my room I'll deal with them." Arguing in public? That didn't sound like Mark.

"Thank you," the manager said. "I would appreciate it if you could get them to moderate their volume."

"Certainly," I agreed. I had absolutely no control over either of them, but I was willing to promise miracles.

CHAPTER FOUR

I started down the stairs to collect Mark and Phillip and met the manager, Mit Sandhu, escorting them to my room. He stood between them, not holding onto their arms, but definitely shepherding them. Mit was taller than Phillip and shorter than Mark, He was about thirty, thin but wiry. I expect he was strong enough to deal with difficult guests. He marched the two men firmly up the stairs, a determined guard dog to two recalcitrant goats. I turned and led them up to my room on the top floor.

Mit ushered them in and stared intently at me. "Will you be all right?"

"I will. Could you bring some snacks?" I checked the tray in my room. "And another cup?"

"Will do." He looked past me at the men. "Will the new person be staying?"

"Yes. Inspector Evans will share my room. Add what you need to my account."

"No charge," he said, staring hard at Mark and Phillip. "You keep those two quiet, and I might even pay you."

I grinned at him. "They'll be fine." Mark was a professional police officer who dealt with the anxious, disturbed and violent people of our country. He would cope.

Mit gave me a salute and left.

I plugged in the kettle and directed Mark to one seat and Phillip to another. I sat on the bed.

"What's up?"

"This idiot!" Mark exploded. The reasonable professional I was counting on had disappeared. His voice almost bounced off the walls. His voice was one of the things I admired about him: a resonant baritone, capable of beautiful songs but, right now, much too loud.

"Mark," I said, "you're going to have to keep it down. The manager is only letting you in because you are with me. So, please."

I could see his chest expand as he took a deep breath and waited a moment.

"All right." He modulated his voice. "This idiot. This 'Phillip,'" he emphasized the name, "attached himself to your tour and put you in danger."

Phillip leaned back in his chair and spoke quietly. "The more you talk, the more *you* put her in danger."

"You think she's safe if she knows nothing? Think again."

There was a knock on the door. I opened it to see Mit with a tray containing croissants, scones, specialty preserves, butter, extra cups, water, a bottle of brandy and, of course, chocolate—Mit's idea of a snack that might appease angry men.

"Thank you, Mit." My gratitude was heartfelt. This might just help.

The kettle was boiling by then. After Mit had deposited the goodies on the dresser and left, I poured the tea. Coffee in the mornings, tea in the evenings. Tea, the panacea for all ills. I settled everyone with a cup and offered brandy and goodies. Phillip didn't eat. Mark helped himself to a couple of scones with jam.

"Okay, Phillip," I said when we had all settled back with our cuppas. "Who exactly are you?"

He looked at Mark, his eyes watchful.

Mark licked the jam from his lips, took a sip of tea and waved the cup toward Phillip. "Detective Inspector Hartley Ferris, The Metropolitan Police, Net Operations."

Scotland Yard? I stared at Phillip. "I thought you were a chemist."

"I am a chemist; I'm also a detective." He'd slumped back in his chair, annoyed.

"Not French?"

"English, but I grew up in France." He answered me with a clipped tone.

I was a little stunned and not thinking clearly. It'd been a difficult day. I struggled to make sense of Phillip.

"So," I said. "What are you doing on my tour?"

He shrugged—now *that* was a French gesture—and helped himself to brandy. "I'm following a drug connection."

"On my tour?" I was shocked. I mentally pictured my clients. Not one of them looked like a drug dealer or a drug baron to me.

"He might not on your tour," he said. "Just following a lead."

By himself. He wasn't letting the local police know the scope of his investigations or Fawthrop would have known about him. Maybe, he did.

"Typical Scotland Yard," Mark burst out. "You keep all the information to yourself, never cooperate and can't understand why you run into problems." I'd guess Fawthrop and the local C. I. D *didn't* know Phillips's reasons for being on my tour.

"Restrain yourself, Mark," Phillip said. "I wouldn't be talking to you in any case because this isn't your jurisdiction."

"God help us," Mark ranted. "A dozen different silos working on the same thing all over the country." His voice rose.

I held out my hand, palm down and dropped it in a sweeping gesture—the dog command for "down". Mark's eyes glinted with humor, and he dropped his voice a few decibels.

"What are you doing investigating on your own?" he demanded of Phillip. "Aren't the NCA supervising you?"

I nodded a thank you for his modulated tone.

The NCA was the National Crime Agency which should be responsible for drug investigations. Were they connected to Jason's death or the chocolate factory? I thought about the business of making and distributing chocolate. My mind roamed over the possibilities. Like many businesses, it had a distribution system that was efficient and systematic. Chocolate was best fresh, so the distribution system must be organized to be sent all over the country quickly. If a criminal organization could infiltrate that system, they would have a read-made distribution line, probably assisted by innocent employees. I probed that idea for faults. There would be challenges in getting the drug into the factory and into the chocolates and in identifying which chocolates were targeted for the drug markets. How would the recipients identify the batch that belonged to them? Such a distribution system would be difficult to set up, but once it was, it could operate smoothly. It wouldn't take much to keep it going. How did the Yard fit into this? I remembered Mark and his Major Crime Investigation Team had been involved in finding an illegal drug smuggling operation a few months ago. He'd complained about the way the country's police didn't work together at that time. It sounded as though it was no better now.

"Jason?" I hadn't forgotten someone had died today.

There was silence, then Phillip said. "He was an informant."

I didn't understand. An informant for whom? He was working with Phillip? "He asked me to keep you out of the factory. Didn't he know you?"

Phillip didn't answer me.

Mark did. "Of course, he didn't know him. It's part of Scotland Yard's need to keep everything secret. Jason probably reported to someone else who reported to Ferris."

Ferris? Hartley Ferris? I couldn't think of him that way. He was still Phillip to me.

He moved restlessly, one foot tapping the floor. "It may not have been a good idea this time," he admitted.

Mark snorted.

"Do you think the drug organizer—distributor—manufacturer, found out Jason was double dealing?" I asked. Had Jason been working for the distributor and reporting to Phillip? If so, that turned out to be dangerous.

"Looks like it," Phillip admitted. "He wasn't an employee, just a casual informant."

I thought about that. "You mean, he wasn't trained."

"We don't train casual workers."

"He was what about twenty?"

"He wasn't supposed to infiltrate any gang" Phillip sounded aggrieved as if Jason was an amateur. "He was just pass to on what he saw or overheard."

"He was young and thought just maybe he could have a career in Scotland Yard."

Phillip shrugged.

"So, he overreached. He wasn't trained, as you say." I know my voice was cold, but I was shocked. "And you aren't telling the local police anything?" Inspector Fawthrop was trying to solve Jason's murder without the information he required. No wonder Mark was frustrated.

"Not at the moment." Phillip said.

I mentally pictured Jason lying on the stairs. My mind poked around at the edges of the scene. Was I able to think about this without crying or screaming? I waited for a reaction. Nothing. I was fine. I explored that picture a little more. Jason had been lying with his hands flung out.

"No phone," I said. "When I saw him earlier, Jason had a mobile in his hand. He didn't have one on the stairs. Did you take it?"

Phillip rolled his head a little as if uncomfortable and shot a look at Mark.

Mark shrugged. "I told you she was smart."

Phillip answered me. "Yes, I took it. He had incriminating numbers in it."

I mulled over the significance of the phone. "I suppose he had contact numbers, including your people. He might have had the murderer's number on it as well. If I have this correctly, you aren't trying to solve Jason's murder, just get whoever is producing and distributing drugs around here."

"That's right."

"So, you took his mobile and impeded Inspector Fawthrop's investigation in order to achieve your aims."

"I suppose." He seemed to think that was a perfectly justifiable position.

"Not happening," Mark said. "If you don't tell Fawthrop, Claire will."

I glanced at Mark. He did know me well. I would tell Fawthrop. I was shocked that Phillip would ignore justice for Jason so he could pursue his case. I could see that there were at least two aims here: the rooting out of a deadly drug distribution organization and one man's death. It wouldn't be easy to decide what was the right thing to do. But there should be an investigation into Jason's death.

Now, Phillip was angry. "This is all your fault, Evans. If you hadn't insisted on talking in front of your girlfriend here, she wouldn't know any of this. It's *you* who's putting her in jeopardy."

"Rubbish," Mark said. "She'd have worked out a lot for herself. She's not stupid. She knew there was some connection between you and Jason."

I haven't worked out exactly how Mark sees me. Sometimes, as now, he gives me credit for being an intelligent partner and sometimes, gives me no credit at all and refuses to tell me anything about his cases because I'm not an officer. It's confusing. I concentrated on Phillip.

"I followed you into the chocolate factory," I told him. "I was sure you went down the stairs. Did you kill Jason?"

"No, no. He was dead when I got there."

"And you kept going?"

"He was dead," Phillip insisted.

"You didn't stop to be sure." The blood had been spreading. Jason might have been alive. "You didn't try CPR? What kind of person does that? Just steals the phone and leaves? Don't you have any compassion?"

Phillip shot me a look of contempt. I wasn't impressed. He hadn't even *tried* to help Jason. I remembered Deidre talking about the legal "duty of care" where if people were related to an injured person, they had a legal duty to help them. If they weren't related, they didn't have such legal duty. But there was a moral duty of care to consider as well. Phillip had ignored that.

He was not concerned about Jason, just his investigation. "There is someone in that factory who's directing doctored chocolates for distribution. We don't know who is doing it or what distribution company is taking them all over the country." He used his hands when he spoke, the way many Frenchmen do. His passport was British; I fancied Phillip had a French one as well, and perhaps others, not necessarily legitimate.

Mark was interested. "Someone in the factory puts what— cocaine? crystal meth? fentanyl? —into chocolates and sends them out in a special delivery system?"

"That's right. Or they put the drugs into the packaging the chocolates are in."

"Wouldn't there be a concern the doctored chocolates would get into the regular delivery line and go to the wrong places?" I could imagine small children getting poisoned. My brain almost froze in shock. People would die all over the country because they would innocently eat those chocolates. Addicts all over the country would die if the chocolates contained fentanyl. Both categories of deaths would be tragic.

"Hasn't happened yet." Phillip was confident that the drug trade would remain within the drug using community. "Too much money involved. Whoever picks up those chocolates is paying big for them. They want the right batch. That's one of the reasons we think it might be in the packaging."

"All the batches are numbered." I remembered that from my tour.

"That's right," Phillip said. "And the batches with the drugs in them must have a particular number or code. That number is attached to a distribution company. We haven't figured out which company. There are twenty different distributors taking chocolates from that factory. In spite of the scope of this operation, we think it is part of an even bigger distribution system."

He had gathered some information. I wondered if Jason had supplied it.

"If you cooperated with other police jurisdictions you might get some help in investigating the distribution companies," I said.

"The minute we did," Phillip shot back, "we'd alert the criminal organization we want, and they would shut down here and pop up someplace else. We want the operators, the guys on top. The ones directing the project."

"That's the job of the NCA," Mark said.

"I'll cooperate with them if I have to. Right now, I don't have to."

"And Jason was just a minnow in your big fishing expedition." Sadness washed over me. Jason probably thought he was important. He was young enough to think his spying and reporting to Scotland Yard was exciting and young enough to believe he'd live forever.

"You're not to tell Fawthrop about this," Phillip directed me.

"Tell him yourself," I said. "Then I won't have to."

Phillip shook his head, obviously disgusted and glanced at Mark who raised his eyebrows and said nothing. Phillip rolled his head from side to side as if loosening muscles, then gazed at his shoes for a few moments, giving him time to consider the problem. "All right. I'll do that. I'll tell him. You realize you are risking this venture with your insistence." He sounded pompous.

I felt a little pompous myself, but I held to my resolve. "I think Jason deserves justice. He's not insignificant."

Phillip turned away and was quiet for a moment, then he asked. "Do you think you can treat me the same way you have been so no one on the tour looks at me suspiciously?"

Until he asked me that, I'd thought he would be leaving my tour. I was conscious of feeling disappointed that he was planning to stay. Could I treat him the same as I had? I thought about it. The men waited for my answer. The house was almost silent except for the creaking of old wood. I let out a long breath.

"I can do that. You often take off without telling me or anyone else where you are going…the others now expect that. I complain about your lack of consideration…and I'll continue to do that. You always turn up for meals, though. You might want to stay with that pattern. Otherwise, text me that you are elsewhere, and I'll report that to the group. They already think you are a little strange and not a regular tourist."

"Hmm." Perhaps it didn't matter what the others thought of him. Except, if he was looking for someone on my tour to be involved in this drug trade, he wouldn't want to arouse suspicion.

Mark and I greeted each other more enthusiastically after Phillip left. After some time, we decided to leave the hotel and walk around the Minster. I waved to Mit at the desk and thanked him again for the snacks. We headed toward the spires of the York Minster not far from the hotel. That magnificent edifice dominated the city.

"Beautiful," I said. "So beautiful. I never tire of it."

The Minster was lit with strong strobe lights anchored in the ground and aimed at the walls, making the already majestic cathedral look even taller and more regal. The center block held the light near the top where it almost glowed, reflecting off the honey brick. The side towers soared into the dark sky.

Mark pulled me close. "Amazing, isn't it?"

"It is. It truly is." It had stood there since the sixth century, symbolic of the endurance of the Yorkshire people through wars and politics and religious change. They were a strong people, sure of themselves, capable of withstanding tragedy, poverty, persecution and hardship. I gave myself a mental shake. *Get some perspective here, Claire. People from Yorkshire had to endure invasion, rape and pillage. You only have to endure Phillip, his investigations, murder, Inspector Fawthrop and a wandering Norma.*

"Have you been to evensong here?" Mark asked me.

I shook my head.

"It's magical. The music soars to the heavens. I'd like to sing here someday." He has a beautiful baritone voice and sings with the Hampshire Constabulary Choir. I hoped it happened. It would be a mystical experience to sing in this cathedral. I'd like to do that myself one day.

We walked down Petergate, enjoying the dark houses and well-lit restaurants. Light spilled from the windows of the pubs. People ambled past us; there was little of the bustle of London or other bright cities. York at night was a sedate old lady. It suited us tonight. We cut across Stonegate and back up Blake Street.

"Does Phillip think someone on my tour is the big boss of this drug organization?" I asked Mark was what on my mind.

"Hard to tell with Ferris. He might think that. It's not likely, but Ferris has a reputation of producing out-of-the-box ideas. Sometimes, he's right."

"How do you know him?" I zipped my puff jacket to the top, keeping out the cool March air.

"We did some university courses together. I see him occasionally at conferences. I knew he was with the Yard. I didn't know he was on your tour. That's *tamping*."

I took a moment to translate from Welsh. *Disgusting*. I'd agree with that.

Mark turned to me. "If he does suspect someone, who do you think it might be?"

I reviewed my list of clients. "Not the ladies from Arizona."

"Why not?"

"For one thing they *are* from Arizona and that seems too far away to manage such an organization. Do you think an American could do this?"

Mark slipped his arm around my waist and pulled me closer to him. We managed to walk comfortably without bumping hips. "They're probably experts over there."

I laughed. "Okay. I agree. But a woman? An older woman?"

"Claire, are you prejudiced? Don't you think a woman could handle the job?"

I considered that. "Maybe I am prejudiced. It didn't occur to me the organizer of an illicit drug company could be a woman. Anyway, I don't fancy those particular women as drug lords. I *like* them."

He let that comment hang in the air. Of course, the fact that I liked someone had nothing to do with their ability to deceive.

"Allan White's company orders chocolates from that factory for export. Sheilagh said so. He's in shipping in Bristol. Distribution from his company is possible." I evaluated others on my tour as fit for the position of a drug lord.

"And?" Mark asked.

"And Grady buys chocolates from that factory. Lots of people do. Evelyn ordered some to be sent to her estate company as gifts for the buyers. Could be any of them. Perhaps, it's none of them," I said. "Phillip might be wrong."

"He's been wrong before," Mark said, "but he isn't a fool. Be careful."

I hated the idea of a drug boss on my tour. I supposed drugs and depravity were everywhere, but I dealt in positive holidays, leaving troubles behind, looking for joy and edification away from an everyday life where clients could revel in the world of pleasure and satisfaction. Mark lived in a world of crime, deceit and the manipulation of the vulnerable. We needed him and his colleagues. Nevertheless, I didn't want to be involved with that side of life. I preferred to listen to his problems, not be an active participant in them.

CHAPTER FIVE

We were both up early on Thursday morning. I'd told Mark about Kala and the fact that she might be visiting us.

"Beatings at an elite junior school? Junior school? That's pretty young. But gangs are recruiting them younger every year."

"For heaven's sake! I never thought of gangs."

"Young girls are trained by gangs on how to intimidate others. This girl might be on of a gang or just your garden-variety bully."

"Why recruit such young girls?"

"*Because* they are young, the men can hand off drugs to those kids if the police are closing in, and the kids don't go to jail."

"They're scapegoats," I said, a little stunned.

"They are. And," he hesitated. I gave him my complete attention. "And boys and girls, can be groomed for prostitution."

My stomach roiled.

Mark dropped a quick kiss on my cheek and left me, driving back to his conference in Manchester for its last day. I was left wishing the world was a much better place for the young. Mark was going to return to York after his conference and talk to Inspector Fawthrop. It would probably take him all day, even two days, to get the permissions required from his Major Crime Investigation Team, his own superintendent and from Scotland Yard, so he could be involved officially. If he didn't get permissions, he might just let Inspector Fawthrop know his connection to me and his background and be invited to help unofficially. His superintendent wouldn't like that. She'd think his time and talents should be concentrated in Hampshire where she had plenty of work for him. The problem with being a member of the Major Crimes Investigations Team was he could investigate anywhere in Britain, but he was paid in Hampshire. I'm sure it was efficient in terms of service. It must be a nightmare to fund. Mark said the team wouldn't last. I could see why. I dismissed his world from my mind.

I organized small bags of treats for each person on the tour containing a bottle of water, a coaster souvenir of York and some chocolate, as well as the itinerary for the day and a map of the Yorkshire Dales and Moors. We didn't have to leave until nine as we were only traveling about forty minutes to our B & B. I had time to call Deirdre.

"Is Kala here in York yet?"

"Yes, Michael drove her up last night. You can call her any time."

"I will."

"What's going on with you now?" She was abrupt. Typically, she was short with me when she was busy.

"Do you have to be in court right now?"

"No, but I have a client coming before court, and I have to be ready for him."

She was preoccupied. I understood that. "Nothing much to report." I wasn't going to tell her about Phillip. "The local inspector seems to have finished his interviews. I'm off the Dales for a couple of days."

"I don't suppose you have room for Kala on that tour."

I thought about it. "No, I don't have room for her. I'll try to see her before I go and when I get back."

"I understand. Call in at night if you need to talk."

"I will. Thanks." I disconnected. Deirdre was my solid backup when life was hard, but she was also a busy barrister, a worried mother of two, and a wife. She didn't have spare time. I wish I could help Kala. I'd put her problem in the back of my mind and think about it later.

We were delayed only twenty minutes as Constable Poole brought our statements to sign. He must have had a late night at the nick to get those statements ready, probably drinking the station's dreadful coffee, but he looked alert. He'd changed his uniform for one that was crisp and pressed with the shiny shoes I had come to expect from the police.

"I need only the witnesses," he said.

The English contingent waited in the lobby as they didn't have any pertinent information to give the police. The rest of them moved with me into the snug, the small room off the lobby, to read our statements and sign them. The Tucson ladies went first. Their statements were short. I wondered if Charlie had edited out all their speculations.

"Passport number?" Evelyn raised her eyebrows.

"Yes, madam," Charlie said, not explaining why he wanted them.

My statement took a little longer. I read it and signed it.

"Driver's license number," Charlie said to me.

I had that memorized and added it under my signature.

I had time for a quick call to Michael's brother, John. I'd come up with an offer of help for Kala. He agreed to drive Kala to our B & B near Northallerton where she could join in the activities of the farm without being a part of the tour group. I gave the address and phone number of the farm and suggested she arrive about six—if she wanted to come.

John asked her. She said she did. I wasn't sure how this was going to work, but it was all I could think of doing.

Everyone loaded into the van quickly. Even Phillip. No one spoke about the police, Jason or murder. They examined their gift bags as I drove west from York. Geraldine was appreciative. Sheilagh also. Norma acted as if I'd given her a birthday present.

"Will we have much time in Harrogate?" Evelyn was sitting in the front right seat of the van today. I wasn't sure if she liked her gift bag as she didn't comment on it.

"We'll have the morning there. We can visit the museum, the Turkish Baths, the Royal Pump Room, St. Peter's and the art galleries." I rattled off some choices.

"I hear the waters at the Royal Pump Room are really stinky," Norma said.

"Yes, sulphur, but it is supposed to be good for you."

"I think I'll pass on it. I'm too old to worry about what's good for me." Geraldine sat back in her seat.

Evelyn sent her a baleful glance. "Never too old to look after yourself."

Geraldine let that remark slide by without comment.

I engaged the mic and gave them a short commentary on the mystery writers of this area. "Francis Brody set her stories in Leeds just south of us. Clara Benson lives in this area, although she set her Angela Marchmont series for the most part in London."

"Brody set at least one story in the Yorkshire Dales," Geraldine said. Remember *A Death on the Dales*? Kate came to a village near Settle."

"That's right," I said. "I stand corrected."

"Where does Sara Rosett set her stories?" Evelyn asked.

"I love those 1930s ones," Norma commented.

"London, I believe. At least some of them. Her *Murder on Location* contemporary series is set all over the country." At least, I thought it was. I'd have to check that out. I had to be accurate with these ladies. They knew their mysteries.

"Does she live around here?" Sheilagh asked.

"Texas." I was sure of that.

"No kidding?" Geraldine laughed. "She sounds so British."

"She understands the culture and the language," I agreed.

"There are a lot of thriller writers from Yorkshire, not Brody who is in the cozy genre, but others, aren't there?" Amanda said.

"I've noticed that,"

Sheilagh had thought about it. "I wonder why? I mean the people aren't any more bloodthirsty here, are they?"

"Certainly, no more than people in my area. The mean crime rate in Tucson is 120% higher than the crime rate of the whole country," Geraldine said.

"Goodness." I glanced back at her. "What a statistic. Lots of scope for writing about it, I suspect."

"Yorkshire has Stewart Paulson, Cassandra Clark, Kate Ellis and John Wainwright." Evelyn offered the information.

"And to balance off thrillers, they have Nicolas Rhea." Geraldine said.

"Well, he's lovely," Norma agreed.

I heard a murmur of voices as the ladies discussed authors in lower tones. I noticed Phillip was rapidly texting. I truly wish he hadn't come. He ought to make some effort to appear as a tourist. If he was trying unobtrusively to observe someone, he wasn't doing a good job of fitting into the tourist mode. He appeared to be a busy executive, or someone on a job. Just as I thought that, he snapped his mobile shut.

"Sorry about that, everyone. I thought I'd left all my work behind. What's on the itinerary for today?"

"Harrogate in the morning," Amanda kindly informed him of what he could read for himself in his brochure. "Afternoon driving to Skipton and back, and tonight north of Harrogate to a farm."

"We will be staying the night at a farm," Sheilagh said. "You'll like that, Allan."

"Blimey. Is that right?" Allan showed interest.

I glanced in to the rear-view mirror. Allan was leaning forward. Obviously, Sheilagh had been the one to plan this trip as Allan didn't seem to know where we were going.

"They'll have animals there?" he asked me. "They aren't one of those farm B & Bs that *used* to have animals?"

"Yes, goats, cows and, of course sheep." I assured him. He was right that there were many "farm" B & Bs that had no livestock at all.

"Is it far from Harrogate?" Phillip asked.

"No just a little north. We'll stop at Harrogate as we're scheduled for a short tour of the Old Swan Hotel and tea at Bettys."

"Really?" Geraldine almost squealed. "The Old Swan. Where Agatha Christie hid out for those missing eleven days."

"That's right."

The ladies, including Sheilagh and Amanda, happily discussed Agatha Christie and her escapade in 1926 until I pulled into a parking spot on Cornwall Road in Harrogate near the Royal Pump Room.

I, also, was fascinated by those missing eleven days in Agatha Christie's life. Any number of people had written about it. Christie maintained a silence about the days she ran away from the world and hid in the Old Swan in Harrogate. The press was ruthless and blamed her for a publicity stunt or an effort to charge her husband with her murder. Any number of theories were trotted out for scholars to study. I was studying them myself and was actively trying to find any correspondence I could on internet sites and in libraries—when I wasn't touring. Not everyone was as fascinated as I was with Christie's life, but these women were, at least, interested.

I glanced at the Valley Garden Park across the street. Gulliver would have loved to explore that. I might bring him the next time I came this way. I took my group on a tour of the main rooms of The Old Swan, comparing it to the pictures taken in the 1920s. It looked exactly as it did in Christie's day. Some newspaper clippings on display in the lobby and hall reported her stay and the hunt that occurred when she disappeared. My group studied them, moving from cabinet to cabinet, reading about the notoriety Christie had incurred. When they had had a surfeit of Christie culture, I herded them toward the Royal Pump Museum just down the small hill and across the road, made sure they each had a map of the town, that Norma had her escort and that all agreed to meet at Bettys on Parliament Street for the afternoon tea I'd booked. They scattered.

The lack of the apostrophe in "Bettys" bothered me. I'm with Lynne Truss on that point, but this establishment was determinedly "Bettys".

Two hours later, they met me as planned, chattering away about what they had done in Harrogate. Bettys is everything anyone yearning after a 1930s experience could imagine: wait staff dressed in black and white formal uniforms, wood-paneled walls, soft gray patterned carpets, cushioned seats, silver tea sets on display and silver cake stands with displays of delicate macaroons. There were stained glass windows and carriage lights at the entrance. We passed through the first room which had tall white pillars with ornately decorated tops, giving the room a grand aura. We followed our black and white clad waiter down the stairs, and since I had booked ahead, into a niche off the main room where we could see the other patrons, but where we had some privacy. We had our choice of elegant coffees, like those in any high-end coffee house. The food was uniquely Bettys: crustless sandwiches with watercress, an egg and avocado dish that looked as if an artist had arranged it, and ribs in sauce for those who were very hungry.

My group was impressed with the Edwardian elegance of the tea room, at least the American women were. The English contingent was probably used to it. I noticed that both Phillip and Grady were comfortable with the tea cups and delicate plates. Allan looked a little nervous but cheered when the waiter arrived with his hearty meal of cutlet, cheese and chips. We tucked in with enthusiasm and made short work of the fabulous food.

For dessert there was an overwhelming choice of pastries and cakes from the tiers of cake stands and plates displayed at one end of the room.

"Look at those cookies," Norma said. "They look like ladybugs."

So they did, with their black-dotted red icing, antennae and cheerful grin piped with white icing. It was impossible to choose with confidence because everything was enticing. We all indulged, even Evelyn.

After our lunch experience, I loaded their packages into the back of the van and they settled in for the short ride to Skipton.

Skipton is one of my favorite spots to stop but, on this trip, we only had an hour. I parked, handed out a map of Skipton and showed them where Bizzie Lizze's restaurant was on the Leeds-Liverpool Canal. The canal ran through the center of town, making it a point of orientation. It should be easy for them to find their way back to me. The sun was shining, although it was a little cool. The canal was beautiful and the streets different enough for the American tourists to find quaint and busy enough for the English tourists to find the shops they wanted.

"This would be a perfect place to stage a murder mystery," Evelyn declared.

"Absolutely," Geraldine agreed. "There is a canal handy for dumping bodies, winding streets for a chase scene and chimney pots and brick houses for atmosphere."

I stared at the three who had stayed behind the general exodus and were gazing around the town.

"Are you writing a book?" I asked, a little astonished.

"We are," Geraldine declared. "Norma will come up with the characters. Evelyn will organize the plot and I'll do the writing. Evelyn will edit and Norma add ideas."

I shouldn't have been surprised. These women had accomplished a lot in their lives; they weren't going to stop now they were retired.

"Well, that's the plan. We haven't actually started yet," Geraldine admitted. "This trip is our inspiration. I think Skipton might be our setting, though. We're here such a short time. Can we come back?"

I mentally scrambled my itinerary. "Leave it with me, and I'll see what I can do." I doubted I could arrange for the group to return. However, I could help them adjust their plane tickets so, with extra days, the three could return here after the end of the tour.

Phillip had walked away quickly. Either he was tailing one of the tour members or he was trying to find Wi Fi. Amanda and Grady had headed for a toy store they'd spotted, and Allan and Sheilagh were strolling down the street looking at the buildings. I was going to take a long walk. I wanted a private trail where I could stride quickly and burn off some nervous energy. When Gulliver was with me, I *had* to take walks. It took more effort to find the time when I was alone.

I hiked the tow path along the canal. The sun warmed the stones and glinted off the smooth flowing water. The canal was built to facilitate the transport of coal from the Leeds district to the port of Liverpool. In the eighteenth and nineteenth century, they didn't seem to worry much about what harm they might be doing to the environment when they dug the canal. Even without protests and environmental assessments, it took fifty years to build and was completed in 1816. It's in use today, but moves pleasure boats, not coal. I walked alongside it, enjoying the sun and the warmth of the March day. I felt some relief from the concerns of my tourists and the need to keep track of Phillip. Kala's problems niggled at the edge of my thoughts. I skirted the castle and entered the Sawmill Entrance of the Castle Woods Walk. Huge sycamore trees blocked the direct light from above. The dappled light filtered through, highlighting the new, bright green growth of the overhead trees and the hawthorn and bluebells below, lightening what might otherwise have been a dark wood. I moved quickly, relishing the activity and clearing my mind of anything but the greenery, the fresh air and the smell of damp growth. I heard the loud call of a chaffinch and the chatter of a blue tit. I spotted the flash of a chaffinch's wing near the ground far ahead of me. While I couldn't see many birds, I could hear them. It felt wonderfully calming to be surrounded by the busy life of the forest. I could hear the Eller Beck rushing past occasionally, although it's a wide stream and usually moves sedately. I did a quick circle of the wood and was back at Bizzie Lizzie's in time to greet my returning group.

The three ladies from Tucson arrived together. They'd been plotting their novel.

"Great spot. We are going to get our protagonist to come from Skipton to Tucson." Norma enthused.

"Why?" Evelyn asked.

"Why what?"

"Why should he go from Skipton to Tucson?"

"We'll figure that out. Then he can join the homeless in the ravines in the center of Tucson. You know, the tent city that grows up there in the winter?" Norma was creating her plot on the spot.

"Maybe, he'll meet the romantic interest at the school where they hold the health clinics," Geraldine added her idea.

I left them to their communal plotting, made sure they had ordered their tea or coffee—no one wanted much after that amazing meal at Bettys—and moved to the other table where the two couples were quietly chatting. Phillip, of course had not yet arrived.

"What did you see?" I asked them.

Sheilagh gestured toward Amanda. "They went to the Castle."

"Yes," Amanda said. "It's a charming little castle" Then she laughed. "That sounded patronizing. But when you have seen as many castles as I have, you can be a little critical of them."

Grady smiled in agreement. "It was charming."

"We," Sheilagh gestured toward Allan, "went looking for bats in the Castle Wood because it's supposed to be famous for them, especially the pipistrelle."

"Should be there at dusk if we want to see them." Allan was dismissive.

"We might have spotted them sleeping upside down." Sheilagh was not going to admit that hunting for bats in daylight was bound to be disappointing.

"It was pleasant in the wood. I was there as well," I tried to smooth over the small disagreement.

"A bit wild," Allan said.

"He likes his animals domesticated." Sheilagh excused her husband.

At that point, Phillip rushed in full of apologies for being late again but smiling as if he knew we'd forgive him.

He gave no explanation of where he'd been, but started a conversation with Grady about the engineering expertise necessary to build the ninety-one locks on the canal. Allan leaned in to add his comments and Evelyn, also, was interested in the vast undertaking it must have been, the many indispensable workers and the increase in the economy of the country once the canal was in use. I had to commend Phillip for his masterful manipulation of the group. They became so interested in their conversation, no one questioned him about the way he'd spent his time in Skipton.

CHAPTER SIX

W e headed north to the B & B in the late afternoon. It was an hour's drive. The fields stretched on either side of us lined with hedges. Ash and sycamore trees dotted the rolling landscape beyond

"We're in James Harriot country now, aren't we?" Allan asked.

"We are. This is the area where he worked. We are driving past Thirsk where he both lived and worked. We can come back another day to explore the area."

"He was Alf Wright, really," Evelyn said ever-ready to elucidate. I didn't mind. She was knowledgeable and a voice different from mine was probably welcome. She did tend to think only she knew the facts—which, in time, might grate. So far, the group had been tolerant. "He had to have a pseudonym because the veterinary association thought writing books was a form of advertising, and he couldn't advertise."

"Against professional ethics?" Geraldine asked.

"Yes, and I suppose he didn't want to let his community know about his writing. He wrote under the name of a football player he admired."

"He's more famous than the football player now," Grady said.

"Wonderful country," Allan was almost enthusiastic. We'd come to a small rise of land and could view the farmland around us. "Look at those sheep. Swaledales, I think. And that green grass. They must have at least 15% protein there."

I could see Sheilagh in my rear-view mirror, smiling at Allan's interest.

Geraldine gazed over the farmland. "My grandparents left here as young adults. There were too many children for the farm to support so they came to the US."

"To Arizona?" I asked.

"Oh, no. I think that would have been too much of a contrast for my grandmother—cacti and snakes, you know. No, to Oregon—lots of grass and productive farms. I think she was happy there." She studied the green fields and the dry-stone walls. "She must have missed this."

I remembered Geraldine's age from her passport and concluded that her grandparents probably left Yorkshire in the mid-1920s. There would be no quick flights home for a visit in those days.

The B & B, called Ambleside Farm, was located in the rolling land near a stream. Grey, stone walls enclosed small paddocks containing sheep, grazing as if imported for an artist's pose. I was hoping Allan would enjoy it here as it was a working farm and had, as well as sheep: goats, pigs, llamas and, naturally, dogs and cats. I hoped Kala would like it, as well. To look after all this livestock were parents, two teenagers and their grandmother. The teenagers, a boy of about 16 and a girl about 12 hustled our luggage into the renovated Old Stable block where the accommodations were luxurious. My room had an enormous bed with memory foam, my own bath *en suite*, a beautiful view of the farmlands and a tray of coffee and chocolates. Lovely.

I talked to Aelwen Yowlet, one of the owners of the farm, about a small room near mine for Kala. We were lucky. She had one vacant. I would share my room if I had to, but I preferred privacy, especially if Mark joined me.

We disbursed to various activities. Phillip went to his room, no doubt to contact important people on his mobile. He must have a method of protecting the calls in the arcane ways available to techies and beyond my ability to even imagine.

Allan and Sheilagh headed for the barns. Grady and Amanda set off for a walk up behind the house on the hillside. The three Tucson ladies were attending a baking demonstration that I'd arranged for anyone who wanted it. Mrs. Yowlet Sr. was going to teach them how to make the local bread.

"I'm throng, but it'll be a change," the older Mrs. Yowlet had told me.

I translated that to mean she was busy but willing. I found the local dialect difficult to understand. Unlike Cornwall, where the words made sense to me and comprehension came easily, in Yorkshire, I found the words very strange. Many came from the Norse language and not the Celtic. The eccentricity of the dialect was fascinating—a linguistic challenge.

"I appreciate you taking the time," I said.

She beamed at me, obviously in her element. Dressed in a bright blue track suit and covered with a voluminous apron, there was no sliding into old age for her. She was active, busy and happy to be cooking and teaching here in the farm kitchen she had managed her whole life. Her daughter-in law, Mrs. Yowlet, Jr. had left to deliver her mail route, a second or possibly third job. The children were attending to the stock and Mr. Yowlet Jr and Sr were on the hillsides checking out the sheep.

"They be 'avin' a look for t'ticks," Mrs. Yowlet Sr. informed me. "Mind, 'tis early yet. You don't see them till May in a usual year. 'Tis the climate change, you see. Too warm by half this winter."

I nodded solemnly. I understood there was a connection between the temperature and ticks. I'd pay attention. My tourists would need to be warned against inadvertently picking up ticks when they were walking in the countryside. I left Mrs. Yowlet and joined Alan and Sheilagh in a tour of the pig paddock.

Freya, the twelve-year-old daughter of the house, was feeding grain.

"Yorkshire crosses?" Allan asked her.

"Yes, they be Yorkshires crossed with Berkshires. That's why you get that black in the skin. Put on weight something fast, they do. Dad's that pleased."

"Brilliant," Allan said, a little wistfully, I thought.

He'd told me he'd grown up on a farm. Now he worked in an office, shipping and importing products. A desk with a stack of papers was a long way from a farm.

"Would you like to give me a hand with the watering?" Freya asked him, recognizing his interest.

"I can do that." He responded quickly.

Freya handed Allan a brush and directed him to scrub out some water troughs and then refill them. I left Allan happily scrubbing. I noticed he stopped every so often to scratch the back of an inquisitive pig. I liked the smell of pigs, a kind of musky, spicy smell. However, I didn't want to clean their pens.

John arrived with Kala in his late model BMW. He's an accountant in York. His wife, Fiona, is a teacher. I'd met them several times but didn't know them well. Kala jumped out of the car, pulling her rucksack with her.

"Hi, John," I said. We shook hands. I turned to Kala and hugged her. The skin around her eye was an interesting shade of purple and red. I raised my eyebrows but said nothing about it. "Hiya, Kala. Want to see some pigs?"

She brightened and even smiled a little. I left John to take her luggage to her room and shepherded her to Freya who continued to direct the trough-cleaning operations. When I left, the two girls were chattering—a good sign.

I spoke to John for only a few minutes. He wasn't staying as he had to get back to York. He said Kala hadn't told him anything about the fight. She might never talk about it to any of us. I checked back with Kala and told her I was going for a walk and Freya would show her where her room was. I couldn't hover over her, and it might be better for her to form bonds with someone her own age. She might talk to Freya.

I wandered down to the beck and found a bench to sit on. The water gurgled past. I could almost hear music in it, a basic melody with sparkling overtones. Soothing. I examined the area carefully for snakes. Adders will find a patch of sun and bask in it from March to October. They were Britain's only venomous snake but weren't aggressive. Still, I didn't want to surprise one. I settled on the bench. The trilling, rolling song of the curlew hung in the air. I couldn't spot the bird.

I called Mark. No answer. I left a message. "*Ambleside Farm near Northallerton. Going out to dinner soon and will be back about ten. Call you then.*"

I took a deep breath and lifted my face to the spring sunshine. House sparrows determinedly chirped in the low bushes. I heard a barn owl rasp its distinctive call from a tree. I imagined a forest full of birds, all playing their own part, looking after their own families and flitting in and out of the trees in family groups—a parallel world to mine.

I stayed for a half hour, hoping for peace but thinking of Jason. He'd hardly started his life's journey. It was both sad and unfair. The innocent and the righteous were being attacked by the wicked—as a preacher I once heard put it. I know that's simplistic; life is more complicated than stereotypes describe, and there are graduations of crime and criminal intent, but I *felt* as if there was a wave of nastiness rising up around me. Even Kala had been abused in spite of the care of her family. The world, at least, my corner of it, seemed uncontrollable.

Ambleside Farm didn't cater for dinner. I had reserved a couple of tables at a restaurant close by. About seven, I loaded my tourists into the van and drove to The Crosby Village Inn and Restaurant. I left Kala behind as I didn't want her to have to be polite with adults she hardly knew and arranged for her to have dinner with the

Yowlet family. She appeared to be happy with that. It was possible she was glad to escape from parental and even aunt scrutiny. She must be aware of the questions in our minds.

The Crosby Village Inn was an old pub established in the 1750s and advertised as "aching with history and character". I hoped my tourists liked it. I usually herd groups from one carefully planned activity to another, getting satisfaction from their pleasure. Today, in spite of the appealing restaurant, it all seemed a chore. Sadness over Jason's death plagued me periodically. I didn't know when it was going to happen, but it descended on me and made everyday tasks difficult. I reminded myself that every job had times when it wasn't enthralling, and you simply had to buckle down and do it. *Disciple, Claire. Be responsible.* I knew I would enjoy the meal once everyone was settled.

I hadn't eaten here before, but the menu was intriguing. They had Free Range Breast of Chicken Wrapped in Dry Cured Bacon, Derbyshire Stilton, Aged Port & Spring Onion Cream which sounded delicious and the old standby of Haddock and Chips with mushy pea. I ordered a couple of bottles of cabernet sauvignon. Phillip had added a bottle of merlot. We should be a happy group. Allan was the only one who drank more than he could comfortably handle. He was sober tonight and animated, telling Phillip all about the pigs.

"They're grand creatures," he told Phillip, slipping into a hint of Yorkshire speech. "Gaining fast and smart. They are brainy—smarter than a dog."

He leaned toward Sheilagh. "You know, Sheil. In our retirement, we could buy a small holding like in 'Escape to the Country.'" He named a popular television show that took buyers into the country to find them their dream homes.

"Do you think so?" She studied him seriously and, I think, with some alarm. "Do you want to live in James Herriot country?"

"You bet." He beamed at her. I could imagine him in overalls and a woolen cap, seriously discussing pig feed with the locals. I could not see him as a drug lord. I honestly couldn't. I suppose a criminal isn't defined by his crime. He must be more than his occupation. A drug lord might love to play the violin, raise horses, dote on his children and not care about anyone else. I couldn't know if the Allan who loved farm animals, also ran an illicit business. Personal character was complex. I could see him as a farmer. I had a harder time imagining Sheilagh in a farming environment. She seemed efficient and given to planning and controlling her space. Farming was a chancy business. She might find it unsettling.

Philip and Grady dropped into a discussion of mysteries on the moors.

"Did you hear about that man, true life story," Phillip said, "who walked onto the moors to die and no one knew who he was, and still don't?"

"I heard about that. It was a little time ago, about 2015, wasn't it?" Sheilagh said.

"It was," Phillip agreed. I wondered if he had been assigned to that case.

Evelyn turned to the men. "Patricia Hall. A mystery writer who set her books in Yorkshire, used that to start her mystery *Death by Election*. She didn't quote it directly but it's such a similar story I expect that's where she got the idea."

"But, Evelyn," Geraldine objected. "Patricia Hall was writing in the 1980s. Maybe this man who wandered up to the moors to die got his idea from *her*?"

The conversation moved from true crime, where I think Phillip wanted it to go, to mystery novels. He'd have to accept that. He was on a mystery book tour, after all.

When we returned, I collected Kala from the family TV room. We had hot chocolate in my suite before she went to bed. Freya had lent her a dog to cuddle, a small, border collie puppy they had great ambitions for on the farm. It was sound asleep on Kala's lap.

"Right now," Kala said. "It needs cuddling because it hasn't been away from its mother very long." I expected Kala craved some cuddling as well.

"What's the puppy's name?"

"Tuffy," she said and caressed its ears.

"Tell me about the big fight," I said, "if you want to."

Kala was quiet for a moment, then said. "Mom gets too intense, you know?"

Passionate, I would have said, but intense was also accurate.

"She'd make everything worse."

I didn't explore that. "What's this girl like, the one or the ones who hit you?"

"She in a gang," Kala said. Mark was right. There were gangs in that school.

"What kind of gang? One just in the school or one outside the school?" I was trying to be careful with my questioning. Too many questions and she'd stop talking.

"Outside. Guys with big cars wait for them after school. I don't know where they take them but they come back with stuff."

"Stuff?"

"Like mobis and clothes and concert tickets and stuff. Just stuff."

"They aren't a kind group of girls who are just preoccupied with things." I wanted to be clear about the threat to her safety.

She snorted. "Not kind at all. Mean and bossy." She looked down at her hands. "Scary. Right scary." Then her head jerked up, her eyes widened and she stared at me.

I opened my arms and she flew into them, clutching the puppy and burying her face on my shoulder.

I stroked her back. The puppy wiggled, then settled. "Tell me about it."

"There were three of them," she hiccupped then sniffed, keeping her face snuggled into my neck and shoulder. Her voice was muffled, and I had to strain to hear her. I hugged her close and didn't ask her speak up.

"They pushed me into a corner in the library. In the library!" Her voice took an indignant turn as if violence in the library was obscene. Any place else might be a possible venue for assault, but a library should be immune. I understood that and kept stroking her back.

"There was no one else there. No teachers. No kids. No one. They crowded me into the corner with shelves of books at my back. I couldn't get away. I couldn't push past them, and there was nowhere to go. Then they started smashing my face with their fists." Her breath caught and she stuttered. "It h..h…hurt."

"Oh, my darling. That was horrible."

"It was. They'd have killed me, I think. But fussy Mrs. Peterson waddled in right then and started scolding them for making a noise."

"For making a noise? Not for beating you?"

"I don't think she even noticed me. She's old, and she doesn't see very well."

"Did she wait until they left."

"She did. They left me there. I was on the floor by then. It was dark in that corner. Mrs. Peterson just shut off the lights and left."

My blood ran cold. I did not think this was a normal school-girl fight, if there was such a thing. This was a fight with intention to harm and harm badly.

"What did you do?"

"I crawled to the door and just stayed there for a while. I didn't want to come out into the hall and find them waiting for me. The bell rang, and I figured they would be rushing out to meet their boyfriends after school, so I waited."

"They're cruel."

"I think they're barking mad."

"That too."

"And horrid with it." She hugged me tight.

I imagined her waiting by that library door. "It must have been terrifying to wonder if they were lingering in the hall."

"Waiting, was the worst part, well, almost the worst part. Getting hit was the worst, but waiting, ugh, that was really beastly."

"I'm so sorry, honey." Fear would have almost paralyzed her as she waited for some sound from the other side of the door.

She pushed away from me. The puppy slipped to the floor where it circled and settled. Kala stared straight in my eyes. "I left the blood on the floor in the corner. I didn't clean it up. Let Old Lady Peterson do that."

I bit my lip, determined not to find any amusement in this recital. She looked ferocious, defending her rebellion at not cleaning up after herself.

"I don't blame you," I managed to say.

She sat back and moaned. "They don't care, you know, Auntie Claire. They're nasty, those slags. They don't care about anything. My dad says you should believe there is good in everyone, but I don't think Judith, Amy and Stephanie have any good in them at all. They're as mean as a bag of ferrets."

"Sounds like it to me," I agreed. But they're young, so young.

She took a couple of deep breaths, sat at the edge of the bed, leaned down and scooped up Tuffy who had started to paw at her feet. She snuggled the dog against her chest and stroked him. He licked her face with eager puppy enthusiasm. Kala smiled.

I put my hand over hers. "What's your biggest worry now?"

She sighed. "Those guys the girls go with? They're really narse. Like telly criminals. And Judith said they'd kill my mum if I told."

I stared at her. Dear God! That might not be an idle threat.

"They would too." She held my gaze.

What could I say? I could not make this go away. "It makes it hard for you to do anything." It made it impossible for her to do anything.

"I don't want to go back to school, not there, anyway."

"I can see why. You might have to tell your mom the whole story. She thinks you're just embarrassed by her."

"Sometimes I am," she admitted. "This is worse."

"Much worse." I agreed. I was far past my competency level here. "I would like to tell Mark about it."

"He's the police." She was alarmed. "They'll kill me for that."

"It's not his jurisdiction," I said. "It's not his area of responsibility. He'll just give us advice, or he'll drop a hint to someone but without naming you. Would that be okay? I don't want to get you killed." I had to be very careful. I believed her. She might be killed.

She bit her lip. I could see she was torn between trusting Mark and me with her fears and keeping them to herself. She'd already told me. How far did she want this to go?

"It's too big a problem for me to deal with," I confessed. "I need some help and you need some help."

"I just hope we don't make it a huge, ugly horrible mess. It could be a proper muck up."

"It could be a gruesome mess," I said.

"Horrific," she said.

"Dreadful."

"Monstrous."

We smiled at each other. We'd played that word game since she had been about six. It felt normal to indulge in it again. I tucked her into her bed in the room next door to me, patted the puppy and kissed Kala good night. I think she was glad she'd told me. However, I recognized her real fear that she could start retributive action from the gang. She was only ten years old. How did our society deteriorate so badly that a ten-year-old had to deal with this?

I called Mark that night and talked to him from my suite. I sat in the bay window where I could look out on the fields behind the farm. Sheep were lying in a congenial bunch near the gate, their white coats picking up the light from the moon, glinting like spots of silver on the dark field. Beyond them, the woods were black.

I told him about Kala. He rumbled soft curses over the air waves then said he'd think about it.

We were both silent for a few moments. Kala's problem would take some deep thought.

"Did you tell Fawthrop about Phillip?" I asked Mark. Somebody should have—if Phillip didn't do that himself.

"I did. It will probably get me into trouble with my superintendent and with Ferris, but Ferris can't wander around the country like he's a separate law department operating without supervision or without boundaries."

I wondered about Phillip's loyalty to his Scotland Yard bosses and about how strong that loyalty was. "Do you think *he* killed Jason?"

Mark was silent for a moment. "I don't think so. Jason was useful to the Yard. They had him on the payroll. The Yard doesn't go around killing informants." I noticed that Mark had to think about it before he answered. Phillip might be a loose cannon.

"No, of course not." I murmured reassurance. I wasn't convinced. Phillip struck me as someone who liked to run in the shadows and make up his own rules. I suppose that was a lot to conclude simply because he didn't come to meals on time or fit into my tour.

"How did Jason die?"

"Knifed. Very quiet. Could have been accomplished quickly without any noise at all. We don't know how long he was lying on the stairs before you found him. Probably no more than twenty minutes."

"Knifed?" I felt sick.

"We don't have a lot of gun violence, but plenty of knife violence."

I knew there were laws against carrying a knife. I supposed that was because many were used to harm others. I didn't want to think about it. "I suppose Fawthrop had to tell the family."

"Indeed. He said it was brutal. A mum who was proud of him and two sisters. A girlfriend too, wailing in the kitchen. Never easy."

We gave Jason a few moments of silence. I thought of the pain spreading out from Jason's death.

"Did he fight to defend himself?" I asked

"No evidence of it."

"So, it was someone he knew, then?"

"Or someone he found so nonthreatening he wasn't defensive." I heard his sigh. "Is Ferris still with you?"

I did a quick translation from Ferris to Phillip.

"He is. He's constantly texting his contacts which is very annoying, but otherwise he seems to participate in the group enough to be civil. I can't tell who he thinks is a suspect. They all seem unlikely."

"Just keep in mind he had enough information on someone there to justify spending this much time keeping tabs on him or her…or them."

I thought about Geraldine, Norma and Evelyn.

"Not my ladies," I said firmly.

CHAPTER SEVEN

The soft bed and the quiet had allowed me sleep deeply through the night, but the morning fresh air woke me. When I peeked into her bedroom, Kala, wide awake, looked a little better. Her bruise had faded to a greenish yellow and she was more alert. Tuffy, the puppy, gamboled about her feet, demanding attention. She deposited Tuffy in the back yard where he hurriedly marked a fence post before rushing over to tumble against two other sheepdogs near the kitchen door. Kala and I joined the tourist group at the main house for breakfast. The Yowlets had adapted the morning room with its many windows as the breakfast room for guests. The rest of the large farmhouse was dedicated to the private lives of the Yowlet family. Tourists slept in the Old Stables and the Old Barn which had been renovated to luxurious standards. It was an interesting contrast: the hundreds of years old stone outside the buildings and the modern tile floors with their underfloor heating and shiny porcelain baths inside.

We assembled at the buffet and helped ourselves to as much of the freshly boiled and no doubt freshly laid eggs, home-made breads and muffins, scones and jams that were available. Mrs. Aelwen Yowlet Jr, an athletic looking forty-year-old, delivered coffee in carafes to the tables, took orders for tea and for poached, fried or scrambled eggs. There were rashers of bacon and sausages that looked delicious. Freya added scones and another jug of milk. I took my full plate to a table where Sheilagh and Allan were sitting. I wanted to make sure Sheilagh had given Allan his surprise package. I could see the brochure for a two-day lambing adventure beside his plate. He caught my eye and beamed.

"I'm going to spend two days mucking in with the lambing. Shiel here arranged it." He smiled at his wife.

Sheilagh grinned at him and turned to me. "He was gobsmacked. He didn't know we were coming to a farm much less that we were going to spend two days helping with the sheep."

The farm offered this two-day experience for only a little more than the regular fees so, after consultation via email with Sheilagh, I'd organized it.

"It means you will miss out on our trip to the Dales today," I said to Allan. "You'll simply have to come back on another trip."

"We will," Allan said. "We will. I suppose you are going to see James's Herriot's vet clinic?"

"We are," I said.

"Ah, well," he glanced at the brochure on the table. "I will be content. I will for sure."

I conferred with Kala and then in the kitchen with Aelwen and arranged for Kala to have a private two-day lambing experience conducted by Freya.

"It will do Freya good to plan and implement a session. Good training," she said.

Freya who had just arrived with an armful of dirty plates for the dishwasher, glanced over at her mother.

"What chore are you thinking of now?" She sounded reluctant. Aelwen explained.

"That'll be fine," she said.

Her grandmother hmphed. Freya shot her a look from under her dark eyebrows that said as clearly as if she'd articulated it, "Back off."

Her grandmother watched her leave. "She'd start an argument in an empty room, that one."

Aelwen shrugged. "She's fourteen, Mum."

"Ah, true, I remember you at fourteen. 'Hedgehog' I called you back then."

Aelwen raised her eyebrows at the reminder, and turned to me. "She'll be right."

Kala thought it a great idea. "Lambs are cute, cuddly-like, but they're a lot of work," she informed me.

"I'm sure you'll do a good job," I said.

The rest of the group climbed into the van. Amanda was alongside me this morning. We headed for Thirsk, the site of James Herriot's life and work and only twenty minutes away. We'd passed through Thirsk yesterday, but today, the groups would have time to explore it.

"The name of the town, Thirsk, comes from the Viking for fen or lake," I informed them.

"A fen is different from a lake," Evelyn said.

"It is, although they both describe a watery place."

"Is there a water there? A lake?" Geraldine asked.

"No lake," I said. "Just the Cod Beck running through the lower end."

"It does make you wonder why they'd call it Thirsk," Evelyn said.

Norma's voice rose from behind me. "Some historic wanderers, desperate for a drink, managed to scramble to this place and were so grateful for the water they named the place for it." In the rear-view mirror I saw Norma bobbing her head to emphasize the probability of her story.

Evelyn snorted but with some indulgence. She must be used to Norma's imaginative flights of thought.

We were again lucky with the weather and were able to view the fields around us in the sunlight. Lambs, bright white in their newborn coats, skipped around their mothers in the fields, contributing to the picture-postcard look of the Dales. The stone fences fascinated the Tucson women, and I obligingly stopped at a layby so they could get out and examine them. Surprisingly, it was the urban Grady who explained how stone fences were built without mortar and with the expense of a great deal of time.

"A team of two men can build about twelve yards a day," he said. "When you calculate the cost of labor times the yardage in a stone wall, you can see that it would be very expensive to build and even repair these fences."

"Oh, I hope they won't disappear," Norma said in some consternation. "They are beautiful."

Grady smiled. "They are indeed beautiful. I expect there will be some kind of government subsidy to keep them repaired. They are a tourist attraction, as well as a practical way to control sheep."

We stayed at the layby for a few minutes. The tourists clicking pictures of the tranquil scene. I took some deep breaths and enjoyed the pastoral vista—green fields, white sheep and gray stone walls trailing over the hills into the distance.

We climbed back into the van and I drove to Thirsk. I handed out the tickets I'd bought online for the James Herriot Museum. I'd seen it before and found it charming. I'd read every book James Herriot had written and now remembered his descriptions of veterinary life with the farmers of this district. It had been a hard life, but rewarding. Farming continued to be a hard life as far as I could see.

We met for coffee and tea after the tour. Grady and Phillip had remained at the farrier site which was part of the tour. Apparently, the tools of the forge fascinated them. We sat in the sunlight looking down the dale toward the rolling hills on the other side.

"It is all so peaceful," Geraldine said.

"It's March," I said, then wished I hadn't commented. Tourist like their romanticized version of the country. I was supposed to satisfy that notion.

"Meaning, in July and August it's teeming with tourists?" Evelyn queried.

"That's right." Summer in the Dales took patience. "This time of year, it's perfect."

"It looks fresh and tranquil," Norma said.

"The world just stops here for a moment, doesn't it?" Amanda said.

We waited for her to explain.

"I mean, it's as if troubles and care never could reach here, like Brigadoon."

It was a magical place. Peaceful, and as Amanda observed, timeless. I loved the Dales, especially at this time of year.

"I need some advice," Amanda said, quite cheerfully. It didn't sound as if she was going to ask us for anything too challenging.

"What kind?" Geraldine leaned forward, ready to help.

"Clothing advice," Amanda said.

Evelyn glanced down at her own jeans and hoodie and shook her head. "Not from me, I wouldn't think." I studied her for a moment. It was true she wore only casual clothes on this tour, but she was an estate agent from Arizona. She showed and sold properties. Surely, she had another wardrobe. That intrigued me. Did she have two closets? One for business attire and one for her normal personality? Which one *was* her normal personality?

Norma looked interested, as did Geraldine.

"What's wrong with your clothes?" Geraldine said. "They look fine to me."

"But definitely not *haute couture*," Evelyn said. I winced. She was blunt.

"Grady says I need to buy conservative clothes that are classic and 'good.'"

"Old-fashioned, is he?" Evelyn criticized.

"A little, I think. He sets a high value on looking respectable."

I had a quick thought that was because he *wasn't* respectable.

"He says he wants my clothes to look ...expensive."

"Is that because he wants you to look like an asset?" Evelyn asked, again critically. I had held back that question because I'd thought it offensive. Evelyn had no such inhibitions.

Amanda frowned. "I don't think so. I think he just wants me to have the best. Grady's a caretaker. He lived with his mother for many years and looked after her. She just died last year. He's used to protecting and caring for someone he loves. It's my job to let him. I don't worry about clothes. I mean I had to support the kids for so long with only minimal help from my ex that I've been used to not buying much. And I can't see the point in it most of the time.

Grady has a different view of clothes. It is as if they give me value. I can't see any harm in buying the clothes he likes--especially when I don't mind."

"And Grady's paying," Evelyn added.

Amanda smiled. "That too."

Geraldine eyes brightened. "We can go with you. Maybe schedule a buying trip to a local town."

"Northallerton," I said. "We can do that." I doubted if the men would like to come. I'd see that they had something to do while we shopped.

Amanda smiled. "That'd be a treat."

"Fun, too," Norma said. "I love spending other people's money."

We laughed and Amanda smiled at her husband as he joined us. They had the air of newly-weds. It made me smile.

Norma requested another half-hour in Thirsk. She had spotted some children playing near Cod Beck, the small river running through the town, and wanted to sketch them.

"You draw?" I said.

"Norma was a kindergarten teacher," Evelyn said. "She can do anything." That was the first fulsome compliment I'd heard from her.

I'd been told that infant school is the most challenging and that teachers of children who could not yet read have to use creativity and innovation to guide their learning. Norma certainly appreciated art and beauty; it wasn't a surprise that she could also sketch.

"Where are you going? "Geraldine asked. "*Precisely,* where are you going?" When I remembered that Norma been lost twice already on this trip, Geraldine's concern seemed legitimate.

"Not far. Just to the end of this street. I'll turn right and the stream is only half a block away. There's a bridge. I'll sit near the bridge."

"Half an hour," Geraldine said.

"Half an hour," Norma promised solemnly.

"Let me draw the map of how to get back here." Evelyn reached for Norma's sketch book.

Norma obediently handed it to her. Evelyn drew a map with the arrows indicating the direction Norma should turn to retrace her steps. If Norma couldn't navigate her way such a short distance where the topography indicated she should go uphill, her sense of direction was definitely deficient. Or perhaps, Evelyn and Geraldine were a little overanxious.

The day was cool without being cold and everyone was agreeable to wandering around the market and into the museum. Evelyn said she was going to investigate the history of the town. She consulted the brochure I'd given her. "According to this, there was a settlement here about 500 BC. They can trace the history of the town through the Doomsday book."

"That was 1086," Geraldine contributed.

"That's right, and it was part of a manor for centuries. Should be lots to look at." She headed off to the museum. The others dispersed. I decided to keep an eye on Norma. She'd shaken me when she'd disappeared in York, and I didn't want that to happen again. From the top of the road I saw her sitting at the edge of the beck. The bridge had a high railing. There was no place there for her to settle, unless she stood. She left the bridge and sat on a rock wall a little apart from the children. They ignored her as she sketched with the book on her lap, looking up occasionally and gazing at the group of three children playing at the edge of the beck. Two of them were about seven-years-old. The third was an older girl of about ten, and all were intent on sending boats into the stream below the weir. They'd attached strings to their boats so they could reel them in if they floated too far away. The current was strong there, stirred up by the turbulence of the weir. Their little red boats with white sails bobbed in the ripples and waves. While this was an attractive park, with green grass on either side and a paved pathway, there was no one else around. I didn't want to disturb the children or Norma so stopped some distance away to watch.

It was an idyllic setting and could have been typical of any time in the past several hundred years: the weir on the beck, the chestnut trees acting as a backdrop that blurred out the nearby houses and shops.

"Lady, do we have to stay still?" the little boy asked Norma.

"Not at all," Norma said. "Move all you like." She smiled at him, and he returned to his play.

"You talk funny," the smallest girl said. "Like the telly."

"I suppose I do," Norma agreed.

"She does not," a bigger girl with dark hair and pale skin said. "She's nice. She gave me a pound. A pound!"

"You have to share, Joanie."

"Nowt for you, Margret" the boy teased.

"I want my share." The smaller girl gave the boy a push.

"A'gate." That was an emphatic "Get away". He pushed back and in seconds the little girl was in the water and out of her depth.

"Now see what you done." Joanie was indignant. "Our mum is going to be right narked. She'll wallop us sure." She was berating her brother and ignoring her sister's plight.

I started to run. The little girl in the water was not swimming.

"Margret," Joanie shouted to her sister. "Stop larking about and get in here. You'll be nithered if you stay there."

She'd be more than cold if she was pulled into the current; she'd be dead. Little Margret was bobbing in the water and traveling downstream.

Norma was on her feet, running past the two children on the shore and alongside Margret whose head was just above water. Norma left the path, dashed across the grass to the edge of the beck and waded in. She grabbed Margret by her jumper and pulled hard. I was a minute behind and waded in after her. The water was icy. We would all be 'nithered' as Joanie suggested. Margret was coughing, but Norma had her safety in tow and managed to pick her up and stagger back to the grass with her. She flopped down; Margret motionless in her arms. Margret's eyes were open and she looked alert. I'd been holding my breath and, now, breathed again. It must be fright that kept Margret rigid. Finally, she stirred.

"There, there, my sweetie," Norma crooned. "You're safe now."

"My boat," Margret wailed. "It be gone."

I looked up and saw the white sail disappear around a corner. In her struggles, Margret had released the string.

"Yes, indeed" Norma said, "it's gone. But aside from being cold, you're all right."

Margret sniffed. "It was proper cold," she said and stared at Norma.

"And scary," Norma said.

Margret nodded solemnly. "Just so." She sniffed.

Norma refrained from pointing out to Margret that she had to be more careful. Margret hadn't fallen into the beck because she had been carelessness; her brother had pushed her. Of course, she'd pushed him first. We didn't get into it.

When the boy trotted up to us, his eyes were huge. "She 'int dead?"

"No," Norma said, "but she could have drowned."

He looked a little sick and retreated to silence.

At that, Margret start to howl.

"Stop your mitherin,'" Joanie bustled forward and barked at her sister.

Margret stopped as if struck mute. I wondered what habitual discipline Joanie used to get that instant response.

"We're goin' yam," Joanie snapped out more instructions.

I translated that to mean they were going home.

"Good idea," I said as I assisted Margret in getting to her feet. "It's too cold to let Margret stand around."

Joanie let out a huge sigh as if the weight of the world was heavy on her ten-year-old shoulders. It probably wasn't the first time the trio had been in trouble.

"Perhaps you could all learn to swim?" I called after them.

Joanie turned to me and then to the shivering Margret. She nodded and trudged up the hill. Norma and I watched them for a moment.

Norma shook her head in wonder. "Intrepid, aren't they?"

"Margret owes you her life."

"That's true. Luckily, she doesn't realize it. You weren't far behind me." Norma returned to the bridge and picked up her sketch book which she had dropped in her dash to the rescue.

I watched her for a moment. She wasn't staggering or shaking. "Let's get you into some warm clothes and find a hot cup of tea. Would that be enough? Are you okay?"

"I'm 'nithered.'" She smiled. "Tea should help. You got wet as well."

"Just my shoes and the lower part of my trousers." I had another pair of shoes in the van, I hadn't gone in the water above my knees—and I wasn't over seventy. I watched Norma carefully, but she appeared unaffected by her dip. I was grateful. I didn't want Norma to suffer, and I didn't want to deal with a shaken elderly woman who required a doctor's care, a trip to the hospital and constant attention. I'd do it all. I'd do whatever Norma needed. I was glad it wasn't going to be necessary.

We walked to the nearest café where I asked for towels and tea. I established her with the tea and darted out to buy her some trousers, a T-shirt, a warm fleecy, underwear and a pair of sandals. She changed at the cafe, I bundled her wet clothes into a bag, and we were only five minutes late meeting everyone at the van.

Norma related her adventure to the group. The subsequent talk acted as a debriefing for her. She seemed to be physically fine after her exposure to the beck, and I supposed incidents of rescuing children were part of the life of an infant school teacher. I imagined fights, falls, insect bites, poisonous plants and the various hazards of childhood. She'd probably seen it all and survived with an inner serenity. I didn't expect any psychological repercussions. In any case, even with her fanciful imagination, I had rarely met anyone so mentally well-balanced as Norma.

CHAPTER EIGHT

We left Thirsk and drove to the Wensleydale Creamery. I'd changed to my Wellingtons which I kept in my van. I don't like driving in Wellies but it was better than wet shoes. I put my shoes, socks and Norma's shoes and socks under the heater. I established Norma in the front of the van where she, also, could get warmth from the heater. She was her usual calm self, contented and happy to observe the countryside.

It was beautiful. The Dales fell away in verdant folds of land with stone walls separating the paddocks. The few clouds in the sky interrupted the sunlight which painted the countryside in light and dark. I stopped several times to accommodate those who wanted to take photos.

Wensleydale Creamery is located near the village of Hawes which is a quintessential Yorkshire village with uniformly historic, stone houses clustered along the road and the Church of St. Margaret slightly up-hill off the main road and hovering over the village. The Tucson ladies were ecstatic.

"So English," Evelyn said.

"So Yorkshire," Phillip corrected.

"Oh, true. All villages aren't the same," Evelyn agreed. "You have to admit it is pretty".

"I do." Phillip smiled at her. I was relieved to see he was making himself agreeable.

"I should have asked my grandmother more about this country," Geraldine said.

"Did she ever return?" I asked.

"Once. I wish I had gone with her on that trip."

"I bet it hasn't changed in centuries," Norma said.

Grady caught Phillips's eye. They grinned at each other.

"It's too old for you?" Geraldine had seen that exchange.

"We like to go with the times," Grady said.

But not, I thought, where Amanda's clothes were concerned. I fancy he wanted her in a twin set and pearls.

I drove thorough Hawes to show my group the picturesque town. "It's been here since 1307," I said. "It's quite high for an English village, 850 feet."

The Tucson ladies laughed. "850 feet? My goodness, that's hardly even a hill."

I thought about the Rocky Mountains, even the Cascades near Seattle. "True. Not high compared to the mountains in your country." Mt. Snowdon in Wales was certainly higher, about 3,500 feet. But 850 feet was enough height to give us a wonderful view.

I pulled into the car park at the Wensleydale Creamery. "This is a must for tourists," I said. "They give samples of cheese, and there's a gift shop."

"Is there anything in it for children?" Grady asked.

I saw Amanda give him a grateful smile. That was one of the things that bothered me about those two. She shouldn't be grateful. That's a dangerous attitude in a relationship. I wasn't grateful to Mark for his love and attention. I enjoyed both. It was a mutual exchange. Gratitude came into it, but gratitude to the universe that allowed us to meet. Not gratitude to Mark. Then, I reminded myself, I wasn't an expert on relationships.

"There are a few things," I told him. I remembered a teddy bear in the gift shop. There might be other appropriate gifts.

The Creamery did excellent tours, and I sent them ahead with their tickets. I detoured to the gift shop and picked up my eight pre-ordered gift hampers. They held substantial samples of cheese, flatbread, chutney and fruit cake. I mixed different articles, so they were not all the same in case the guests wanted to trade items with each other.

They spent more than two hours in the Creamery and joined me for a late lunch in the café. It is located at the back of the production area where the view is spectacular. I sat with my coffee, enjoying the green rolling hills. Black cattle roamed in the higher fields, and white and black sheep dotted the lowers ones. It is always a shock to me to find in this era of manufacturing, fast travel and factories that the world stopped centuries earlier right here. I'm sure the people who live here have tablets, mobiles, TV and on-line shopping. They must have their fair share of quarrels, illness and vice, but they lived in beauty.

I stopped many times on the drive back to Ambleside Farm. The scenery was wonderful and, occasionally, the two men wandered off to check out a stream or a small village while the women gathered around me to hear about the mystery writers of the area.

"Patricia Hall who was really Maureen O'Connor set her novels in Bradford. That's quite a bit south of the Dales."

"She's a bit gritty," Geraldine said.

"Yes, but she has wonderful descriptions. She uses words like a master." Amanda was defensive. "I like her books. Her characters have big flaws."

"The way we all do, hmm?" Evelyn said.

"Yes," Amanda agreed. "They seem more real for that, like someone you might know."

"What about Stuart Pawson?" Evelyn asked. "He's from Yorkshire."

"Yes." I'd read his work. "He is from Yorkshire but from Fairburn which is south of York. I expect these Yorkshire Dales produced farmers and vets and not many writers."

"What about Kate Ellis?" Geraldine asked. "She sets at least one of her novels in Yorkshire. "

"In what she calls Eborb." I said. "I'm afraid that's York".

"Ah, well. The Dales are beautiful and worth seeing." Norma broke up our conversation about writers. "We're going to the moors, aren't we? Lots of writers there."

The men returned from their explorations, seemingly in good spirits and happy with each other's company. It must be Allan Phillip suspected, because Allan wasn't here and Phillip looked relaxed with Grady. Although, I suppose a good detective wouldn't look at someone he was investigating with obvious suspicion.

The afternoon sun lulled the group into soporific mood. Norma dozed in the front seat. I expected from the quiet behind me that everyone was copping a nap.

Out here on the Dales, it was hard to believe in Jason's murder. Even harder to believe any one of my tourists had anything to do with it. Grady was simply getting out of town and enjoying himself. Allan was back at the farm working with the livestock and not interested in much else as far as I could tell. I refused to consider my Tucson ladies.

Everyone who had been on the Dales tour dispersed to their rooms when we returned to Ambleside Farm.

Kala ran towards me. "It was fab, Auntie. You should see the little lamb that was born today." I accompanied her to the barn and duly admired the tottering, spindle-legged, snowy-white lamb.

"They don't name them, because they are not going to stay here long. The ones that stay here get names."

I listened to her chatter and thought how working with animals was healing. I hardly recognized the subdued girl who had arrived yesterday in my lively, enthusiastic, talkative niece.

I caught up with Sheilagh and Allan in the kitchen of the big farm house where they were drinking coffee and reviewing their day.

"You've got a good man, 'ere," Mr. Yowlet, Jr said to Sheilagh. He was about forty-five, almost bald and ruddy-faced. His mother fussed around the table with more coffee and some scones. She put a cup in front of me.

"He be right handy so they tell me," she said nodding at Allan.

Allan appeared tired but happy. "I recalled so much from my boyhood," he said. "How to catch the sheep, calm them, and like Brian said, be handy."

"I was good at bottle feeding the weak ones," Sheilagh said. "It was satisfying. They're cute, little things, and they wriggle."

The work gave them purpose and satisfaction. I admired that about farming. It satisfied the farmers. They probably worried all the time about financial solvency, but they seemed to like their work day to day. Perhaps, the ideal farmer would have enough pension to survive—and farm for the joy of it.

"I learned a lot about the breeding program here," Allan said. "I'll check into the kinds of sheep I want."

"Better get some land first," Brian Yowlet said.

"First, catch your hare," Mrs. Yowlet Jr. said.

I must have looked blank because she explained. "It's from Mrs. Beaton's recipe for rabbit stew. It means …" I nodded. I understood. If you want rabbit stew, you had to first catch your hare. In order to farm, the Whites had to buy one.

The Whites showered and changed and joined us for dinner at The Crosby Inn, the same pub as the night before. I stashed Kala in the back seat which was not as comfortable as the rest, but we weren't going far. We had the same excellent food and everyone enjoyed themselves.

Allan talked more that night than he had on the whole trip. Sheilagh just relaxed and basked in his enjoyment. Phillip was sociable, particularly with the men. Kala was full of her experiences with the lambs and the group included her. Grady asked her intelligent questions, treating her like an adult. I expect he was an attentive father to Amanda's children.

He laughed at some of Kala's descriptions of her mistakes in farming. She'd tried to feed a lamb as if it were a baby, cuddling it against her instead of letting it stand and drink from a bottle held at lamb height.

"Learning takes time," I heard him tell her.

The men abandoned the table at the coffee stage to play billiards in the adjoining room. Kala went with them to watch. The women pulled their chairs closer together.

"Well, done, Sheilagh," Geraldine said. "You've worked a miracle."

"I'm chuffed," Sheilagh agreed. "I thought he was going to disappear into depression."

"Amazing," Amanda said. "You must understand him well."

Sheilagh stared at her for a moment. "You know, I'm not sure I do. I'm surprised that this day of farming has made such a difference. I knew he'd like it. I didn't know he'd... embrace it the way he has." She was worried.

"What's wrong?" I asked.

"It's just...what happens when we go back to Bristol? I'm retiring soon. Our mortgage is paid off. Allan's retiring. We're sound, financially, if we're careful. We can't afford to leave all that...."

"And buy a farm?" Evelyn finished the sentence for her.

Sheilagh looked stricken. "It's not the plan."

"Change," Norma pronounced the axiom, "is always scary."

"It makes me think I might be more flexible with Grady," Amanda said.

"How so?" Norma asked.

"He wants me to quit my job. I'm a paralegal in a solicitor's office. It's an excellent job, and it has allowed me to look after my children. Grady says I don't need the job now, and he would like me to be on hand when he wants to travel. He has outlets for his products all over the country and visits them."

"His chocolates?"

"He distributes more than chocolates. I'm not sure what else. I know he distributes ceramics and linens and souvenirs—you know the kind you see in the tourist shops. It would be fun to travel, but the kids are still young,"

"How young?" Evelyn asked.

"Ten and eight."

Evelyn nodded. "Too young."

Amanda sat back a little abashed. "Too young?"

"Well, too young to leave for long."

"How long have you been married?" Geraldine asked.

I sat like a spectator at a tennis match, my head turning from Geraldine to Evelyn. I could not imagine British women of this age asking such personal questions. Amanda looked a little surprised, but she answered willingly enough.

"Six months."

"Not long enough," Norma said.

This time Amanda stared at her. I don't think she counted on getting advice when she asked for it.

"Give it a few more years. Keep your job. When Grady wants you to go off on a jaunt and you want to stay with your kids, you can say the job won't let you go. It doesn't have to be because of the kids. That way, they won't get in the middle."

Amanda was thoughtful for a moment, as we all were, trying to untangle this advice. Then she said, "I might lose Grady."

Evelyn cocked her head, obviously considering the idea. "That might happen," she said.

I could tell that, as far as Evelyn was concerned, it wouldn't be a great loss. It made me wonder what kind of relationships Evelyn had experienced. Nevertheless, she couldn't expect Amanda to feel the way *she* did. I changed the subject and asked who wanted to go to Northallerton in the morning.

"Shopping?" Norma asked brightly.

"Oh, yes, we have to dress Amanda," Geraldine said.

Amanda smiled. "I'm up for that."

"I'm lambing tomorrow," Sheilagh said. "Sorry to miss it."

The men returned and fetched themselves another cup of tea.

"We are going to buy a farm, Sheilagh," Allan announced.

Sheilagh bit her lip. "I know you love the land and the animals, Allan, but we've never farmed before. We've both worked for a salary, my nursing career and your job with Fanshaw's Imports. We'll have our pensions but...." She hesitated.

I think she suddenly realized she was disclosing her finances to strangers, not something she was comfortable doing.

"I know. I know," Allan said. "I've been talking to Grady here. He's got a head for business. We can plan, so we'll do fine. I want to look into it."

"Planning and management," Phillip contributed.

"Oh," Sheilagh said. "Certainly. We could do that. Look into it, I mean."

She appeared a little dazed with the consequences of her actions. She'd offered Allan two days of farming experience, and he was leveraging it into a life-style change.

"I played billiards, Auntie Claire." Kala leaned on my shoulder and reported on her evening.

"Did you?" I glanced at the men. That was kind of them.

"Mr. Corbett showed me how."

I was grateful for the attention they were paying Kala and grateful that she was her usual, cheerful self in spite of the fading multicolored bruises.

The men decided they'd like to rent a couple of mopeds from the young Yowlet boy who ran a bike and motorbike rental business from the barn. They would explore the countryside in the morning and join us for a late lunch.

Grady was the one who asked me about the mopeds. We were a little apart from the others, and I assured him that I would arrange it.

"That Kala, she looks like someone beat her up."

"It was unfortunate. She may not want to talk about it."

"Do you think that's common? That teenagers beat up on one another? At good schools?"

I thought Grady might have a naive view of "good" schools, but I wasn't going to discuss it. I understood that Grady had children Kala's age and probably wanted to find out what went on in the world of the young so he could help them. Nevertheless, it wasn't my story to tell.

"Hmph," Grady said. "A girl gang?"

"Are there such things?"

"I think so. Now I'm a father, I'm trying to get more educated about the current situation for kids."

"Worrisome," was all I said.

"We haven't had to deal with that yet." He shook his head as if to say, 'What is the world coming to?"

Amanda had had years to plan for her children and to accommodate them. Grady was getting an overwhelming package all at once. I gave him credit for trying hard.

Everyone loaded into the van, and we drove back to Ambleside. Now that we were away from the city, and barring a few minor arguments, the tour was going well. Norma did not seem unduly affected by her dip in the beck. She didn't regard her rescue as anything particularly unusual, and she had the satisfaction of having saved Margret. Her friends seemed to think this was normal for her. I hadn't been around Kala and Josh much when they were that age, but I imagined rescuing was part and parcel of looking after children. It was a relief that Norma had no repercussions. I was happy with Grady and the others. I wished Phillip wasn't with us. He was playing the tourist today, joining in on our activities. I didn't trust him to stay in that role.

CHAPTER NINE

M ark's car was parked outside my room when I pulled into the Ambleside Farmyard. Since we were the only guests at the farm and had filled the rooms, my tourists gave the car their attention.

"Who's that?" Grady asked. "Do you know?"

"My significant other," I replied. "You might remember him from York."

"Oh, yes." Grady said. "I do." He smiled, and I returned the smile. He would welcome Mark, I was sure. Grady had an ability to bond with the men in the group.

I headed to the main farmhouse to check with Mrs. Yowlet Jr., Aelwen. She was at the front desk near the door when I entered.

"Hello," she said. "You be having another with you then? I sent him to walk around the farm while he was waiting."

"My man," I said, using the vernacular of Yorkshire.

"No trouble, luv. Just add his particulars to the registry, would you?"

I wrote in Mark's name and address. "Can you put it all on my bill?" I asked. "It's just easier."

"Aye. T'is no trouble."

Her mother-in-law came through from the breakfast room where she had been laying out the crockery and cutlery for the morning.

"Got a lover have you, then?"

I wondered if she was being critical or just curious. "I do."

She leaned against the banister, delaying her progress to the upper floor.

"Is he satisfactory?" she asked. I wondered what she meant by that. My mind skittered around the many ways Mark was satisfactory. "In what way?"

"Well then, is he a drinker? Does he arse around with your money? I see you're paying for his room. Jammy for him." I glanced over at Aelwen. She had her head in her hands as if she couldn't deal with her mother-in-law one more minute. For some reason I thought that was funny and began to enjoy myself.

"I make him pay for other things. It balances out."

"He has a job now, does he? Mind you, a lot of jobs don't pay."

"He is a detective on the Major Crimes Investigations Team. He gets good pay."

"Oh, aye." She nodded. "A copper. That's exciting. Should ginger up life a bit for thee."

"Sometimes," I agreed.

"And he doesn't spend it all on t'booze, does he? I heard you tell Aelwen here his name. That's Welsh. He's Welsh."

"He is."

"They drink, you know."

I nodded solemnly. "He does, sometimes. But not to excess."

"Imagine that. A moderate Welshman." She shook her head. "Wonders never cease." She stated her prejudice without any awareness of its offensiveness. "You're a lucky woman then, luv." She proceeded up the stairs almost majestically.

Aelwen and I waited until we heard the door shut to her bedroom. I caught Aelwen's eye and burst out laughing.

Aelwen joined me. "Aye, she's a trial sometimes. She's also a dear one."

"Your B & B keeps her young." It certainly kept her interested in the lives of others.

Aelwen closed the registration book. "You're right there, luv. It does, and she's that hard a worker. She makes life easier." She glanced up the stairs, and I could see the affection in her eyes.

I walked back to my deluxe room and was chuckling when I opened my door and met Mark. He swept me up in his arms as if he hadn't seen me in weeks. We had just started to enjoy ourselves when there was a knock on the door.

Mark cursed.

I laughed. "Hey, I'm a tour guide. We are on duty 24/7 like an officer of the law. We're lucky it isn't Kala. She wouldn't knock." I opened the door to Phillip.

I rolled my eyes. "You'd better come in." I hoped Mrs. Yowlet Sr. wasn't looking out her window and putting a salacious slant on Phillips' visit.

"Ferris." Mark said with obvious ill humor. "What do you want?"

"It is more to the point for me to ask what you're doing here?" Phillip said belligerently.

Uh. Oh. "Tea, "I said. "We are all going to sit down and have tea. You will discuss things and not yell at each other in my room."

Mark's lip quirked and his eyes lit with humor. "Yes ma'am. Sit, Hartley. Be civilized."

Phillip sat.

Mark passed around the tea, and we stared at each other for a moment. Two officers of the law, taking up space in my room. I could almost smell the testosterone. Images of strutting roosters and goats butting heads flitted through my mind and were gone. Phillip wasn't staking a personal claim on me. He wasn't the least bit interested in me as a woman. He must be staking a police jurisdictional claim. Now, that was ridiculous. Why wouldn't they cooperate?

"Why are you here?" Philip asked Mark.

"Claire is here and you are here. Obviously, she needs protection."

"Not from me. I agree there are people who might want to lean on her, but I'm here. That's enough protection," Phillip said.

Mark took a sip of tea and stared at him. "Not in my book."

Phillip snorted. "You don't know what you're dealing with."

"Drugs," Mark said.

Phillip said nothing.

"I don't think whoever is behind both the murder of Jason and the drug business is the usual neighborhood gang," Mark said. "They seem more like the Vancouver model."

"What's the Vancouver model?" I might as well learn. Years ago, I'd lived in the beautiful city of Vancouver, Canada, for a few months. What unique role did that city play in the drug world?

"In most of the world, gangs are organized around racial or geographical lines—everyone comes from a certain neighborhood. The Vancouver model is set on the lines of an organized business. The members are recruited for their value to the organizations and, for the most part, racial or neighborhood affiliations are not important. That means, it's hard for us to pinpoint who they are."

I nodded my thanks for the explanation and drank my tea.

Phillip frowned and put his tea down on the end table. "Of course. We know that. It's happening all over Britain, changing the nature of the gangs. Have you found out anything?"

"I did a Holmes search on the men on this tour," Mark admitted, referencing the information resource for police. "And nothing comes up. They seem to be what they say they are. Allan White is an executive in an import-export firm in Bristol and has no criminal record. Corbett is in the same business, but he is a distributor of foods and souvenirs. Does well."

"Does he live beyond his means?"

"Doesn't seem to. He may have Swiss bank accounts or pounds parked in real estate all over the world, but I can't find it."

Phillip was quiet for a moment and then offered, "I did a search myself and didn't find anything. If either of them is managing a drug business, they're hiding it well. I didn't find any consistent travels to the continent. Did you?"

This questioning of each other made me wonder just how separate the different police forces were. I remembered hearing about the problems the police had in finding evidence to convict Peter Sutcliffe, the Yorkshire Ripper, because five different police forces didn't have a system of talking to each other. They fixed the communication problem with the Holmes computer system, a central data bank accessible to all jurisdictions. Someone had a sense of humor to call it the Holmes system after Sherlock Holmes. Still, if no one on this tour had a previous investigation or conviction, they wouldn't appear on that system, and both Phillip and Mark would have to resort to searching social media servers. It could take hours. At least, their animosity had abated, and they were cooperating.

"No. Corbett travels quite a bit. He checks into his suppliers and his distributors. It seems legitimate. White doesn't travel. Stays in Bristol. He could run a business from there. It would make sense to send minions out to check on the business and to enforce it."

"It might be one of the women," Phillip said.

I wasn't having that. "No. Really. Amanda has a job and two kids who keep her busy. Besides, she's far too retiring and . . . I don't know. . . meek to be a drug lord."

"You'd be surprised what good actors some of them are," Phillip said.

"And the Tucson ladies simply couldn't," I persisted.

"Unless they're in it together," Mark said. "What about Mrs. White?"

"Sheilagh," Phillip said. "She has drive and organizational characteristics. I noticed that. I haven't seen or heard anything from her that's suspicious. Not even when they're alone."

Not even when they're alone? I had a sudden, shocking thought. "Have you been listening to conversations?" I demanded. "How could you hear them if they were alone?"

"I have a device, naturally," Phillip said. "I listen in the evenings. I do my job."

"You what?" I shot out of my seat, spilling my tea on the tile floor. I put the cup down on the end table and turned to Phillip. "You have a listening device, and you are spying on my guests!" I held out my hand palm up. "Hand it over."

Phillip looked at Mark.

"Hand it over," Mark said. "It's quasi-legal anyway."

Phillip reached into his pocket and passed me a tiny device that looked like an ordinary ear plug. I located the battery cover on the underside and removed the tiny battery. I put the battery on one pocket and the device in the other. I'd get rid of them when I could figure out where to dump them, safe from inquisitive children. I narrowed my eyes at Phillip.

"Don't *do* that," I said. "My guests are entitled to their privacy." I understood Phillip was looking for a murderer, probably a murderer many times over, but he was unlikely to find such a person on my tour, and my guests wanted their privacy. I felt fiercely protective of my group. Did he listen to Mark and me? The thought of his eavesdropping on our lovemaking made me furious.

Phillip noticed. "I'm out of here," he said. "I'll contact you tomorrow, Evans."

He left and I was shaking with anger when Mark gathered me into his arms and patted my shoulder.

"It's so intrusive," I said into his shirt front. "And on my tour. It's disgusting." Phillip had left me livid. I shook myself and stepped back. "At least I confiscated his device."

"I hate to tell you this, *cariad*, but he probably has another."

When I calmed down, we talked about Kala. Mark listened to my report of what was behind the fight at school. "She's right to be worried about consequences from the gang," he said. "I suppose you don't know what started it?"

"She said she 'smart-mouthed' a girl named Judith."

Mark knew about this. "Disrespect. The gangs are high on disrespect. It can get you murdered. She might have to change schools and stay a long way away from that Judith."

"That seems such a severe consequence. She has so many friends in the school."

"They aren't worth her murder."

He had a point.

In the morning, I ignored Phillip. After breakfast, he and Grady took their mopeds and roared out the driveway, heading for the hills beyond the farm. Mark drove his own car to Northallerton where he had promised to check in with the local police. He'd decided not to ask for official blessing on his investigations from his superintendent back in Hampshire because it would take too much time and involve too much paper work. He had a week off to be with me. He hoped he wouldn't have to let Superintendent Addison know what he was doing. She would not approve of him investigating a murder that occurred in York and for which she had not received an official request for help. Of course, the Northallerton police might ask her for it.

The ladies, minus Sheilagh who was working as a land girl for Brian Yowlet and Kala who was doing the same for Freya, herded together to assist Amanda in her shopping. We wandered through a few shops but ended up at the Edinburgh Woollen Shop which is one of a chain. The styles suited Amanda. She didn't want to spend a lot even if Grady did.

"Buy a conservative cut," Evelyn said. "but a lively color."

"Yes. Brighter than you usually wear." Norma picked out a magenta jumper. "This sweater would be a wonderful color on you."

Evelyn gave more advice. "Look modern in the colors you choose but old fashioned in the style." I was surprised to find such detailed advice from someone who insisted she wasn't stylish.

Geraldine approved. "That's right. Let the colors express your personality."

We picked out a few jumpers and two pairs of trousers for her and wandered down the street to find a small dress shop, very expensive, very exclusive, where the proprietor offered assiduous attention.

My Tucson ladies all talked at once. The proprietor, a Yorkshire woman with an elegant air, sorted out what Amanda required. She went to her racks and pulled out a cherry red suit that made Amanda's skin glow.

Amanda tried it on.

"Perfect." We breathed the accolade together.

Amanda passed over Grady's VISA and charged it.

"Enough shopping," she said as we left the store. "That was a month's rent when I was on my own. It feels strange."

"You can get used to it," Evelyn said.

"I need some souvenirs," Geraldine told us. We hunted through the stores and found a souvenir shop that had the usual ceramic souvenirs as well as some more artistic ones. I thought the ceramic birds were exquisite, and I knew Kala would like one. Typical of Yorkshire were the black grouse, the reed bunting, sky lark and the grasshopper warbler.

I found a set of salt and peppers in the shape of the black grouse, dramatic and skillfully made. I picked them up. Lovely. Good price, I'd take them. I turned one over to see if it was locally made and saw a London maker's name fired into the mold, and an inked stamp of a raven on top of it. Interesting.

The ladies were busy at the other end of the shop when I brought my selection to the clerk.

"That's a lovely set," he said with the professional shopkeepers need to flatter the taste of the purchaser. He was a young man of about twenty-four, and very polite.

"I'm interested in the stamp on the bottom. Is there any significance in it? Does it indicate who designed it?"

He turned the bird over and stared at the stamp. He stayed very still for a moment. I eyed him curiously and noticed sweat on his forehead.

"Those are not supposed to be out on the shelves." he said. "That was…it was a special order. I'm going to get into trouble."

He held the birds in one hand and looked past me. "They were at the end, weren't they?"

"Yes, at the back."

He left the till and marched down to where I'd found the black grouse. He picked up a different set. They were exactly the same. He turned one over and grunted.

"Phew. Here. I will wrap up these for you." He put the original set in his pocket.

"What's the difference?" I asked.

He took a moment to answer, returning to the till and reaching for tissue to wrap my purchase.

"Not a lot, but the stamped ones are part of a set I'm sending out as a wedding present. We stamped every piece so we would be sure to get it all together. If you hadn't noticed this, the customer would be missing their salt and pepper."

"Oh, I see." No wonder he was worried. "And you would be blamed?"

"Indeed," he said. "I definitely would be blamed." Then his posh veneer slipped a little. "They'd think me a right git."

In Yorkshire, that was an imbecile.

"It makes no difference to me," I said, trying to reassure him. "They look exactly the same."

"Thanks for letting me know about the stamp." He found his posh accent again. "I would appreciate it if you didn't tell anyone else, because I'm going to slip these into the wedding package and not own up to my mistake." He gazed at me with the appeal of a puppy.

"All right," I said. "My lips are sealed." Some employers never forgot the mistakes made by their employees. Vastly unfair as we all blunder at times.

"Thank you," he said with a sigh of relief.

The men had disbursed to the books store, the priory, the museum and various pleasure of Northallerton. They all had my mobile number if they needed me to chauffer them. We met for dinner at the Tithe Bar and Brasserie where Mark joined us.

When he walks into a room, my shoulders ease. It`s as though he surrounds me with a protective bubble of warmth. I can look after myself; I`d been alone for years. I manage life quite well— except in emergency situations where I tend to freeze, and I'm content. But I *feel* safer with Mark. It was inexplicable. I smiled at him and received an answering smile that lit his eyes. I felt lucky to have found him.

He slid onto a chair beside me and joined our conversation about the souvenir stores. I'd liked to have added my story about the mix-up with the wedding present. Since I'd promised the clerk not to say anything, I refrained.

"You distribute souvenirs, don't you, love?" Amanda asked Grady.

"I do. I usually try to drop into the stores when I'm traveling, to see how well they display them. I can tell by my receipts at the office how much they sell, but I like to know why the souvenirs do better in one store than another. And sometimes I can only understand that by observing."

That comment stimulated Allan to talk about the way imports and export goods sold in waves and then receded.

"Some countries order tons of Vitamin K for some reason. And then they stop."

"You sell pharmaceuticals?" Grady asked.

"Among other things," Allan said. "I don't personally sell them. I just see the orders are filled."

That sparked Evelyn to talk about the way in which mystery

books burst out in sales along a theme. "Cupcakes. Who would have thought you could have a mystery series on cupcakes."

"That series sells very well," Geraldine said.

"I agree," Evelyn said. "But I never would have predicted it."

We left the restaurant together. Mark put the mopeds in the boot of his vehicle tying it down with bungee cords. That way, Phillip and Grady didn't have to ride home in the dark. We drove to Ambleside Farm about ten in the evening and dispersed to our respective bedrooms.

Mark put his mobile on the charge on his bedside table. I put mine on a charge on the desk. I peeked in on Kala. She was asleep. The puppy lifted its head then snuggled back to Kala's warmth. All was well there. I'd give her the black grouse set in the morning.

I had a bath and thought about the day. It was a little strange to find that ceramic salt and pepper set with the raven stamped on the bottom. What did I know about the symbol of a raven? I spent a few minutes after my bath on the internet, looking up the raven as a symbol. In Greek mythology, it meant bad luck, a messenger bringing a prophecy to the receiver—usually not an encouraging one. Would that mean that anything stamped with a raven contained a message? Some cultures saw the raven as a bringer of good fortune, particularly food. Norse mythology attributed the raven as the eyes and ears of Odin. Were the stamped articles meant to tell the recipients to supply information? That was possible. From my years on the west coast of North America, I knew the raven was a mythological figure in First Nations legends. It was a trickster, an instigator of mischief and had the ability to change people's lives. I clicked off the computer with explanations for the raven symbol tumbling around in my mind. Poor clerk. He was definitely upset. I was just going to join Mark in bed when an idea hit me with the impact of a mallet. Another name for raven was corbett. Grady's last name was Corbett.

CHAPTER TEN

In the morning, I was too busy to concern myself with the meaning of anyone's name. I had gift bags in place for each person in the van. I'd checked the reservations for supper, and I'd answered four emails from people interested in my next tour. I called Kala's Uncle John to make sure he was coming to get her today. I gave her the grouse set, which pleased her immensely and said my goodbye to her.

The dark green hue around her damaged eye had faded to a puce color. Her eyes were brighter, and she looked more cheerful than she had when she'd arrived.

"Thanks, Auntie Claire. It was great here. Freya's going to text me and send me pictures of the new lambs. Maybe I can come back sometime?"

"Absolutely," I said. I'd talk to her mother and see she had a chance to return. "Possibly in term break." Deirdre could arrange for the whole family to come. I tried to image Deidre in Wellingtons wading through muck. She'd do it, but she wouldn't like it.

Mark was up early. I hadn't asked him what he was planning, but he said he might join us for our picnic on the moors. Holiday time. He'd said something earlier about taking holidays.

"Where are you planning to stop?" He rubbed my shoulder and caressed my neck. It felt warm and comforting. I had to get used to being touched with such affection. Mark did it casually when we were alone. I wasn't quite as spontaneous, but I might learn. "I know you have a definite plan."

Of course, I had a plan. "At the Cross."

"Ralph's Cross?" he said.

"That's right. It's a good place for a picnic. I know it's on private land but no one ever bothers us."

"Good spot. Great views and about half-way to Whitby. I'll get a picnic box from Mrs. Yowlet."

We would cross the Yorkshire Moors on our way to the seaside town of Whitby. It was a spectacular trip. I wouldn't rush through it.

"I'll take my time, stopping to let them get pictures of the moors. The new grass should be greening up and the heather might be in bud. I hope it isn't too cold."

"Always cold on the moors."

There were miles and miles of windswept country, hills and dales, with no mountains or ridges to restrain the weather. I thought of Emily Bronte and her bleak view of the undulating moors, hillside and dales inhabited by sheep, cattle, rabbits and voles. It would be too isolated for me. Not that Emily Bronte had lived out on the moors. She'd lived in a nearby village, but she understood the moors. They certainly feature in *Wuthering Heights*.

Allan and Sheilagh were the last to load into the van as they had to check on the lambs they'd been feeding the previous two days.

"Everyone's doing well," Sheilagh said.

"The farm is very busy right now," Alan said with what sounded like worry in his voice, as if the farm couldn't get along without him.

I checked my rear-view mirror before I pulled out of the yard and noticed how eager and alive the Whites were today. Their faces were more relaxed and they looked ten years younger. Maybe Allan should retire and buy a farm. It might even suit Sheilagh, once she was used to it.

I headed south toward Thirsk and then east onto the moors.

Norma was in the front right passenger seat today. She was fascinated by the landscape.

"Emily, Charlotte, Anne and Bramwell. Imagine living in all this wonder."

I did not correct her perception that the Brontes had lived on the moors. I read a study that reported tourists were satisfied with their trip if their experience met their expectations, no matter how inaccurate or inauthentic. This experience of the moors where Norma thought they'd lived was matching her expectation of the Bronte's world. Perfect.

We arrived in the North York Moors National Park where heather and grass sit on top of thin peaty soil. It is a huge track of land, the biggest moor in the country. At some points, there was such a broad vista that it was like looking at a sea of heather. It reminded me of the tundra of northern Canada where I once visited. Except in Canada, if you headed off over the tundra, you might be lost in thousands of acres of wilderness and never found. Here, the National Park is about five hundred square miles. That's just the park area. More wild moors are in private hands, so it's huge but possible to navigate. If you were lost on the moors and kept walking downhill, you'd eventually find a village.

In the fall, the vista is a deep purple. Today, it was variegated green with the moss green of the heather and the bright chartreuse of the new grasses, periodically broken by pockets of blue water.

"I wouldn't want to slip off the path into that bog," Evelyn said.

"Not a good idea, I agree." I'd never wandered on the moors, and I didn't plan to.

"You can disappear into some of those bogs," Phillip said. "They can be deep."

I smiled to myself. There is nothing like a bit of danger to add excitement to the day—when you are safely inside a vehicle.

"I bet Heathcliff could wander over this country without falling in." *Wuthering Heights* was a classic. Norma knew her literature.

"That's such a melodramatic tale," Geraldine contributed. "Full of passion and obsessive love. You wonder how such an innocent as Emily Bronte could have dreamed that up."

"Thousands have wondered," Evelyn said.

I'd wondered myself. How did such a protected, restricted and isolated young woman come to understand sexual passion? Was it simply imagination? Observation? Doubtful, but just possible.

My tourists stared at the vast panorama.

"Gorgeous," Amanda said. "I haven't seen anything like this before."

"You've never been here?" Grady asked, sounding surprised.

"Never," she said. "Much too busy, and it isn't a trip I thought the kids would like." She stared out the window again. "I might have been wrong about that."

It often surprised me how many people in England didn't travel far from their homes. In America, people would travel a hundred miles for a concert or to visit some site. Not here. Not usually.

"Have you been here before?" I asked Grady.

"A few times. Not the route we're going. I skirted the moors to the south and just went north to Whitby."

"That is the way most people travel when driving up from the south," I said. Today, I was driving east through the north part of the moors.

"I am seeing much more on this route," Grady said.

"Who are the authors who wrote about this area, Claire, besides the Brontes who aren't strictly speaking mystery writers?" Norma asked.

"More like frustrated romance writers," Evelyn said.

I burst out laughing. "I take it you don't care for Victorian novels?"

She shrugged. "No, not that kind. I guess that's obvious. Who set stories in this area that I might like?"

"How about Nicolas Rhea, the name Peter Walker used when he wrote the Constable series. Remember. *Constable on the Hill*? *Constable Around the Moors*?"

"Wasn't there a TV show set on those books?" Phillip said.

"Yes, *Heartbeat*."

"I've seen that," Grady said.

"There you are. Something we've all experienced." Norma was pleased.

"Oh, yes," Geraldine said, "And *Constable around the Park*. That one was set on these moors as well. Didn't he find a body up here?"

"Strictly speaking, he found the body in a shed, but the shed was on the moors." Evelyn corrected her.

"Lovely," Norma said. "We'll look for bodies."

Grady laughed. "You ladies are surprising. To look at you, no one would think you ever even thought of murder."

I'm not sure if my Tucson ladies heard that as a compliment. Was he implying they looked staid?

"I agree it's hard to consider murder when we are surrounded by such beauty," Norma said with a slight stiffness in her voice. "It's incongruous somehow."

"I expect it's the puzzle of the solution to the murder that you like," Allan suggested.

"It is." Norma agreed. "And the motivations of the perp."

We stopped several times for pictures. The breeze was brisk, so we didn't linger. The pictures would be beautiful as the periodic sunshine created landscapes of sun and shadow on the heather, grasses and rocks. The road climbed to Ralph's Cross. I pulled over and turned off the engine. The cross stood stark against the vast sky, dark and dramatic.

"I will tell you about this cross, before we get out of the van," I said "because the air might be cold, and we may need to picnic quickly."

"What is the significance of this cross?" Norma asked, settling back in her seat as if waiting for a bedtime story.

"There are a couple of different legends about it, but the one most commonly held around here is that a farmer named Ralph found a body here of a traveling man who had starved to death, since he had no money for food. Ralph felt such a compassion for him that he erected the cross with a depression on the top of it so travelers on horseback could leave shillings for those who didn't have any, and thus prevent another death."

Norma stared at the cross more than six feet above the ground. "How do those poor, weak, hungry travelers reach the top of that cross to take a penny?"

"Good question," I said. "I have no idea."

They gathered around the back door of the van while I handed out thermoses of coffee, packages of sandwiches, pickles, cheese and sweets. It was a little chilly but not freezing. They took their lunch and wandered along the trails near the cross. Some of those trails dipped into hollows. I couldn't see them all the time, but I didn't think they'd go far. The warning about dropping into a deep bog and disappearing should act as a caution. As usual at many a British site, there were no warning signs about dangers. Tourists were supposed to act sensibly. I tried to keep one eye on Norma in case she decided to meander away, but she blended in with the other tourists and I soon lost sight of her. I hoped either Geraldine or Evelyn paid attention so we wouldn't have to drag Norma out of the bog.

A bus pulled up and disgorged about twenty-five people, all with quilted down jackets and cameras. The tour guide for the bus walked over to me. He was about thirty, well dressed in cold-weather gear and friendly.

"You have just a small tour?" he asked.

"Yes. My preference. I have them for two weeks. What about you?"

"I have them for two weeks as well, and they're a handful. They are always polite, but very demanding."

I scanned his group. "Do you speak Japanese?"

"I do," he said. "Essential for this tour."

"Good for you." I was restricted to English, although I could probably stutter through Italian.

Another small van pulled up and disgorged twelve tourists. I heard them speaking English. It was probably one of the day trips from York. I'd taken one of those when I was a teenager and enjoyed it. The guide, a young woman this time, was also dressed in cold-weather gear.

"Hi. I'm Jane."

We introduced ourselves. The big-bus guide was Aaron.

"Which story did you tell about the cross?" Jane asked me.

"The dying traveler one," I said. "And you?"

"I have a lot of older ladies in this tour so I opted for the monk and the nun romance."

"I told that one as well," Aaron said. "It generates a lot of talk as my group tries to figure out what a monk and a nun are, and why they were having a romantic liaison here at the cross."

Jane glanced around. "It's an uncomfortable spot for a liaison, that's certain."

I tried to find my tourists in this now populated hill top. I saw the three Tucson ladies and the Whites. Good. Norma was safe. They were taking pictures of the cross and the rolling vista behind it. I moved over to watch them follow Phillip down a short trail to the peat bog. The two tour guides ambled off to answer questions from their guests.

I spotted Mark's car inching in behind the big bus. He parked, locked it and walked toward me, pulling up his collar. He wasn't wearing an insulated jacket.

"Hi," he smiled.

"Busy morning?"

"So, so." He came closer, slipped his arm around my shoulders and gave me a quick hug. We stood companionably watching the scurry of tourists wandering over the site, their colorful jackets mixing and moving like a kaleidoscope. I saw my group, or at least most of them climbing back up to the car park.

I heard a chatter of voices like disturbed starlings, rising in volume and then a scream. I stared at people at the bottom of the slope. Several of the Asian tourists were grouped around something on the ground hidden by a tall clump of heather. As I watched, they streamed back toward the bus. Mark bounded down into the hill toward the spot they had just vacated. I trailed a little behind him. My tourists stood watching from the top of the hill. I counted them. Phillip was missing. He was always missing.

Mark stood transfixed for a moment beside the bush, looking down. He dropped to his knees.

I hurried to join him. The heather was not yet in bloom. There was no purple on that bush, just the green leaves and white buds. Beyond the heather and beside a small wet section of bog lay Phillip. Mark flipped him on his back, felt for a pulse at the carotid artery and pulled back Philip's head.

"Can you do chest compressions?" he demanded.

I stood stock-still for a moment. This can't be happening. I stared at Mark stupidly, then focused on his question. "I can." I'd trained for this when I obtained my guide license. I knew how. I hadn't helped Jason. I would try on Phillip.

Mark breathed into Phillip with regular bursts of air. I kept up steady compressions at a rate of about 100 a minute, stopping after 30 to let Mark breath into Phillip's mouth then continuing. It was hard work. I expect it made more sense for Mark to do the compressions and me the breaths, but I didn't suggest we change.

"Can I help?" I heard a voice behind me. It was Sheilagh.

"Call 999," Mark said. "And keep everybody back. It might be a crime scene." Phillip had been his colleague if not his friend.

"Mark," I said gently, puffing a little with exertion. "There've been at least ten tourists milling around here." There wouldn't be much for the CID forensic team to find.

"Yes. Yes. That's right. Even so, better keep people back. There might be something for the SCOs."

Specialist Crime Operators. I didn't think they would be the ones to respond. I didn't put any energy into trying to sort out the British police system.

While I putting my weight on Phillip's chest, Mark was searching for a viable pulse.

"Nothing?" I asked.

"No."

"We called 999." I heard Allan behind Sheilagh. I was too busy to turn around and look.

"I'm a nurse." That was Sheilagh behind me.

"Take over from Claire," Mark instructed.

Sheilagh slipped into my place and continued the compressions. I stood back and took the position of protector, ready to keep the curious away should they come too close. I was exhausted and took a moment for a couple of deep breaths.

Sheilagh and Mark kept the CPR going for what felt like an hour but was probably about fifteen minutes until the police arrived and, quickly after them, the medics. Mark and Sheilagh stepped back and let them take over. They loaded Phillip into the ambulance. They weren't doing CPR when they reached the ambulance. That wasn't a good sign.

Mark looked wooden as if he was storing away ideas and emotions. I glanced around. The Asian tourists and their bus were gone. The small van and her tour had left as well. The rest of my group stood together around the cross, watching and waiting. They were all there. I turned to the two police officers who had answered the call.

"Dead?" I said to the nearest officer.

"Looks like it." He pulled his notebook from his jacket pocket. "Can you tell me who he was?"

"He was a member of my tour. D.I. Evans can tell you more."

The constable directed a sharp look toward Mark. I doubted Mark was going to make a secret of his detective inspector rank or of Phillip's deployment by Scotland Yard.

"I'll get back to my tour. I'll get them into the van. It's cold."

"I need your names and addresses, starting with yours, madam." He nodded at Sheilagh.

We gave him the information.

"Don't leave. I'll want to interview your tourists."

"All right." I moved slowly toward the cross.

"Thanks, Sheilagh," I said.

"Sorry we weren't successful." She kept her head down. As a nurse, she must have had years of experience with death and dying. It was probably frustrating for her to be unable to revive him, and sad.

"Me too." I hadn't liked Phillip, but I hadn't wished him dead and was shocked by it. He'd been white and silent. No snapping black eyes, or searing intelligence left to him now. I shuddered.

"I suppose we'll have to stay around to be interviewed by the police," Sheilagh said.

"Yes. We'll have to stay." I concentrated on Sheilagh. While used to death, she might need a little comfort.

The constable had acted properly. He was likely cursing the tours that got away. I could tell him the names of the tour companies and the first names of the guides. He could send someone to intercept them. Phillip could have died a natural death. In that case, no one would go to much trouble to hunt down witnesses.

No, I was wrong. They wouldn't just let it go. Phillip worked for Scotland Yard and, even though there was rivalry between the different police forces, all forces would consider Phillip one of their own and give extra care and attention to this investigation. "Officer down," is what they called it in American films. The British police had a similar solidarity with their own. They would investigate even if only to *prove* Phillip died of natural causes.

I herded my group into the van and produced another thermos of coffee, started the van and turned on the heater. In about ten minutes, we were warm enough to be comfortable with the engine off.

Mark was sitting in the police car with one officer. The other came over to the car. Norma spotted him and rose from the passenger seat. She gestured to him. "You can sit there. I'll get in the back."

"Thanks."

"Get in, constable," I said. "It's cold out."

"Ta," he said and took Norma's place.

"My name is Constable Mike Patel. I have Ms Barclay's and Mrs. White's name and address. I will need all your names."

They gave their names and addresses and waited in silence for more information or more questions. When he had finished, he put down his notebook and turned to look at the group.

"Did anyone see anything suspicious around Mr. Ferris?"

They looked at him blankly

"Phillip," I translated. "He had another name."

They absorbed that information, then Norma spoke. "I saw him go down the hill toward the pond at the bottom. Well, we all went down, didn't we?" She turned to check with the others.

Geraldine leaned forward from the back seat. "We did. We wanted to see a real peat bog up close, but we didn't want to fall into it. Phillip guided us."

"He had his camera out. He was always taking pictures," Evelyn said. "He told me that in the spring you could sometimes get good pictures in a boggy spot. Flowers, I think".

"Yes, he showed me some kind of pink flower," Grady said. "I left him to it. Flowers are not an interest of mine."

The constable half-smiled. I suppose they weren't passion of his either.

"Did anyone see him collapse?" Constable Patel continued.

They exchanged glances and shook their heads.

"He often went off on his own," Evelyn contributed. "He liked his own company, so as Grady says, we left him to it."

"Wasn't his death natural?" Geraldine asked the question we all wanted answered.

"It could be, madam. There were no signs of obvious foul play. We won't know until the autopsy and toxicology reports come to us. We treat all sudden deaths as suspicious until proven otherwise."

"If he had two names," Evelyn observed. "It's highly likely to be 'otherwise.'"

CHAPTER ELEVEN

When Constable Patel left us in the van, we sat for a few minutes in silence, then I turned to the group. "Would you like to go back to the farm?" A death is upsetting. Personally upsetting to them and to me. At some point, I was going to have to think about how it might impact my business. Death on a mystery tour is not the best advertising. I'd consider that later. Right now, my guests had had a shock and needed my attention. Most of them were elderly. They were so lively, I often forgot that. They might want to rest.

There was silence.

"Or," I said, "we could continue on to Whitby where we're scheduled to go this afternoon."

"It was a natural death, wasn't it?" Amanda asked. She was expressing the wish of most, I was sure.

Sheilagh spoke calmly. "We don't know how he died. He might have had a heart attack. There didn't seem to be any signs of injury."

"No blood, knives or gunshot wounds, you mean?" Geraldine said.

Sheilagh was silent for a moment, then said, "That's right."

Evelyn offered her opinion. "I lost a lot of friends in their forties. It seems to be the time when underlying medical issues fell quite a few. When you get past that, you have a statistically greater chance of living a long time. It's natural to lose some." Evelyn certainly appeared to be tough and destined to hike into her 90s.

"That's true enough," Norma said. "Death is tragic, but natural."

They may think it had been natural, but Mark was going to treat it as murder.

 Evelyn said. "I'm sorry the poor man died, but I didn't know him well, and I would like to continue." Her voice was decisive.

"What about the rest of you?" I asked.

"Let's go on," Geraldine said.

"I'd like to continue," Amanda echoed Geraldine's opinion. Grady agreed with her.

Allan spoke slowly. "I could return to the farm. I'd spend all my time there, if I was honest. But this is a tour, and I say, 'Let's tour.'"

"I've never been to Whitby," Sheilagh said a little wistfully.

"You don't live that far away from it, do you?" Norma asked her.

"Not by American standards. I've just never had the occasion to go there. I'd like to."

The consensus decreed that we continue to the sea. I turned on the ignition and prepared to leave for Whitby. Mark tapped on my van window. I lowered it.

"I'm going to be tied up at the nick in Whitby." His voice quick and crisp. He was in officer mode. I mentally pictured the police station in Whitby.

"I thought so."

"Catch you back at the farm tonight?"

"See you then," I said, and we left.

The moors were beautiful and the vista wide and wonderful, but the joy had left the day. Had Phillip been murdered because he was from Scotland Yard and getting too close to the gang leader? Was simply being a member of the police force enough to entice someone to murder him? If that was so, Mark was in danger. I felt hollow as if a huge abyss of worry had opened. Threats to Mark that I had previously kept away from conscious thought crowded in now. He walked in danger every day. I swallowed. Phillip's death made that obvious. I had to face it. I took a deep breath and let out a controlled exhale. I was driving. I could not fall apart. Now was not the time to consider the precarious nature of Mark's job. I pushed my mind to plans for the afternoon and tried to salvage the tour. I activated the mic when we were about twenty minutes from the Whitby Riverside Car Park.

"Whitby as you may know is spread on either side of the Esk River. Captain Cook grew up nearby and his ship *The Endeavor* was built here. It was a flat-bottom collier, a coal ship, and ideal for his explorations as he could beach it and repair it fairly easily. There's a Captain Cook museum here containing much information."

"He was killed in Hawaii, wasn`t he?" Norma asked.

"He was, and that always seemed to me to be ironic, because he was one of the enlightened captains who respected native peoples of the lands he visited."

"That's sad," Norma said. "Unfair, even."

I'd always felt that way. Fate could have knocked off several bigots before it got around to Captain Cook.

"What else is there to see in Whitby?" Amanda asked. "Is there a wool shop?"

"Probably. I'll look it up when we arrive and get you the address."

"Feeling the need to calm yourself, love?" Grady said.

"Yes. Knitting is soothing, and I could use that today."

"I feel that way about bookshops," Geraldine said.

"There's a bookshop on Church Street." I knew where all the bookshops were in any town or city I'd ever visited.

"There is also a castle...well, rather a ruined Abbey... on the hill overlooking the town. It was built in 657 by King Oswey of Northumbria and suppressed in 1539 by Henry VIII. The abbey's celebrity is St. Hild who organized a Synod for the Church where they decided to follow the Roman philosophy rather than the Celtic. So, it is an important site and there is a fabulous view from there."

"Hild, not Hilda?" Geraldine asked.

"That's right." Every county in England has its own particular saints—some of them never heard of outside that county.

We left the wide expanses of the moor behind and dropped down from the low hills into farmlands and into dales. Green fields divided by stone fences surrounded us as far as we could see until we approached the mouth of the river Esk at the edge of the North Sea.

I pulled into the car park near the river and shut off the motor. The ruins of the abbey in crumbling antiquity rose before us with the old town squatting at its base. As I remembered it, the old town bustled with Yorkshire folk, tourists and dogs. I found the address for the wool shop and texted it to Amanda.

"You have two hours to do whatever you want to do here and then, please, meet at the Magpie Café. It's on Pier Street. They have excellent food, and it's near the river. You should enjoy the view."

They agreed to meet at the appointed time and dispersed. I slipped into Sherlock's Cafe, and texted Mark. Surprisingly, he was free and the nick was only a half block from the restaurant. I suspected the proximity to the police station was why it was called Sherlock's Café. I ordered coffee from a passing wait staff as Mark slid onto the bench across from me.

"I suppose the local constabulary called in Scotland Yard." Since Phillip had been an officer of the Metropolitan Police, the real name for Scotland Yard, they would want to be involved in the investigation. As usual, there would be several jurisdictions engaged.

"Of course. They had to. And, they wanted to. For all they know, Hartley was on the track of an international criminal, and the Yard needs all the evidence it can get."

"I suppose they'll be searching his room at the farm. Scotland Yard, I mean." I wondered if Phillip had bat ears listening devices tucked away in a drawer.

Mark agreed. "He might have left information there. I searched his pockets before they put him into the ambulance and gave everything to the local constable. I didn't see anything worth keeping."

"Did you find a listening device?"

"I gave it to the constable."

Mark had been right. Phillip had had more than one.

We were quiet for a moment, thinking of Phillip and the end of his life.

I took in a deep breath and let it out slowly. "Mrs. Yowlet. I should let Aelwen know about this."

Mark jerked his head up. "Shit. I should have thought of her earlier. Whoever killed him might go to the farm."

"I'll call." I did so and reached Aelwen. I told her that Phillip had died on the moors and that the police would likely be coming to search his room, because a sudden death had to be investigated.

"Tell her not to let anyone into the room without a warrant card," Mark instructed.

I told her that and then listened.

"She says," I told Mark, "that there's a man there right now, insisting he is a police officer, but he won't show her his warrant card."

Mark grabbed my mobile and spoke to her. "Take a picture of him and send it to me quickly."

I heard my mobile ping. Mark glanced at the picture and said, "Now, tell him you just sent his picture to me. and that I am the police on the line."

She must have done that because Mark half-smiled and handed the phone back to me. I stared at the picture. I'd never seen that man before. I put the phone to my ear.

"What happened, Aelwen?" I tried to imagine her being threatened by someone impersonating a police officer.

"Our Ma came down the stairs and started scolding him as if he were a young'en. He'd tracked in mud, and she gave him a right wigging. He stared at her and at me, then I couldn't see his face for t'dust," Aelwen said. "Strewth! I've never seen a man move so fast, even with a bull chasing him. It was a treat to see the speed of him."

Mark gave instructions. "Tell Aelwen I'll ask the Whitby police to contact her local station and send a constable out there to guard the place until Scotland Yard arrives."

Even when I knew the convoluted policing system, I found it hard to understand. I concentrated, relayed the information, then queried, "Do you know your local bobby?"

"Oh, aye," she said. "It's Brandy Cawson's son, Aiden. He's doing right well for himself. I'll give him a call."

"That might be faster," I said. "Keep yourself safe, now."

"Oh, for certain I will. Tarra." She said a quick goodbye.

I disconnected and reported to Mark. "She's going to ask the local constable, whom she knows, to come out for a chat and stay with her until Scotland Yard or a directive from his chief comes through."

"Smart," Mark said. "Send that picture to my mobile, will you?

I did that. I thought about how quickly the criminals showed up at the farm after Phillip's death. That was chilling.

"Someone knew Phillip was Hartley and a Yard agent," I said.

Just then, Mark's mobile rang.

He checked the ID and answered. "Ma'am?"

It must be Superintendent Addison, his boss.

He listened for a few moments, then said. "Right away. Who do I report to?"

I mentally corrected his grammar. 'To whom do I report.' But few people used that form any more. Another piece of archaic grammar that has disappeared. "Such as" and "as if" have been replaced with "like" which is not as precise. Did that mean that, as we lose precise expressions, we become lazy thinkers? I wrenched my attention back to Mark.

His eyebrows rose as he listened. He didn't respond until his superintendent stopped speaking.

"Yes, ma'am. I can do that. I'll let the Whitby Chief Superintendent know if I find anything and I will let you know as well. Do you want to inform the Yard?"

Whatever the answer was it caused him to roll his eyes.

When he disconnected, I said, "Your superintendent?"

"Yes. Addison. She told me to report to Chief Superintendent Simon Whelan of North Yorkshire who is in Whitby and who will communicate with Scotland Yard."

"So much for your intention of doing this investigation without her knowledge. How did she know you were here? You didn't tell her you were involved in this, did you?"

He shook his head. "Fawthrop did."

"She won't be best pleased."

"She isn't."

Mark officially reported to Superintendent Addison in Hampshire. He was also on the national Major Crimes Investigation Team, so he could report to a Chief Superintendent or the Chief Constable in any county who would outrank his superintendent. The inquiry here was being headed by the Yorkshire Constabulary. Chief Superintendent Whelan would head it. It was confusing.

"It sounds as though it's a perfect way to lose information and time."

"It is. *Cywir.*" I knew that word. It meant correct. He stared at his coffee cup and frowned. Hartley had been, if not a friend at least a long-time colleague. I don't suppose Mark was comfortable with the way the investigation into Hartley's death was being organized. The chances of its being a natural death, in spite of my tourists' fervent wish, were slim.

He sat there for another few minutes then punched in a number on his phone. He seemed to have to wade through a phone tree and receptionists before he connected with the person he was calling.

"Sir? D. I. Evans here, Major Crimes investigation Team, Hampshire Constabulary."

He listened for a moment.

"Yes sir. I was traveling with Ferris, but I was not on the same file he was investigating." He listened again then said, "I'm staying at the farm where Ferris was staying. Would you like me to search his room? I can leave everything where it is so the Yard can't complain I've interfered."

I wished I could hear what was being said at the other end.

"I can pick up some booties and gloves at the station here in Whitby if you will authorize it."

Again, silence then, "Yes, sir, Superintendent Addison insisted I report to you and I will do that."

Another silence then, "Thank you, sir."

Mark stood and looked around for the waiter.

"I'll pay. Just go," I said.

"Claire, I can pay for this. I'm not on your stratospheric income level, but I can manage a coffee."

I felt a flash of anger and tamped it down. Anger would not serve me now. I thought he had accepted my lavish inheritance. Obviously, he hadn't.

"It's just a friendly gesture, Mark. I'm not spending a fortune on it." I held his gaze. "You're in a hurry, I'm trying to be helpful." His problem with my legacy was nothing I could fix. I wasn't going to constantly apologize for it.

He closed his eyes for a moment and then stared straight at me. "Sorry. You're right."

I let him go.

CHAPTER TWELVE

I hiked over the bridge to the old town of Whitby where the streets wandered in a medieval design. Narrow streets followed the old footpaths in curving and sometimes bewildering ways. The brick streets were cambered to let the rain drain away, and the flagstone sidewalks gave the old town the distinct flavor of the medieval days. Fast walking dissipated my anger, and I was soon back to a relatively calm state. The streets were full of people, even at this time of year, and there were dogs everywhere. I wondered why there were more dogs here than anywhere else. Whitby must love their dogs. There was even a sign outside a teashop that said "Dogs are very welcome inside". I'd bring Gulliver the next time I came.

I was amused by the social dance dogs performed when they met. A particularly inquisitive and self-confident Miniature Schnauzer was trying to get acquainted with a tall Dalmatian. The difference in size could lead to frustration. The owners moved their dogs around each other without any complaints. It was surprising how many people and dogs could intermingle without incidents. My Gulliver had not been with me a year yet, and he was still learning how to safely interact with others. All these dogs made me miss him. I nipped into the Whitby Pet Shop on Station Square. I understand why parents buy presents for their children when the parents are on holiday; there is a little frisson of guilt for leaving them behind. I found a raincoat I thought would look charming on Gulliver. I drew the line at the matching booties.

I crossed back over the bridge and wandered down Pier Street where I sat on a park bench, keeping an eye out for my tourists as they made their way to the Magpie Café. Pier Street had shops on only one side and the river on the other. A guard rail separated the strollers from the water several feet below. I sat on a bench hanging out and watching the people like one of the ubiquitous gulls perched on the railing. I smiled at a particularly handsome gull who was strutting along the rail, looking a little pompous. He stopped, ruffled his feathers and stared at the ground in front of him. Then, he dove to the pavement and snatched a chip that had fallen from the hands of a passerby. He had gobbled it and was on the wing again before the man could react. I laughed and watched the gull hop back on the rail. Tour boats chugged in and out of the harbor across the river, loading and unloading their passengers after a jaunt out to the ocean and back. The toots of the boats, the revving engines of the diesel busses, the occasional bell from a church mixed with the shrill cries of those raucous gulls slipped over me like a coast folk tune. It was lively, colorful and busy.

I had my hands in my pockets as it was also a little chilly. My cold fingers found the listening device I'd taken from Phillip in one pocket and the battery in the other. I rolled them around my fingers a little absently and then with more interest. I wondered it could pick up conversations from nearby or from some distance. I didn't know these people on the street. I saw Grady and Amanda going into the Whitby Gift Shop. They should be far enough away that I wouldn't hear them. I fitted the battery inside the device and put the plug in my ear. A cacophony blasted my senses. I almost jumped off the bench. I pulled the plug out and looked around. No one was paying any attention to me. Cautiously, I put it back in and concentrated.

"Now don't do that, Sydney." I heard a querulous voice. I gazed over the pedestrians and found a mother scowling at a child of about three. That must be Sydney.

"I want to,"

"No. No." The mother was emphatic, and Sydney gave up.

"Too much brass." I heard a deep voice. I placed that with an older man peering in the window of the gift shop. His wife beside him said something in a quiet voice, but I lost it as the man overrode her with, "I'll not be partin' wit' brass for that bit of nowt."

I smiled to myself. This was fun. Then, I clearly heard Amanda's voice. "Grady, darling, why are we in this shop?"

I heard Grady laugh. "I can't help checking on my merchandise, darling. I like to see if it is properly placed and the clerks here are doing a good selling job."

"You have people to oversee this, Grady. Stop working so hard."

I pulled the ear plug out. I wasn't going to eavesdrop on Grady and Amanda. That was truly an invasion of privacy. This little device must have an amazing range. Grady and Amanda were *inside* that shop.

I stuffed it back into my pocket. I wasn't going to eavesdrop on them. I joined Grady and Amanda as they exited the gift shop.

"Checking on your wares, Grady," I asked. Oops. Was I supposed to know he distributed souvenirs? Yes, Amanda had told me, and Grady had told me himself.

He answered me without any obvious suspicion that I'd overheard him. "Amanda gets cross with me because we're on holiday, but I like to know how my merchandise is doing."

He turned and gestured toward the gift shop. "They sell my ceramics and vases and chocolates, and they do very well, very well indeed."

"They do well because you oversee every bit of it," Amanda said.

Grady patted her hand. "I'll learn to let go, love. Give me time."

"It's a challenge?" I asked "to keep the souvenirs flowing I mean?"

"It's a challenge," he said, "and I like to think I'm doing a service to the tourists who come to our country. As well, tourism brings millions of dollars into the British economy. I'm doing my bit to keep the economy going."

I smiled, showing some interest. I'd never thought of souvenir distribution as a service industry. When I thought of service, I thought of police, firefighters, medics, nurses, doctors, teachers and social workers. I didn't think of manufacturers or sales people. I gave my brain a twist. Service was in the mind of the person doing the work. I served my tourists. It wasn't noble, but it did demand expertise, and I tried to do it well.

I gave a quick thought to where my legacy came from. My step-father Paul, had been someone important in the steel industry. Perhaps he had bought and sold it. I'd never asked him for the details. Was my legacy based on sales?

I smiled more genuinely this time. "Tell me about it."

From the gift shop to the restaurant, Grady held forth on the challenges and joys of sales and distribution. He was particularly proud of the ceramic salt and peppers in the shape of birds like the set I'd bought for my niece Kala.

"Many people won't spend money on art," he said. "They think it's frivolous—particularly here in Yorkshire where hard work is esteemed. If you give them something utilitarian such as the salt and pepper shakers and make them beautiful, they get art without bruising their conscience."

"How fascinating." It really was.

Everyone had gathered outside the Magpie Café except the Tucson ladies.

"Where are they?" I asked Sheilagh. *And are they together?*

"They went to the Cook Memorial and probably lost track of time," she informed me.

"All three of them?" I asked her.

"That's right."

I was relieved. "Go on in and get settled. I've reserved a table under 'The British Mysteries Book Tour.'"

They nodded and entered the café. I hiked the two blocks up and over a small hill to the memorial. The three ladies stood around the plinth dwarfed by the statue of James Cook. They did not look happy. I stood silent for a moment, anticipating trouble.

"Is something wrong?" I asked quietly.

Evelyn snorted. "Norma here wants to conduct some kind of woo-woo memorial to our departed Phillip. We hardly knew him."

"You could embrace a remembrance ceremony, Evelyn. Let a little humanity into your soul." That sounded a little sharp for Geraldine.

"It's hypocritical," Evelyn insisted.

"Evelyn has a point," Geraldine turned to Norma. "He wasn't a friendly man."

"It doesn't matter," Norma said. "He was a fellow human in the journey of life which stopped much too early. We should commemorate that. It adds to our humanity."

Geraldine bit her fingernail. "Norma has a point, too."

"You want to have it here?" I asked, looking around. The river was below us and, across the river, the town on the other side clung to the base of the cliff which rose up to the abbey on the bluff where the ruins watched over the sea. It was quite beautiful.

"Of course," Norma said emphatically. Evelyn rolled her eyes.

"You could extend your sympathy to someone else," Geraldine said to Evelyn.

That sounded provocative, tantamount to accusing Evelyn of being selfish. I intervened. "Why don't the two of you," I indicated Geraldine and Norma, "have your ceremony while Evelyn and I return to the Magpie Café. Do you know where it is?"

"Oh, yes, we passed it to get here," Norma said. I glanced at Geraldine, checking that she knew where it was. She nodded.

"Good. We'll join the others at the café. You can conduct a short ceremony here then join us. I'll order you a drink. It will be ready when you arrive." *In other words*, I said mentally, *don't take much time.*

"That would be wonderful. I'll have the local ale," Geraldine said. "Just a half-pint."

"I'll have a pink lady," Norma said.

I grinned to myself. No one I'd ever met had a pink lady. It was a combination of gin, egg white and grenadine and was a gorgeous light pink color. Very old-fashioned and elegant. I wondered if the bartender at the Magpie knew how to make it.

Norma was reciting poetry, Tennyson, I think, as I left her to join Evelyn who waited impatiently at the edge of the grass. We walked down the road to the café while Evelyn complained.

"I can't stand that sentimental claptrap," she said.

"Not your style?"

"I don't think it will make any difference to Phillip."

I gave a thought to Phillip, so alive this morning and gone this afternoon. He must have liked danger to work undercover for Scotland Yard. He probably thought he would always be able to extricate himself from any problems. Not this time. I gave my attention to Evelyn.

"I don't suppose it does, but it makes Norma feel better about Phillip's death, so that makes it legitimate."

She was silent for a moment, then said, "I have a friend at home. His name is Max. He is a dear man, really. Gentle, kind, taught art history at the university. We golf."

I said nothing and waited.

"He wants to marry me. That's what Geraldine was on about. She thinks I need to be involved with other people, in particular with Max."

"What does she say about it?'

"She says 'You should extend your empathy,'" she quoted.

"And what do you think?" I wondered how Max had managed to get past her prickly defenses—or if he had.

"I'm not capable of being a generous partner. I like my space. I like my life. I like my schedule. I wouldn't consider someone else's needs. I had trouble with that when I was married twenty years ago and I haven't changed. Max would end up hating me, or I'd end up hating him. I'm not tolerant. Look at the way I criticized Norma. All that sentimental stuff. I don't care that much for people. It's not me." She rapped out her self-analysis succinctly.

I studied her for a moment. "It doesn't mean you're unfeeling, Evelyn. The British understand that. Most of them would rather be stoic than sentimental."

Surprising me, she smiled. "That's me. Generations of the stoic British behind me that never assimilated American sentimentality. Naturally, I'm not going to feel sympathy for Phillip."

I suppose it could take generations in a new country to change the habits of the old.

"I'm sorry about Phillip," she said. "No one, even one who was up to nefarious activities, deserved to die out there on the moors without any loved ones around him." She turned the conversation away from her feelings.

Nefarious activities? What did she know? "Do you think he was into something illegal?"

"Something secret, in any case. It might just be industrial espionage. He used to dictate into a recorder when he didn't think anyone was watching. I caught him doing that twice, although I was careful to make sure he didn't see me. I didn't want to be a part of whatever he was doing."

"How did you manage that?" Phillip was observant. It was part of his job. Like Mark, he must notice what others were doing. How did he miss Evelyn's scrutiny?

"I saw him in a distance, put my camera on him and zoomed in. I could see quite clearly."

Her surveillance was that easy. I'd tell Mark about this. My anger at his discomfort with my money had dissipated. I hadn`t forgotten it, but I wasn`t angry now. Disappointed perhaps. Frustrated that my income bothered him. I`d still do what I could to help in his investigation. If there was a murderer around, I wanted him away from my tourists.

Evelyn continued her ideas about Phillip. "He might have been a spy for another tour company. Do you think so?" She turned to me.

I shook my head. "Possibly, but I doubt it. He didn't seem interested in the itinerary. He didn't even seem to know it half the time."

"True. Maybe a criminal or a police officer." Evelyn was getting too close to the truth. She was intelligent and she read murder mysteries. We moved into the café, and she greeted the others. Norma and Geraldine joined us just as their drinks were delivered. Everyone studied the menus.

"The fish pie is wonderful," I recommended.

"The fish probably jump from the river into the pan," Allan said.

"Nothing beats fresh fish," Evelyn agreed.

"What," Geraldine asked, "is Yorkshire Gammon with Free Range Fried Egg?"

"Ham and eggs," I said.

"Well, I think I'll pass on that in spite of the enticing description. It sounds as though the gammon and eggs galloped onto the stove."

We laughed.

"I'll have the homemade lasagna," Sheilagh said. "Anything homemade sounds wonderful."

"I agree," Amanda said. "The best part of the holiday is not having to cook."

"Deep-fried whitebait, 'headless and gutless," Geraldine read. "Do they serve it sometimes with heads and guts?"

Geraldine had the whole table laughing and some people at the adjoining tables. She was doing her best to smooth over the contretemps at the Cook Memorial.

"Grady has some great ideas for our farm," Allan told us.

We looked at Grady.

"Just some sound business practices."

I glanced quickly at Sheilagh. This farm was becoming more than just a pleasant idea.

"He thinks we should join a local farmer's organization before we buy a farm and get their advice," Allan said.

That sounded reasonable. In my business, we'd call it researching the market.

"He thinks we should look at specialty sheep and alpacas for fleece and progeny because you can make living on superior stock."

"And," Sheilagh said hesitantly. "It would make sense to put everything on a spread sheet and work out our expected income and expenses before we start. It's the chancy nature of it that makes me nervous. I'd love a spread sheet."

I'd been right about her organizational abilities. It sounded as though Grady had spent time considering their prospects and had really helped them. The spread sheet might even tell them to avoid farming.

"I have about two years before retirement and Grady here says I should take night courses on farm management." Allan smiled at Grady.

"Good idea," Evelyn said.

"All good ideas," Norma agreed.

Grady must have a lot of experience with running companies. A farm is a small business, so most of his experience could apply. It was generous of him to share with the Whites. It was the challenge of a business that kept small operators like me fascinated by the work. It would be the same for Grady and the Whites. Business people like us tried to organize what worked best and kept tweaking our plans until we made a profit—or at least kept our business going.

I'd ordered two bottles of French viognier to accompany the meal and everyone was relaxed by the time we finished. I planned to drive home to Ambleside in the late afternoon when the golden light of dusk would give a magical view of the moors. Everyone agreed to wander for another hour and meet at the van.

After we assembled and loaded into the van, I took the northern route, through Danby, then Osmotherly and west to Northallerton.

We did catch the sun as we went through the moors, but we drove through the dark for the last half-hour. All my passengers dozed, but woke when I shut off the motor at Ambleside Farm.

"My, my," Norma said. "That was quite a day."

Since it included murder, that was an understatement. She might be very tired indeed. She was so engaged and energetic that I sometimes forgot that she was also over seventy.

"Have a rest," I said. "I've booked us into The New Inn, but not until nine. Would that suit everyone?"

It did.

Mark's car was parked near my cabin. Mark. I wrenched my mind from my tourists to Mark's investigation. I should tell him about Evelyn's observation of Phillip speaking into a recorder. He must have stashed that recorder somewhere. He had a listening device in his pocket which Mark gave to the constable. Did he have a recorder that held his thoughts and ideas? Would Mark find it? Could he listen to it? Could I listen to it?

CHAPTER THIRTEEN

I made a quick call to Kala at her uncle's house in York.

"Is all okay, Kala?"

"All's good. I miss Tuffy. Do you think mummy would let me get a puppy?"

I thought of the two energetic Labradors, Pike and Duff, already occupying the house. They had to be fed, watered and taken out for walks twice a day. "Probably not," I said.

"Oh, well." She already knew it was unlikely.

I headed for my room where Mark met me at the door and blocked my entry.

"Sorry, love," he said before I could even say hello.

I stared at him. Oh, his crack about my wealth. He was sorry. Well, that's a start. Maybe his irritation about my income would be like the bumps in a lane, always there, never completely removed, but something we could get used to.

"No more sarcasm," I said as I moved past him into the room. "It's hurtful."

"I agree. I'll stop that." He leaned down and put his forehead on mine. We stayed like that for a moment, just absorbing warmth from each other. He patted my shoulder and rubbed his cheek on mine.

"Direct complaints will be entertained," I instructed, "but not nasty jibes."

"Got it." He stepped back and saluted. I laughed.

He joined us for dinner at The New Inn. It wasn't far from the farm and offered a calm environment. I thought a pub might be a bit too stimulating after the events of the day. The food looked delicious and offered local Yorkshire specialties such as Wensleydale Chicken and Barnsley Chops. The group appreciated the soft lights and quiet atmosphere. Mark took a chair near Geraldine.

Allan scanned the menu and let out a deep sigh. "Ah, curry. I can have curry."

Evelyn was amused. "I don't understand why so many British people like curry."

The four English tourists stared at her for a moment.

"It's true. We like our curry," Sheilagh said. "Many British soldiers were stationed in India in the nineteenth century and had local cooks. They probably brought back a fondness for the food of India."

"Or perhaps," Amanda said, "our cuisine was so bland curry was a wonderful change."

Norma protested. "Your menus seem varied and interesting."

"Now, they are," Amanda said. "My mother tells me stories of mushy peas and chips and not much else. We've changed."

"For the better," Grady said.

Mark grinned at me. He liked mushy peas and chips.

"What's it like in Wales?" I asked him.

"Cosmopolitan," he said. "Some of the best meals in the world are in Wales."

"Of course," I said. "Thousands of the Welsh would agree."

"This looks excellent," Norma perused her menu then sat back and gazed around the room. "This is lovely, Claire. Restful, somehow."

It was an attractive room, cozy without being tacky. The multi-paned glass in the bay window area where we were seated were very old, but not ancient, probably eighteenth or nineteenth century. It gave an ambience of timelessness, continuity and order. Something murder definitely disrupted.

Because we were eating late, everyone wanted a starter. The offerings looked delicious--except the black pudding. No one ordered that even topped with caramelized onions and apple chutney.

"Look at all the vegetarian choices," Amanda said.

"You didn't say you were vegetarian," I was startled. No one on this trip had indicated they had a special dietary need. Evelyn likes vegetarian on occasion, she'd told me, however, she wasn't strictly a plant eater.

"No, but it's usually a healthy choice. On this menu, it's amazing how much healthy food I can choose."

"I think I'll pick unhealthy tonight," Evelyn said almost defiantly and ordered Barnsley lamb chops.

Amanda laughed a little ruefully. "No matter how you say it, ordering vegetarian does sound judgmental about other people's choices. A bit precious, perhaps."

"It could be the tender conscience of the carnivore that interprets it that way," Evelyn admitted. They smiled at each other. What an unlikely friendship that might be. Then again, I am constantly surprised at how relationships form and endure—or don't.

Mark conversed with Geraldine on one side and Grady and Amanda on the other. The meal progressed through the wonderful food and three bottles of wine. I, as usual, could only drink one glass, and I noticed Mark also had only a glass. No one mentioned Phillip.

I could see the lights of Mark's car behind me on the way home. He was already in our room by the time I'd said good night to my guests and opened my own door.

"Mark, can we talk?"

"First things first," he said and kissed me.

After a few minutes, I noticed the radio was blaring. I fluffed my hair, pulled my jumper down and started toward the radio to lower the volume.

"Leave it," Mark said.

I turned in surprise. He motioned me to sit on the bed near the radio.

He sat beside me and whispered in my ear. "Do you have that bat ears device you took from Hartley?"

"Uh huh," I glanced at the radio and around the room.

"Bugged?" I mouthed.

"Maybe," he whispered. "How far can you hear with it?" He must have known I'd tried it. No one with a healthy curiosity could have resisted.

I searched in my pockets and found the device. I plugged it in my ear and listened.

Mark picked up a notepad and pen from the bedside table. "What do you hear?" he wrote.

I concentrated then started to speak. He shoved the pen into my hand.

I wrote, "A horse coughing."

He looked up, probably calculating how far away the horse might be.

I listened, grinned, then wrote, "Mrs. Yowlet Sr scolding someone."

I could hear creaks, sounds like wind in the trees, crunches, then Shelagh's voice.

I wrote, "Sheilagh."

Mark took my hand and led me to the bathroom. He turned on the shower, the steam started to rise.

"Use cold," I said.

He turned the dial. We shut the door and sat in the bathroom with the shower running.

"Now what?" he said.

I concentrated on the receptor in my ear but could hear only muted voices.

"Not much," I said aloud.

"Okay. Let`s speak in whispers. If you have bat ears someone else might have them as well."

This was the most unromantic situation I could imagine. Here I was with the love of my life, crowded into a bathroom, whispering about people and their reprehensible deeds. I gave up on romance and concentrated.

"What do you want to talk about?" I asked him.

"You first. You came into the room saying you wanted to talk. About what?"

"Oh, yes. That. I wanted to tell you that Evelyn saw Phillip dictating into a recorder. Did you find one?"

"No."

"Does that mean someone beat you to it?" Mark had said he was going to pick up protective gear and search Phillip's room. I assumed he'd done that while he'd been on his own this afternoon.

"Not necessarily. He may have hidden it, and I didn't find it. How big was it?"

"Evelyn didn't say, but I expect it was quite small. I have one for recording my choir teacher's instructions and it's smaller than an eyeglass case. In fact, that's what I keep mine in."

Mark was quiet for a moment. "I should look again."

"What did you learn today from Scotland Yard?" I asked.

Mark tried to stretch his legs in the small bathroom without much success. "They think Hartley died of some fast-acting poison."

"Cyanide?" I said, thinking of the many Agatha Christie novels where cyanide had been used.

"No. Probably Fentanyl. Cheap and easy to find. The Yard won't know for sure until they get the toxicology report and that will take a couple of weeks. They're operating on the premise that it was Fentanyl or Carfentanyl. Impossible to trace."

"Who gave it to him?"

"We don't know. It's almost instant death unless you have naloxone immediately available, and we didn't."

I thought of how hard we'd tried to save Phillip and how useless it had been. I should keep some naloxone in my emergency supplies alongside the aspirin I kept for potential heart attack victims.

I considered the problem. "So, since it was fast-acting, it must have been someone on the site of Ralph's Cross. There was a busload of foreigners. Can we rule them out?"

"Maybe, but their driver was local," Mark said.

"Oh, yes, I remember Aaron. Could he have been instructed to kill Phillip? And the driver of the smaller tour bus, Jane and her tourists." I thought them unlikely, but they might have had instructions that went beyond guiding.

"Anything's possible."

"We have to include my tourists," I said reluctantly.

Mark stood, stretched then settled back on the edge of the tub. He had chivalrously offered me the toilet to sit on, so I was reasonably comfortable. He, obviously, was not.

"Allan White is a shipping clerk for an import company. He is in a position of trust there and could be bringing in illegal drugs." Mark started on my tourists.

There wasn't much use saying that I thought he was an unlikely smuggler. He *could* be managing an illicit business.

"His wife," Mark whispered, "could also be doing it. She seems more organized than him and more ambitious."

I shrugged. I didn't know Sheilagh well. She was a nurse. Could she have had access to a drug that poisoned Phillip? I suppose anyone could.

"Grady could be importing and distributing drugs with his legitimate products. All three of them could have moved close enough to Hartley to poison him."

"A man from the bus stopped Phillip to ask a question," I said. I mentally saw the man approach Phillip and speak to him. "I don't think he moved close to him, though."

I could see Phillip standing near Ralph's Cross, gazing at it then going down the hill to show the others the peat bog at the bottom.

"Phillip had a cup of coffee," I said slowly, remembering the scene. "He put it on the ground when he dug into the bog for a sample of peat." I was recalling the scene, trying to work out where people had been standing.

We were quiet. Then Mark said. "Anyone could have put something in his coffee at that time?"

I remembered people from the smaller tour bus and my own tourists walking down to the bog.

"Yes, they were all there crowding around him."

"Or, someone could have injected him while others were crowding him." Mark stood. "I can't talk all night in a whisper with the shower running. I'll go back to Hartley's room later tonight and see if I can find that recorder."

We shut off the shower and went back into the bedroom.

"Let's drive up to the local courting spot and look at the moon." Mark gave an explanation of why we were leaving if anyone was listening.

"You've found a local courting spot?"

"Of course."

I laughed. "Okay."

We shut and locked the door and made our way over to Mark's vehicle. I checked the sky. Indeed, there was a moon.

"Where are we going?" I asked.

Mark put his finger to his lips. What did he mean? Someone could hear us in the car? Was the car bugged?

"To a spot I know," he said.

He pulled off by a burn that trickled through a wooded area. He got out of the car, and I followed him. We walked down a trail about fifty yards. He stopped where there was a park bench. He did know the courting sites. He held out his hand, and I gave him the bat ears.

He plugged it into this ear and listened. In a few seconds, he pulled it out.

"Good. Nothing."

"Did you think someone could hear us in the car?" Obviously, he thought that, but I was shocked it was possible.

"I don't know if my car is bugged. I'll have to check it in the morning."

"Do you have some kind of device that checks it?"

"I'll get one."

The burn widened here and moved more slowly. The moonlight painted it silver. Black reeds were straight silhouettes at the shore line. I heard the wavering cry of a tawny owl as it drifted through the trees behind us, then a low continuous roll of notes.

"What's that?" Mark looked up and over the water from where the sound arose.

"That's a nightjar."

"We have nightjars in Wales. I haven't heard one in years. The woods here are full of life," he said with some wonder.

"They are," I agreed.

I heard a blackbird and a robin. A cow called a loud demand for her calf from a field beyond the woods. The night was cool, but not as cold as I had expected. Spring was definitely coming.

"Tell me about your Tucson ladies," Mark said. "Starting with Evelyn."

I pulled my spirit away from the woods and the magical bird life and concentrated on the problem of murder.

"Evelyn Roberts," I said. "Lives in Tucson. She has traveled a bit more than the others, from what she says. She owns a lot of rental properties and manages them. She is quite wealthy."

"Even by your standards?"

I let the lengthening silence make my reaction clear, then said, "No sarcasm."

It was his turn to be quiet. He was probably evaluating whether he had been sarcastic. He had.

"Okay. Sorry."

I was getting tired of his comments about my money. I ignored my irritation. "She has a son, I think, but no husband. Perhaps, he died. I'm not sure but her ex has been out of her life for about twenty years. She has a gentleman friend named Max. The son is managing the properties while she is away. She checks in with him occasionally. She hasn't mentioned any British connections or tried to go off on her own to see anyone. She's an unlikely suspect, I think."

"And Geraldine? I like her."

"I like them all," I said. "Geraldine Smith, retired upper form science teacher, has a husband at home, Peter who is a retired dentist who golfs and watches sports on the telly. She's good at reading people and making practical plans. She hires a housekeeper to feed her husband while she's traveling. She likes to keep the peace, although she's self-confident. Again, she hasn't made any effort to get away from the group or to contact anyone. I have no idea what she might do in her room in the evenings, though."

"Again, not a likely suspect."

"And Norma? No one could possibly suspect Norma. She is a retired kindergarten teacher, willing to be everyone's friend, has an artist for a husband. Before you can say where does she get her money to travel, he's a very successful artist. I checked him out online, and one of his vases is selling in a New Mexico gallery for ten thousand dollars, that's about seven thousand six hundred pounds."

Mark whistled. "That much?"

"Impressive, isn't it?"

"Yes," he said. "I agree she's unlikely. Mostly, because I can't see her organizing anything."

I smiled. It did defy rational thought to see Norma handling a drug business.

"That leaves us with the English tourists."

We had already discussed them in the bathroom of Ambleside Farm and I didn't want to talk about them any more tonight. I remained silent for a few minutes, looked out over the burn into the woods beyond and said, "About that moon."

Mark laughed and pulled me close.

We tumbled back into the room at Ambleside Farms and were quickly into bed. Mark turned on the radio to mask any sounds we might make. We were enjoying ourselves immensely when the programming changed and a stirring rendition of Rule Britannia blared into the room, totally shattering the romantic mood. I shot straight up in surprise. We stared at each other and burst out laughing.

CHAPTER FOURTEEN

I was awakened by a movement near my bed. I lay there, tense, frozen and listened. Gulliver? No. I wasn't at home.

"Mark," I said softly.

"Sorry. I didn't mean to wake you." His voice was a whisper from across the room.

"What time is it?"

"About half two."

"Oh." I started to settle back into sleep then sat up quickly.

"Where are you going?"

He eased down on the bed beside me, hugged me and whispered in my ear.

"To search Hartley's room for that recorder."

"But it's locked," I whispered back.

There was silence while my brain caught up to my speech. "Oh." Obviously, he had ways of getting through locked doors.

"Don't break the locks," I whispered and settled back to sleep.

I didn't hear the door open when he returned. I felt him slide into bed.

"Did you get it?" I murmured.

"Got it, copied it and put it back."

"Good." I drifted into sleep.

In the morning, Mark ran the shower. He brought his laptop into the bathroom and fired it up

"You were right. The recorder was hidden in an eyeglass case and the case was hidden in a pillow that was on the sofa in his room. I plugged the recorder into my computer and copied the files."

"They have zippers, those pillows. For washing the covers."

"Yes, well, I didn't think of that earlier and, luckily, no one else did either."

He inserted a memory stick and pulled up the audio file. He pushed 'play' and we listened to Phillip set down his observations and conclusions. We sat there with Phillip's voice drifting around us like a spirit from the nether world for about fifteen minutes. Phillip had observed my tourists, made decisions about them and had come to the same conclusions we had. Allan could be the drug lord he was looking for, or Grady. He even considered Evelyn—I think probably because he didn't like her—but I paid attention to his reasons. Evelyn was organized, rational and, he thought, unfeeling.

"I don't agree…that she is unfeeling."

"Everyone has biases," Mark said. "I wish he had more concrete evidence. This isn't much good to us."

"I'm disappointed," I said. "I expected him to make an accusation and be sure of his facts."

"Like a specter from the other side, instructing us." His voice deepened. "Here be dragons."

"Something like that." It would've been helpful.

Mark shrugged. "Definitely unsatisfactory. I'll turn it over to Whelan. I don't think he'll get much more out of it."

"The police might want to interview Evelyn again." That worried me a little.

"They might," he agreed.

He told me his plans for the day. "I'll take my laptop to the station in Northallerton where the internet is secure and send the recording to Whitby. I'll try to return before the locals get here to search Hartley's room."

"Who's going to do that?"

"Whitby is arranging for the Northallerton police to do it. I'd better get moving. I'll get breakfast along the way."

"Right then. I don't suppose driving to Northallerton and working on the computer is going to be dangerous."

There was no point in wasting energy worrying about him in any case. His job was often dangerous. Phillip's death was evidence that whatever they were investigating had a high level of threat. I would keep my anxieties under control or I'd handicap us both with my worries.

"You're the one I worry about," Mark said. "Hartley's dead. Someone on the tour might have killed him."

"Hartley was a Yard man. I'm not with the Yard or any police force. You are, though, and you may be in the same danger as Hartley."

"No one on the tour knows I'm with the police."

Mrs. Yowlet Jr and Sr knew. They didn't seem to gossip with the guests—just me. I wouldn't be surprised if the others were beginning to wonder why he was away from the tour so often.

"The Yowlets know," I said, reluctantly admitting I'd been indiscreet.

He was silent for a moment. "Damn it. I wish you hadn't told them. That was careless."

"It was. Sorry."

He stared at me, his face hard to read. "Let's hope they keep mum."

I hoped so as well and that it was only careless, not catastrophic.

He left for Northallerton, and I joined the others in the breakfast room at the farm house, taking our usual places. It amused me to notice how predictable we were. It was as if someone had allotted us our own spot to sit, and we made sure we sat there every morning. No one had, and anyone could choose a different spot, but they never did.

Aelwen had put out a coffee urn where we could help ourselves as soon as we arrived. There were several different kinds of fruit juice as well as a bowl of peaches, raspberries, blackberries and kiwi along with small tubs of yogurt. Brown boiled eggs, no doubt hard-boiled, filled a bowl. A tray of croissants and scones lay further along on the table.

Mrs. Yowlet Sr. came out to take orders for a hot breakfast.

I was satisfied with fruit, yogurt and a croissant, as long as I had unlimited coffee. Evelyn chose the same. The others ordered the fried eggs, bacon, tomatoes and beans. Allan ordered the black pudding. I suppressed a shudder. I truly did not like it and couldn't see why anyone did, but I kept that to myself.

"Are you sure, me luv," Mrs. Yowlet Sr said to me, hesitating for a moment. "I can get you sommat 'ot in t'shake of a lamb's tail."

"No thanks, Mrs. Yowlet. I'm fine. It's all delicious."

She smiled. "And where's tha handsome lover?" she asked. "Off arresting someone?"

There had been a buzz of conversation; now there was sudden silence.

"No, he's on holiday. He's just gone to get something from Northallerton that he forgot to bring with him." I improvised wildly. "He'll be back soon." I shouldn't have counted on her reticence. I stared at my yogurt, unwilling to meet anyone's eyes.

"You make him relax now, luv. Too many nerves these days. Twiny, they are. Tha group is a bad one for traispin' about in t'nightime. Restless leg, the lot of you. All the men pace back and forth. Enough to wake the hens, it is. Everyone works too hard, I figure. Far too hard."

"You work hard, yourself, Mrs. Yowlet." I tried to divert her. What did she mean, the men paced in the yard at night? Had she seen Mark go out to search Phillip's cabin?

"Well, aye. Tha' goes with the farming, now don't it?"

And having dropped her bombshell she bustled away.

The silence lingered.

Evelyn leaned across the table to me and said, "Your Mark is a policeman?"

"Not here," I said. "He works out of Hampshire. This isn't his jurisdiction."

"Not Scotland yard?" Norma said. "How thrilling to have a British police officer on a mystery book tour."

"No, not Scotland Yard. Hampshire Constabulary. And he's on holiday." I implied he was a low-ranking bobby. Mark would prefer that.

He was going to be furious that Mrs. Yowlet had exposed him. He wasn't happy with me for telling her about him in the first place. I'd been careless. He was right about that.

"Could we meet at my room in about forty minutes?" I said, trying to change the subject away from Mark.

"Where are we off to today?" Allan asked.

"The Thirsk area." I outlined the activities and the conversations broke up into the discussion at the separate tables. I was just excusing myself to Evelyn and Norma when I spotted a police car pulling into the gravelled area outside the breakfast room. For the second time that morning, conversation stopped completely.

We watched as Aelwen went out to meet the constable who had stepped out of his official car and was walking toward her. They conferred, and he accompanied her into the lobby.

A few minutes later, she poked her head in the door. "The police are here to search Mr. Saunders' room. No one else will be inconvenienced." She popped out again.

The group turned to me.

I took a breath, then started the explanation. "It's usual, as you readers of mysteries know, after a sudden death, for the police to investigate. I'm sure that's what is going on here." It would be thorough, as the death was suspicious, but I didn't tell them that.

Mrs. Yowlet Sr. arrived just then with another urn of coffee. Allan stood to help her with it.

"Ta, luv. That's good of ya." She wiped her hands on her apron. "Police in the house. Imagine that. It's as good as t'telly, now, int it."

She swept a few crumbs from the table with her hand and dropped them into the waste basket. "It's exciting that's what tis. Where is that policeman of yours?" She turned to me. "Just like a man. Never there when you need 'em."

Then she was out of the room. The door swung behind her.

"I thought your Mark told me he was a civil servant," Evelyn said. Blast Mrs. Yowlet for bringing up Mark's job again. I didn't want to talk about it.

"The police are civil servants," I said. "Anyway, he works out of Hampshire. He was at a conference in Manchester and took a few days leave to be with me. I hope you can all let him have his holiday."

"Oh, certainly, certainly," Geraldine said. "We are, after all, having our holiday and should be able to let him have his."

"In any case, he wouldn't have any jurisdiction here," Grady said. "The different counties are protective of their authority."

"That's true" I said, grateful for his comments, although in Marks' case it wasn't accurate. Since he was on the Major Crimes Investigation Team, he had jurisdiction anywhere in England. I wasn't sure about Wales and probably not Scotland.

Mark returned as I was passing through the front lobby. He strode over to the officer who was just coming out of Phillip's cabin.

I could see they were talking. I couldn't hear what they were saying. I couldn't walk up to them and listen. I entered my cabin and shut the door. I did want to know what that officer had found. I remembered my mother talking about the slippery slope to perdition. How the first transgression was difficult, but that subsequent transgressions were easier. It only took seconds to get that bat's ear plugged into my own ear.

"A recorder of some kind and various papers." That was the officer.

"I see." That was Mark's voice. "Anything else?"

"Well, we found these big bars of chocolate. Probably not of much interest. There were three of them."

"Seems a little excessive."

"Perhaps." The officer sounded doubtful. I peeked out the window. The officer was showing Mark something.

"What's on the back?" Mark asked.

"Looks like a stamp of some kind. A bird, maybe."

A bird? A raven? I thought of the raven stamped on the bottom of the salt and pepper set. I couldn't see chocolate being stamped as a wedding present.

"Maybe a manufacture's stamp," Mark said. "I'd get that chocolate analyzed. Can you send me the report?"

"Will do. Do you have a business card?"

There was silence for a few seconds. Then Mark spoke. "Of course, the chief in Whitby will need the original report. You can send me a copy."

"And the Yard," the officer said. "Everything we do here, we have to do in triplicate." He sounded tired.

I must tell Mark about the stamp I'd seen on the ceramics in the shop. It might be important.

I didn't get a chance as Mark went directly to his car and didn't return to our room before I drove off with my group. I didn't know what he was going to do today. I was quite sure he wasn't going to spend it with me. We were barely on the road when the ladies from Tucson began to question me.

"Is Mark helping with the investigation?" Geraldine asked.

"I expect the local police want to make sure he didn't see something the rest of us missed," I said. "I don't think they're going to make him work on his holiday."

That satisfied them and they turned to questioning me about the mystery authors in this area.

"Deborah Crombie set *A Share in Death* at Fallowhouse on the Yorkshire Moors." Evelyn informed us.

"That's Duncan Kincaid and Gemma James, right?" Geraldine asked, naming the main characters.

"That's right."

"Any more authors?" Evelyn asked.

"Patricia Hall sets her books in Yorkshire, but not precisely here," I said.

"She's an excellent writer," Evelyn said from the seat behind me, "but if that protagonist of hers doesn't get on antidepressants soon, I'm going to give up on her."

"He does have a few issues," I agreed, remembering the morose and tortured soul of Detective Chief Inspector Michael Thackery.

"I don't know why today's authors can't give us more hope," Norma said. "I read Karen Sharpe's novels in preparation for this trip, but I find the dysfunctional main characters irritating."

I could understand an optimist former kindergarten teacher like Norma wanting to steer Sharpe's characters into a more positive view of life.

I found it hard to bring forth Yorkshire mystery writers with any ease. In Cornwall, authors and mysteries imbued the landscape. It was just a matter of choosing which ones to feature. In Yorkshire, was like pulling the novels from hard rock. Many authors are not writers of cozies, but writers of thrillers or psychological dramas. My group, especially my group from America, did not want to talk about psychological dramas, except *Wuthering Heights*.

"Where are we going?" Sheilagh called from the back seat.

"I thought we'd have a change of pace today and go to a donkey refuge and a farm." It had nothing to do with mysteries, but it was an interesting tourist attraction and I tried to give them variety.

"Fine with me," Allan said.

"We'll see," Grady said.

"They have a gift shop at the farm," I said. That should make him happy.

Did he had anything to do with the raven stamped on the gifts? He'd told me he distributed the beautiful bird ceramics. Was someone in his management or even in his warehouse flagging the products? It might be difficult to find out who was stamping those articles, or if the stamp actually indicated anything of importance.

The refuge for superfluous donkeys was run by a couple of retired teachers who had pooled their resources to provide food, shelter and veterinary care for the donkeys that were no longer being cared for by their previous owners. As Marlene Powers explained, "Either they were sorry they'd bought the donkey and didn't know what to do when the kids grew up and left home, or they ran out of money to feed the poor thing or any number of any reasons you can imagine."

She was an energetic sixty-something woman who tossed bales of hay into a paddock with the ease of long practice. We followed her to the larger padlock to view about twenty donkeys.

"How many do you have?" I asked, looking around to see if I could spot more.

"We have fifty here. There are about 3,000 scattered around Britain."

"Donkeys no one wants?" Allan asked. "That's a lot. I suppose they're cute when they're small and then they grow and eat into the finances." He'd been listening.

"That's right."

We didn't stay long and everyone dutifully dropped a few pounds in the donation box. I saw Grady write a cheque. That was nice of him. I suppose I could do that as well. Perhaps, I'd send a donation in the mail. I didn't want my guests to feel pressured to contribute.

The next stop was a farm near Thirsk. I'd booked this one ahead as well. There was more for the guests to do here. This was a working farm with milking cows, some highland beef cattle, sheep, chickens, geese, alpacas and llamas. They were organized to take tours from companies like mine as well as from schools, and, therefore, included many activities. I'd paid for a guided event, so I handed my group over to Ella the teenaged daughter of the owners and allowed her to take them through the milking barns and the lambing pens which held about ten ewes—some with lambs and some ready to deliver.

"We keep the ewes who are going to have twins in here. It gives them a better start," Ella said.

"Where they are protected from the weather, you mean?" Allan said.

"Yes, they're sheltered there. Also, some ewes aren't good mothers; they don't seem to realize they have two lambs, so they just look after one. We help her with that."

I trailed behind the group, listening to the teen explain the way the farm worked. From what I could gather, it only was successful if the whole family worked all the time.

When we emerged from the last barn, Ella asked who would like to take an alpaca for a walk. Amanda was eager and Grady said he'd take one. The American ladies were anxious to do so as well. I collected all the purses and rucksacks, leaving them free to take their walk unhindered. Allan and Sheilagh decided to go into the sheep pasture.

"We're trying to figure out what kind of sheep to have," Allan said. "I know what kind I'd like to have, but I'll look at what other people raise."

Ella, took her mobile from her jean's pocket and called for assistance. A boy about her own age ambled out of the barn and headed our way.

"This is my brother, Peter. He'll take you out in the paddock. We have Swaledales and some Herdwicks."

"Herdwicks? Really?" Allan's face lit.

All I knew about Herdwicks was that Beatrix Potter of Peter Rabbit fame raised them. I left them all happily engaged and retreated to the gift shop and café where I ordered a latte and spent time checking the reservations for the next two days. The group was occupied for over an hour before joining me for coffee.

Geraldine was enamored of the alpacas. "My girl was called Gertie and she was the sweetest thing. You'd think she had been waiting all day for me to take her for a walk."

"Mine was called Alphonse," Evelyn said "and I think he took *me* for that walk, but I enjoyed it," she added quickly. "Quite an experience walking with an alpaca."

Everyone collected their belongings from around my feet, drifted off to get coffee and returned. Norma was the first one back to the table.

"Did you get pictures?" I asked her.

"Of course," Norma said. "I must have taken about fifty of the alpacas and us and the countryside. I saw a bird I didn't know. I didn't get a photo, though."

"Can you describe it?" I asked her.

"He was the emperor of birds, regal almost. Black and white with a trailing feather from the back of its head".

"Did you hear it call?"

"Yes, it called a kind of too whit, a rising call as if it were asking a question."

"I think you saw a lapwing. Just a minute."

I pulled out my phone, clicked on the appropriate app and scrolled through until I found a picture of a lapwing.

"That's it," she said pleased to have her curiosity satisfied.

I gave them another forty minutes to invade the gift shop, then trailed after them. There might be more beautiful ceramic birds here. I spotted some along the far wall. There would be no lapwings because no one would be able to create those trailing feathers in ceramic, but there might be an owl. Kala would love an owl.

I saw Amanda near the yarn. That would be local wool. She was totally engaged in comparing skeins. She had said it was calming to knit. There were many yarn shops in the towns and cities. She'd be easy to satisfy. I often had no idea what my tourists were going to enjoy. Grady was wandering through the knick-knacks looking

at vases and boxes that promised him "Yorkshire Memories". I
fondled the ceramic birds. There were two owls: a short eared and
a barn owl. I chose the barn owl. I turned it over; I couldn't resist.
No raven stamp on the bottom.

I drove to The Black Lion in Thirsk, advising my tour that it
was as close as I could come to a Martha Grimes pub.

"All her titles are names of pubs, aren't they?" Geraldine
checked with us for confirmation.

"Yes. I like 'The Old Silent'. It makes me wonder who was silent.
How did that pub get its name?" I asked.

"I don't remember. Did she tell us in the book?" Geraldine said.

"I don't think so," Evelyn said. "I'll have to read it again".

"I know that pub is in Haworth which is in the south part of
Yorkshire. The novel was not set right here."

They piled out of the van and into The Black Lion. The meal was,
again, very good. I purchased a Black Lion mug for my nephew Josh.
It was hard to know what to buy him as his interests changed regularly.
When we reached the coffee stage, I passed out printed brochures of
sites to see in Thirsk. There weren't a lot of literary sites except the
James Herriot Museum which most of them had already seen. There
was a Thirsk Bird of Prey Centre and a walk in Hambleton Hills.

"Would you like to decide what you would like to do for a few
hours this afternoon? I can drive anyone who wants to go a little
out of town."

"The James Herriot Museum for me," Allan said.

Sheilagh smiled. "Right then. That should take us a couple of
hours."

"I'd like the Bird sanctuary," Norma said.

Everyone but Evelyn decided to accompany her. I drove them
the short distance to the sanctuary and asked them to give me call
on my mobile when they wanted to be collected.

I met Evelyn on my return, and we wandered through the
museums and gift shops. She seemed content to stop and gaze

around her. She was good company and knew quite a lot about the area.

"It always amazes me," she said as we sat on a bench overlooking the dale.

"What does?"

"The fact that people have been farming these hills and dales for thousands of years. Probably doing it the way their fathers did."

I gazed at the white and black dots of sheep scattered over the green grass in every direction. She might be right.

She continued her thought. "There isn't room for big tractors and the thousand-acre farms all growing corn or wheat. No Kansas-style operations here. Just sheep and some cattle, not huge herds, just enough for the land to support. Amazing, that it continues generation after generation."

"It must be efficient," I said. I knew there were much bigger farms in Norfolk on the flat lands, but I wasn't going to interfere with Evelyn's romance with the landscape.

She smiled. "As long as you don't hanker for Cadillacs or the latest every thing. And no realtors developing the fields into condos."

"Not allowed," I agreed.

My mobile binged. Deirdre. In the middle of the day? I answered. Surely, Kala was in York. Wouldn't she be safe there?

"How are you," she started. "No more bodies?"

"No. All is calm. I assume the police are doing their due diligence," I said.

"Good," she continued. "Things have improved here, as well—at least, for Kala."

"What did you do?" Deidre was a determined woman. I could imagine her taking on the school.

"Nothing. That's the strangest thing. The girl who was the instigator of the fight is in hospital."

"What happened?"

"Apparently, she ran afoul of another gang, and they ran her down with a vehicle. Premeditated GBH."

Grievous Bodily Harm. I was shocked. "You didn't have anything to do with that, did you?" I asked her. Deirdre defended criminals. She knew people who might conceivably kill for hire.

"Of course not."

"Michael?" Her husband was a barrister as well. He might know someone.

"Claire! We don't solve problems that way. We prosecute people who do."

"Sorry." I was instantly ashamed I'd even thought of it. "How is she, the girl who was hit, I mean?"

"Pretty severely injured: broken legs, internal injuries, but she's going to live."

"And you didn't have anything to do with it?" Rats. I hadn't meant to say that.

"I didn't. I swear."

"Yes, of course. Sorry. It does sound as though she offended her own gang, doesn't it? Or was it a rival gang that got to her?"

"Hard to know for certain. I expect she didn't comprehend the viciousness of the organizations she'd joined. She's only fourteen. She might not have known how ruthless they could be, or, more likely, thought they wouldn't direct that ruthlessness toward her."

I was silent. It was a dangerous world for some children. I was abruptly sorry for Judith, the bully. She was, as Deirdre said, only fourteen. I was angry with her, as well. The conflicting feelings were confusing.

"I can't believe you thought I might have sent someone after her." Deirdre complained again.

"Sorry. Sorry. An aberrant thought. Do you think someone sent a hit man because Judith had beat up Kala?"

Deidre must have remembered my past connections. "What about you? Did you send someone? Know any criminals?"

"I don't know anyone who would care about Kala and be in a position to order Judith's attack." I did know a few criminals in my past. There was an ambitious drug smuggler last year and a greedy villager who used poison but I wasn't on speaking terms with them now. I mentally reviewed the members of my tour.

Phillip might have caused someone to die. I wouldn't put it past him, but he wouldn't have cared about Kala's problems.

"We'll have to speculate on who sent someone after that poor girl. Nasty as she was, she shouldn't have paid for her behavior that way." Deidre was committed to justice. She'd want to know who was responsible.

"We'll talk about it later."

She agreed and disconnected. Having Judith in the hospital would mean Kala could go back to her school without fear of being bullied or injured because Judith had been the instigator of the beating. Why would Judith be attacked? For any number of reasons that didn't have anything to do with Kala. She might have tried to bully someone from her gang or another gang and was 'disciplined' by one or the other.

My mobile binged again, and I answered the call for a pick up. Evelyn and I collected Allan and Sheilagh and the others from the bird sanctuary, then headed north to Ambleside Farm for a refreshing twenty-minute stop at the farm.

With Mark following us, I drove north from the farm to The Fleece Inn. Tonight was a change of pace. The pub had live music and a small dance floor. It was noisy—even a little raucous. It was not the environment for wine, but the beer flowed freely.

"I'd be happy to drive anyone home when they want to leave," I said.

"Thank you, I expect we'll stay," Norma said and smiled.

It was a night for dancing. A wiry, elderly man, who looked like my idea of a sheep farmer asked me to dance. I agreed and found myself being whirled around the flagstone floor under the direction of his strong arms. I imagined he threw hundred-pound sheep all day long to keep in this shape. He asked all the women, and while Evelyn declined, Norma seemed delighted to bounce around the floor with him. A few older men sat in a dim corner watching the lively activity around them. Full pints of beer sat before them on the small table. Throughout the evening, those pints rotated through a cycle of empty and full. They must have had about four pints each. I wondered if they were there every night.

A darts competition in the opposite corner hosted four couples. When the music stopped momentarily, I could hear the thud of the darts and the good-natured comments of the kibitzers taking an interest from the sidelines.

A hum of lively conversation vied with the band, each contributing to the general feeling of festivity.

A smorgasbord of food was included in the price of the evening. The beer was extra.

I paid for the first round and Mark came to the bar with me to help carry back the pints.

"Productive day?" I asked him.

"Not so much," he said. "Just reporting in and checking on new information. What about you?"

I remembered I had to tell him about Mrs. Yowlet Sr's disclosure at breakfast.

"The old dear let everyone know you are a police officer. Sorry."

He stared at me for a moment. "Shit."

"My fault this time."

"Careless." He agreed it was my fault. He was right. I already knew I'd been careless. It worried me, but I couldn't do anything about it now.

"What did the police find out today?" I had apologized. I wasn't going to harp on it. A change of subject was called for.

"They found opiates in that chocolate bar, the one with the bird stamp."

"I've seen that stamp before." I told him about the salt and pepper shakers in Whitby and about the stamp the clerk had said indicated it was part of a wedding present.

"The stamp might have indicated the articles contained drugs," Mark speculated.

He picked up the first three of the glasses of beer. I picked up the next two.

"I don't think the chocolate was a wedding present," I agreed.

We made two trips and everyone had a starter beer.

When the band took a break, we helped ourselves to the food. Grady bought the next round of beer and the dancing recommenced. Amanda and Grady flew by in a fast dance I had never seen before. Allan and Sheilagh did the fox trot to whatever music was playing. Mark and I managed a few slow ones. Mark was a shuffler rather than a dancer. I didn't mind. The floor was so crowded, there wasn't much room to dance.

At one point, Norma and Geraldine did a complicated jive much to the admiration and appreciation of the rest of us who stood around, giving them a circle in which to perform. We erupted in cheers and clapping when they finished. They bowed.

No one wanted to go home early. I stopped drinking about ten and we headed home about one in the morning. Luckily, it wasn't far.

CHAPTER FIFTEEN

The bright sunshine seeped around the edges of the blinds, demanding a response. I pushed myself upright, flipped the switch on the life-saving coffee maker and opened my computer spread sheet. I dug out all my receipts from my rucksack and entered the numbers into the program. If I didn't do this at least every other day while I was touring, I dropped into a mess. With coffee, I could do it.

Mark rose, rolled out of bed, grunted at me and silently hauled on shorts, a T-shirt and running shoes.

"Back soon," he said and closed the door quietly behind him. He returned just as I was closing my financial program.

"Good run?" I asked him. He'd told me he used to run a lot over the hills in Wales.

"Nice enough."

He headed for the shower.

I called to him. "Were you a fell runner? One of those who ran every weekend." Those used to be hardy amateurs, mostly shepherds, who competed in marathon events. Now, they were probably all sponsored wearing name-brand fashionable athletic wear.

"No. I just ran for fun."

He beckoned me, and I joined him in the bathroom. I did not want to spend all my conversation time with Mark in the bathroom, but it was the one place we were safe from listening devices. It felt a little paranoid. After Phillip's death, I was willing to be a little paranoid.

"What's your official position in this investigation, Mark?" I tried to ignore the fact that he was showering in front of me.

"Officially," he said, "Whitby Chief Constable Whelan, is in charge of Phillip's death. I am just a consultant."

I tore my eyes away from the stream of water running through his dark hair and down his back. "And Inspector Fawthrop is in charge of investigating Jason's death in York?"

"One hopes to God they communicate with one another." He held out his hand. I reached for the soap from the basin and handed it to him. He took a quick shower and toweled dry. He wandered out into the bedroom and picked up his jeans and shirt. He was wearing the jeans and buttoning up a dress shirt when he returned to the bathroom. The shower was running on cold now.

"Scotland Yard will send an agent to check out Hartley's death and they may be interested in Jason's—if Jason was reporting to Scotland Yard or to Hartley. They may not choose to coordinate the other two investigators, though."

I tried to follow those lines of authority. "That's three different jurisdictions? Where do you come in?"

"Under Whelan." He reached for the brush and smoothed the black curls away from his face. "Officially, the Hampshire Constabulary is not involved and the Major Crimes Investigation Team is acting as a consultant, without authority."

"Could the latter be more involved? Could you direct this investigation?" The purpose of that team was to allow them to investigate homicides in any county.

"We could. Someone has to ask us, and no one has." I could hear annoyance in his voice.

He disappeared into the bedroom again and came back with two cups of coffee. He handed me one. I poured it into my now empty thermal cup. It was lovely, intimate even, to share a morning coffee with Mark—usually. The bathroom setting rather dampened the romance. I sat on the lid of the toilet and thought about the lack of systemic organization in the investigation of the two deaths.

"Officially, you're on holiday."

"That's right. If I find out anything, I'm to report to Chief Constable Whelan."

"And unofficially?"

"Unofficially, I'm working very hard." There was determination in his voice. He must be used to dealing with independent jurisdictions and, often, it must be frustrating. "I'm cooperating with the York, Whitby, and Northallerton Constabulary."

"I forgot about Northallerton. That makes four police forces, and you make five. Who designs a system that inefficient? It's cumbersome."

"It is that."

"What are you going to do?"

"I'm going to get the toxicology report. They put a rush on it. I'll find out what killed him. Then, I'm going to go over all the statements and see if there was anyone that might be remotely connected to Hartley on either of those tour buses."

I thought about our stop at Ralph's Cross. "Check out that man who came and asked him for directions. He could have slipped something in his food, or thermos or even slapped poison on him in some way—perhaps injected him."

"I'll do that," he said.

I was giving the suggestion. He was the one who would have to spend the hours on the phone and reading through reports, following up elusive leads and feeling inadequate when he couldn't find anything.

Mark draped a dry towel over the bathtub edge and sat on it. "Would it take a lot of cash to join one of those tours? If I find that man from the tour bus and he is someone of little means, it would indicate someone else was paying his way."

"It would take a fair amount to join the big tour. Those people probably came over on the same plane, are housed in beautiful hotels together and stay with the tour. That takes money. My tour is a private one as well but much smaller. Only my people are in my van. They pay a lot to have a private tour."

I thought about the third tour group. "Jane drives for one of the tour companies that operates out of York. They'll take anyone. You just have to come to their office in York, book the tour, slap down your thirty pounds or whatever it costs and you have a tour to the moors."

"You can do it on the day, then. You wouldn't have to book ahead. Would they take your name and address?"

"They'd take your name and a phone contact number. They wouldn't be fussy about your address." Those companies take thousands of tourists a year to the Yorkshire Moors. They don't ask for much but money.

"It's the reputation of the company that gets them customers. This murder worries me because it happened on my tour. What if tourists won't book with me because of it?"

He glanced at me. "You don't have to work."

"My reputation matters to me and I need to work. I have *always* worked. I wouldn't know what to do with myself if I didn't."

"Right. Anyway, I'm glad you know about how the tours are organized." He was silent for a moment while the shower continued to pound a background noise. Finally, he said. "I'll look into it. Maybe Fawthrop could do that for me."

"You could hire a private detective, couldn't you? That way you wouldn't be officially involved."

He shook his head. "No, I couldn't. I don't have a private income. Besides, it would smack of a parallel investigation. I want everything I do to be recorded officially somewhere. "

Was that a pointed remark about my private income? "I don't have unlimited funds, you know. I have a nice, very nice, nest egg. Why is it such a problem?" Was I picking a quarrel because

I was worried about my business? Why couldn't he understand that the business and my success with it was important? I'd been on my own a long time and I liked my independence.

"Look, Claire." He shut off the shower. I don't suppose he cared who heard us arguing. "You don't have to charge your people anything. You could run your company at a huge loss and you'd still have plenty to do whatever you wanted to. I don't."

I was tempted to tell him that what he had was a sensitive ego, that the problem wasn't my money but his sensitivity.

"What was your family's attitude to money?"

"We had enough, and we worked for it." He was quiet for a moment. "In Wales, men don't live off their partners."

I doubted that was true. The essential notion here was that he *thought* it was true. If I explained how I felt about my legacy, perhaps he'd understand?

"Mark, my inheritance from Paul came so late in my life that I'd already established how I wanted to live in the world. I'm determined to make my own way. It's important to me that my business is successful and that means it's financially successful. Making it pay challenges my abilities. Paul's legacy is for buying a house, going on fabulous holidays, supporting causes like the retired donkeys or ones that no one else wants to support. It gives me the extras of life, not the essentials."

"Gold-plated essentials," Mark said and walked out.

I snorted. So much for understanding. I was through explaining. He'd have to deal with it.

As usual when I was upset, I called Deirdre.

"He doesn't like what?" she queried, when I had explained my problem.

Obviously, I hadn't been clear. "Intellectually, I know I should just accept the fact that he comes from an old-country background and will need time to adjust to an equal partnership, but emotionally, I think his attitude is ridiculous."

"You didn't tell him that, did you?"

"Of course not. That would be unfair. He feels that way. I can't complain about how he feels. I'm ranting at you so I won't rant at him."

"Always happy to be of service."

The argument seemed to come out of nowwhere."

"It may seem like that, but he comes from some place deep that's been fomenting for a while. Trust me on that."

She had been married more than fifteen years. She had experience.

"Dierdre! I want it all to go away."

"I understand." I knew she did. She didn't always agree with me, but she usually understood me. "It's frustrating."

"It is."

"He's a clever bloke," she said. "He'll figure it out. I am sure he loves you, so he may figure it out sooner than later."

"I hope so."

Nothing much had changed after we talked, except I felt better for talking to her.

Mark wasn't at breakfast. I expected he was off to the police station in Northallerton. Fine! I joined the Tucson ladies. They were sitting at a table for four. Norma had a full plate, including beans which I found a little overwhelming for breakfast. Evelyn had a poached egg, brown toast and coffee Geraldine, yogurt, berries and pastries. There was small coffee urn at the table. Mrs. Yowlet Sr. must be somewhere about as everyone had either served themselves or had been served.

"We had a great time last night, Claire," Geraldine said. "Such a lively crowd. I haven't danced in a coon's age. It was fun."

"Very nice," Evelyn said.

"I felt as if I knew Yorkshire a little better," Norma said.

I smiled, remembering Norma whirling around the dance floor with that energetic farmer. "It was fun," I agreed.

"Where is your policeman?" Evelyn said.

I shrugged. "He went for a run this morning," I said, implying he was still running.

"Ah, well. We can tell him our conclusions later."

"What conclusions?" I started on my yogurt and berries while Evelyn filled me in on the conjectures of the three ladies.

"I know we all had a little more to drink than usual last night," she said. "It loosened up the brain juices, and we came up with some ideas."

"Really?" I asked politely, wondering what in the world they had indulged in when I let them off last night. I'd thought they had been ready for bed.

"We had a bottle of French Bordeaux just begging to be finished, so we started on it last night," Norma said. "Geraldine took notes."

I could see them in my minds' eye sitting around in the biggest bedroom, Norma pouring drinks, Evelyn convening the meeting and, of course, Geraldine taking notes.

"First of all," Evelyn said, "we agree that there must be some link between Jason's death and Phillip's."

"Why?" I asked.

"Mainly," Geraldine said, leaning toward me, "because we don't have a lot of other deaths to account for. The police might have six murders this month to try and solve. We only have two, so naturally, we'll link them."

There was something terribly wrong with that logic, but I didn't criticize.

"You think Phillip's death was murder?" I was sure no one had told them that.

"There's far too much interest by the police in his death to have it a natural occurrence." Evelyn went on, "what do they have in common?"

"Chocolate," Norma answered the question. "Jason worked in a chocolate factory. Phillip was intensely interested in the chocolate making process."

He had chocolate in his room when the police searched it. That did not make chocolate a critical factor. It was a common factor, though and might have some significance. I didn't discourage Norma. If they wanted to weave a suit out of invisible threads, I'd let them.

"We think Phillip was a spy," Norma said.

They were right about that. He was a spy for Scotland Yard.

"For whom?" I asked. If they'd twigged to his connection to Scotland Yard, they might as well work for the police.

"Ah. There are several choices," Evelyn aid. "Our favorite—he was a chemist, correct?"

"That's what he said." I agreed so far.

"We think he was working for a French chocolate manufacturer."

"Stealing secrets," Geraldine said, "That's what we think."

"Why would anyone kill him for that? He could be accused of theft and jailed. No need to kill him." Spying for a French chocolate company wasn't impossible, but it was improbable.

"We don't know some things," Geraldine admitted. "We don't know how ruthless the chocolate industry is. Or how much Phillip's information might have been worth? It, no doubt, boils down to greed as a motive."

"In the absence of jealousy, hatred, fear and ambition." Norma said.

They might be onto something. They'd read a lot of mysteries. They were intelligent and observant.

"I had an interesting experience," Norma said. "I didn't think about it much at the time, just thought Sheilagh was dealing with a work problem. When we started to talk about murder last night, I saw it in a different light."

"What happened?" I said.

"It was when we were at dinner at the New Inn. I had gone to the ladies' room and, on my way back, stepped outside to listen for a nightingale. I've always wanted to hear one. Sheilagh had stopped in the hall outside the rest room and was talking on her phone. I was just beside the door because…"

"Because you didn't want to step too far away and get lost." Geraldine supplied.

"That's right."

"Tell her what you heard." Evelyn was impatient.

"I heard her say…." Norma cocked her head and looked up to the right, obviously trying to remember exactly what she'd heard.

"She said, 'If that doesn't work, you'll have to take more drastic steps. His days are numbered in any case, just do your best.'"

"I thought she had a pet at home that was old and not likely to live long and didn't want to talk about it. She doesn't like to talk about emotional things very much."

"Sheilagh?" I could see how Sheilagh would be good at managing people, planning, and executing plans but was that conversation instructions to a hit man? Or woman?

"I think the chocolate angle is more likely than any involvement from Sheilagh," Geraldine said.

"That's starting to sound likely." I could see how logical this was to them, especially last night when they were finishing the Bordeaux. Someone should look into it.

"We still don't know who did the murders, whether they were committed by the same person or whether they were an ordered killing. We're working on it."

I had a sudden concern that they might end up at the bottom of a cliff or overcome by poison.

"Be careful," I said.

"Oh, we're only talking to you and your Mark."

I thought of the bats' ears in my rucksack. Someone else could be listening.

Geraldine passed me her notes. "You'll let your Mark know, won't you?"

I promised I would, stuffed the papers into the rucksack,

picked up my coffee and joined the rest of the group at their table. The Tucson ladies followed me. I hadn't even considered Sheilagh as a drug lord or lady. I didn't want to consider it.

"What's on for today?" Amanda asked. "It's a treat not to have to organize and plan anything myself."

I smiled at her. "You have choices." I enumerated them. "Clay shooting, a steam train ride to Wensleydale and back, and wandering around Northallerton. There is a wonderful photography gallery here."

"Let's take the train." Norma was enthusiastic. "It will take us back into the Dales country, right?"

"It will," I agreed.

"We'd like to go back to Skipton." She raised her eyebrows at her friends; they nodded. "That's where we are setting our mystery. Maybe Geraldine could channel her Yorkshire grandmother."

Geraldine rolled her eyes.

"Are you writing a mystery?" Sheilagh asked them.

"We are, but we are only at the research and planning stage," Evelyn said. "We don't even have a plot yet."

"Or a full list of characters," Geraldine added.

But they had enthusiasm, and it was stimulating.

"Who takes the notes," Allan asked.

"I do," Geraldine said.

"Who thinks up the ideas?" Grady asked.

"We all do," Norma said.

"Mostly Norma does." Evelyn was scrupulously honest. "It's my job to sell it, once we write it."

"Good luck," Grady said. He turned to his wife. "I'd like to go clay shooting. What about you, Amanda?"

"Love to," Amanda surprised me by choosing this. "I have to warn you I am a very good shot."

"Are you?" He sounded amused.

"I am indeed. My father taught me, and I love it."

"Sheilagh, would you like that?" Allan turned to his wife.

"I would."

I think Sheilagh was determined to do almost anything Allan wanted on this trip. I didn't get the impression that she usually catered to him, but that she was treating him somewhat like a man who was recovering from an illness, possibly depression, and who had to be pampered.

Mrs. Yowlet Sr. bustled in with more coffee and heard our plans.

"I can throw together a snap lunch for everyone, if you like."

Everyone agreed that would be a good idea. I promised to meet them at the van in an hour which would give them enough time to get ready for the day and for Mrs. Yowlet Sr. to put together the lunches.

I collected the brochures I wanted and sat down on the bed to text Mark. I typed out an abbreviated version of the Tucson ladies' ideas and sent it to him.

He replied with a thanks and said he'd pass it on to Chief Constable Whelan at the Whitby station. The Whitby Chief Constable outranked the Northallerton one. It must be a nightmare to decide who received the report. Superintendent Addison had ordered him to report to the Whitby Chief Constable. I expect Mark picked the one who would be the most cooperative with him and kept everyone happy by reporting to both.

When I met everyone at the van, I passed a brochure to each of the American ladies.

"It's a list of mysteries that involve trains," I said, "since you'll be traveling on a train this morning."

"Oh my. This is exciting." Norma opened it. "*Murder on the Orient Express*," she read.

"Naturally, we have to have Agatha Christie," Evelyn pronounced. "*The Edge* by Dick Francis. That was well-written. Very exciting."

Geraldine read her list. "*The Man in the Lower Ten*, Mary Rinehart. That's an old one.

"*The 4:50 from Paddington.* That's a classic Christie." Evelyn said with what sounded like satisfaction.

The clay shooting group did not join in the discussion of the mysteries. Except for Amanda who did know her cozies, the rest of the group were only mildly interested in mystery novels. The Tucson ladies were avidly interested. Everyone might benefit from being separated for the day.

"Thanks." Evelyn said to me.

I dropped the ladies off at the train station first and took a few minutes to make sure they had their tickets with the commission rate for seniors. Then I drove to the Thimbleby Shoot Grounds. I stayed with the two couples until they were welcomed, properly outfitted with guns and ear protectors and were ready to enjoy themselves. I left their lunches with the receptionist who put them in the club house refrigerator. My group could use the club house and have a comfortable place to gather before or between their shooting experiences. They promised to text me when they were ready for pick up.

I spent an hour in the Joe Cornish Gallery, entranced with the beauty of the photographs. I promised myself I'd take more care in composing my photos and try to be more observant about what I might photograph. Visits like this were one of the perks of tour guiding. I experienced some of the best offerings of the towns and cities.

On my way out of the building, I spotted a community events signboard. Front and center was an announcement for a dog show. It was located near the Thimbleby Shooting Grounds. That was convenient. I parked near the entrance as I had to be ready to leave when the two couples called for a pick up. A class was in progress. Tiny dogs paraded around in a large circle. I climbed the bleachers, sat, and watched.

Yorkshire Terriers. Tansey Finn-Smyth's breed. Tansey is the wife of my step-brother. I don't know him at all well as I was an adult when my mother married his father. I'd met Tansey when she had come to visit me with her sister-in-law, Pamela. They were not alike. I supposed the brothers James and Harold were also not alike. My other step-brother's James's wife, Pamela was poisonous just like her husband, but Tansey was a dear. She showed Yorkies. She might be here. I watched the judge examine the dogs and pick out her top choices. And there she was—Tansey with her Yorkie. The audience was silent as the judge moved around the dogs, paying close attention to their ears for some reason.

She picked out Tansey and her dog and indicated the head of the line—a first prize position.

"Hello, Tansey. Congratulations." I caught her as she was heading toward the sheds in the back with her Yorkie tucked in her arms.

"Well, I never. Claire! How lovely to see you. Did you watch the competition?"

"Just the last of it. I don't have much time. I have a tour here. Again, congratulations."

She grinned. "Poppet here is doing very well."

Tansey had no children and spent her time and some of her considerable wealth on her dogs. She worked hard and was generous, helping others to train their dogs.

"When are you going to bring Gulliver to me?" she asked. She'd offered me her services a few months ago. I hadn't called her.

I shook my head. "I don't seem to be able manage to get away. I'll try in the fall when things slow down."

"Right you are, then. Any problems with him?"

I told her of Gulliver's need to bark hysterically when the doorbell rang." Mind you," I said. "That doorbell is raucous."

"Treats when he doesn't bark," Tansey said. "That should do it."

I agreed to try it. I gave her a quick hug and headed back to my car. I wondered how her husband dealt with her inherited wealth.

Mark texted me as I reached for the ignition." Can you come to the station in Northallerton?"

"Sure. I'm not far away. Why?"

"Chief Constable Whelan is here from Whitby and wants to talk to you."

I tried to imagine what the chief wanted as I drove the van to the police station north on High Street. I'd been at the site of the murder on the moors. Perhaps he wanted to get my observations, such as they were, on that.

Mark met me at the entrance and ushered me into an office. It was spacious with two desks, two computers, a coffee machine and a large, paned window that gave a view onto a brick building next door.

Chief Constable Whelan was about fifty-five, tall, with a shock of dark grey hair that stood up on his head. He had dark eyes, a lean face and resolute manner.

"What do you know that could help us?" He didn't waste much time.

"Which murder are you interested in?"

The chief glanced at Mark.

"Chief Whelan is interested in Hartley's murder. I'm interested in both Hartley's and Jason Taylor's."

The chief swung his head back to me.

"I discovered Jason on the stairs in the chocolate factory, and I was at Ralph's Cross when Phillip died," I explained.

"Phillip?" the Chief asked.

"He registered for my tour as Phillip Saunders. I understand his name was Hartley Ferris. I think of him as Phillip."

"I see."

I wasn't sure if Chief Whelan thought I was explaining frivolous details, or he was simply slotting the information into the files in his head. His face told me nothing. It was all bones and shadows.

"Go on. Did you notice anything at the site on the moors?"

I suspected the moors were his responsibility and whatever I knew about Jason's murder could more properly be reported to Inspector Fawthrop.

I mentally conjured the scene at Ralph's Cross. "Phillip was talking to my tour group. He was explaining the role of the peat bogs in the ecosystem. He was an interesting man when he talked about something that interested him. I wasn't close to him to hear this. It is what my tourists told me after he died."

He nodded and waited.

"I saw the group follow him down the hill to the bog at the bottom. I didn't see anything unusual until I saw people gathering around him when he was on the ground."

There was silence while Chief Whelan stared at the papers in front of him. A fly buzzed against the window, making an inordinate amount of noise for such a small insect. The silence lengthened.

"Did you know he was working for Scotland Yard?" he finally asked.

"Yes, eventually."

"How did you know?"

"It was after Jason died. Philip kept disappearing."

"What does that mean, 'disappearing'?"

I glanced at Chief Constable Whelan with more interest. That was a precise question that was looking for a precise answer.

"When we were in York, he was often not with the group. When you travel with eight people, eating together and sightseeing together, you get a sense of where they are, or in Phillips' case, where they are not. It's a bit like a family after a time, because you notice when someone is away. The others in my group noticed as well, but I paid particular attention. I always count my guests going into an activity or site and when we leave. I'm responsible for them, so I pay attention to where they are."

"And you noticed he was often away?"

"I did. After Jason died, I confronted him because I had seen him go through the door to the stairs, then Jason was there, and Phillip wasn't."

"He told you he worked for the Met?"

Mark had told me in front of Phillip but there wasn't any need to be completely honest. I nodded. Phillip had not denied it. I'd better learn some discretion if I didn't want to put Mark into trouble with his bosses or into danger with criminals.

Chief Constable Whelan was silent for a few moments. Then he heaved a sigh. "There are too many detectives cluttering up my bailiwick, too many tour guides at the site of the murder, and too many bloody tourists. What about these women, American women, and their speculations?"

Mark must have given him the ladies' views.

"They are mystery novel fans," I said. "That's what my tour is centered on—mystery novels."

"Old ladies can be observant."

I didn't think any of the three Tucson women considered themselves an "old lady". Retired seniors perhaps, but not "old ladies".

"What do they think?" Chief Whelan was at least respectful enough to consider their ideas. I was surprised that he was interested

He must have understood for he said. "You never know where a good idea can come from."

I told him the ladies' rationale and their conclusions. "There might be something in the chocolate angle. Not Phillip spying for another company, but something about chocolate."

Whelan glanced at the mobile phone on his desk that displayed the time. He had probably given me all the time he had allocated. He turned to Mark. "There might be a link between the Jason Taylor murder in York and my murder on the moors. You look into that and report to me."

"Yes, sir."

Whelan held my gaze. "If you think of anything you saw when the murder of Ferris happened or anything anyone else saw and told you about, report to me."

"Yes, sir." I didn't work for him but I'd support this investigation. He handed me his business card and stood. I was dismissed. Mark escorted me back to my van.

"Lunch in ten minutes?" he asked.

"I can do that." You'd think we'd never quarreled this morning.

CHAPTER SIXTEEN

Romanby War Memorial Park was well-equipped with benches. I watched Mark walk quickly across the green. He skirted the curved flower beds with their purple and white crocuses and bouncing bright yellow daffodils, moving like an athlete with confidant strides and a smooth gait. The smell of samosas reached me before Mark did. He noted my fixation on the bag he carried.

"Do I have to share?" he said.

"At least one," I insisted.

I don't know why we Brits are devoted to Indian food. Sheilagh might be right and it was a hold-over from colonial times, but there you have it, we are. Perhaps, as Evelyn had diagnosed, it was the curry. Mark handed me a cup of coffee and a samosa. The other three and the butter chicken were his lunch. I laid out Mrs. Yowlet's hard-boiled eggs, raw carrots, ham sandwiches and apples on the bench. I was about to encourage Mark to eat some fruit and vegetables then stopped myself. His eating habits were not my affair.

Instead, I asked him, "How did it go?"

"It's pretty frustrating." He answered me around the samosa. "I don't have any authority, but Whelan keeps assigning me jobs, so I'm involved."

"If you want to know what's going on, you're going to have to cooperate?" I asked.

"That's right. He does realize my position. He just wants to get as much as he can out of me without paying my department for it."

"Are you getting paid for this?" I knew he would do it anyway because he was determined to find out who killed Phillip, but he had to pay his bills.

"I'm on holiday pay." He said shortly. I supposed it was none of my business.

I let the subject drop. Personal boundaries are tricky to negotiate, especially, I was finding out, financial personal boundaries.

"I manage financially," Mark said with a defensive tone. "I have savings. Investments. A retirement package. It's good enough."

"I think so." I hadn't meant to sound inquisitive. I needed to be careful. "Actually, Mark, that's admirable. You are reliable and my favorite policeman."

"It doesn't matter to you that I'm a salaried employee of the state?"

I shook my head. "It matters that you're doing what you love, that you contribute a great deal to society, that you are hugely attractive— and you can sing."

He grinned and paused with the samosa halfway to his mouth. "It shouldn't bother me, then."

Finally! I hoped that was the last of the jibes about my money, but it might take him some time to change.

Mark finished the first samosa and started on the second. "If I deal with the Whitby nick, I can pursue my own leads, and Whelan has to work with the time I'm willing to give him."

Mrs. Yowlet's ham sandwiches were delicious. Surely, that was home-cured ham, home-made mustard and some kind of chutney. Lovely. I wrenched my mind back to Mark's case.

He continued. "The disadvantages are: I don't have any back up that I can call on instantly; I can't order officers to work because I'm not from this unit; and any information I need I have to dig for—I can't just assign a sergeant to do the grunt work. The advantage is: Whelan is ahead of me on some of it, so he can give me information I need."

"What kind of information?" I was curious.

"Background info the people on your tour for one. Then the background info on the other tour guides."

I had a disquieting thought that Whelan had checked into my background as well. He wouldn't find anything criminal.

"I suppose the police can hack into my bank account and my mobile." My mobile! What had I texted? Nothing too bad, although I may have given Dierdre my opinion of Detective Inspector Fawthrop. Whelan wouldn't care about that. All this careful scrutiny made me nervous. Would any of this get into the papers? Online? If tourists heard about murder on my tour, they might not book with me. Whelan could look at my accounts and find nothing because there would be nothing in my business account to interest anyone. I put a rein on my imagination. I was getting too far ahead of the situation.

"We can't get into your bank account without cause," Mark said around the last samosa. "But we can get into your mobile."

"What about *your* phone?"

"Mine's encrypted."

Back to the investigation. "What did you find out today?"

"A constable in Whitby found the man from the day tour, the one who asked Hartley about the bog. I'm going over there this afternoon to sit in on the interview. While I'm there, I'll read all the statements from the tour guides and any others they've collected."

We finished our lunch and our coffee and Mark headed back to Whitby. I put in a quick call to Deirdre and caught her eating lunch at her desk.

"Is everything fine with Gulliver?" I missed my dog, but I was determined not to moan about it.

"Thanks, I'm fine." She said.

"Oh, sorry." I should have asked about her first.

"Kala called from York. She seems back in the world of normal."

"I talked to her. She's going to ask you for a puppy."

"Oh, no."

"I told her another dog was unlikely."

"Thank you."

"Did you talk to her headmistress?"

"I did. Kala won't like that, but I did. I didn't threaten legal action, though, and the headmistress was truly worried about Kala and Judith. I think Kala is in better shape than Judith, so I just let it go."

"Odd the way it worked out."

"Very," she said. "Are you sure you don't know any criminals?"

I wasn't sure. "Tell me about Gulliver."

"Gulliver is doing very well. He's getting spoiled by Josh who's decided Gulliver gives him prestige with the girls in the neighborhood. He's walking Gulliver without being asked."

"Remind me how old Josh is," I said a little surprised.

"Almost fourteen. They start young these days."

"Wow. Imagine him thinking of anything but sports."

"I know. It takes adjustment. Any more bodies on your tour?"

"Of course not. Everyone is fine." I heard the alarm ring on her computer. It was her way of keeping on schedule.

"Let me know if you need anything," she said and disconnected.

I pocketed my phone, took one last look around at the beautiful park where the small tete-et-tete daffodils bobbed near the walk ways, the same daffodil Peter Brown my gardener had planted in my yard at home. They were a cheerful promise of a burgeoning spring. Then I headed out to the Thimbleby Shoot Grounds.

"It was fab," Sheilagh said as she climbed into the back seat.

"I really enjoyed it," Amanda said. The two couples arranged themselves on the back of the van, leaving the front seats for the American ladies.

"And Amanda is a proper good shot," Sheilagh praised.

Amanda laughed. "My dad taught me when I was a teenager. My sister and I used to compete."

"I bet you won," Allan said. "You certainly won today."

"I didn't know this about you," Grady said, slamming the door shut. I made sure everyone was settled before I pulled away from the car park. I didn't think Grady and Amanda had known each other long before they married. They were discovering new talents.

"*I* certainly didn't win," Sheilagh said. "Everyone left me in the dust."

"We could practice, if you like when I retire," Allan said. "I used to be pretty good."

"Military?" Grady asked.

"Yes. When I was a lad. I didn't stay in long, but I learned quite a bit. And you? You are a good shot as well."

"Not military. I just like the precision of it, and I practice."

Like any tour guide, I was pleased they had enjoyed themselves and encouraged them to talk about it.

"Did you use shotguns or pistols?"

"Shotguns. Only shotguns. Not much pistol shooting any more," Allan said. "They banned pistols after our one mass shooting."

"In Scotland, wasn't it," Sheilagh said, as if Scotland was a foreign country. The *United* Kingdom was a shaky concept to some.

"That's right," Allan said. "About 1987. No one can legally own a pistol now except the police and the military."

"We haven't had a mass shooting since then," Sheilagh said, "but I bet there are guns out there."

"No doubt," Grady agreed. "Not legal ones."

Allan leaned forward from the rear seat. "We had an inspector from the Home Secretary's office looking at our books about two years ago to make sure we weren't importing any guns. I guess it's getting to be a problem."

"What were they looking for?" I asked.

"Guns, particularly from Eastern Europe, packed as components and then assembled here."

I tried to imagine what the gun components could have been packed in. Bubble wrap? Cushions?

"One of the lawyers in the firm where I work defended a man who had been accused not of importing, but repurposing guns," Amanda said.

"What's that?" I hadn't considered that there might be guns in Britain. I was aware of them when I lived in the US. I had naively thought there were few, if any, in Britain.

"People can own antique guns," she explained, "which are not classified as weapons. Some nefarious souls buy the antique guns which are legal and re-tool them to take modern ammunition. It isn't legal to own a hand gun or a pistol of any kind. A repurposed antique gun becomes a weapon and is therefore illegal."

"You are well -informed," Grady said.

"It's surprising the information that comes my way in the law office when I'm preparing documents or taking notes. I found out that criminals, particularly the ones who are the enforcers or killers in a gang, would rather use revolvers because they don't jam, even though they are bigger than pistols. Apparently, pistols are unreliable."

"I wonder if you met any criminals out there on the clay shooting range, practicing," I said.

Grady laughed. "Not likely. I expect they have their own indoor ranges."

Amanda sounded serious. "I don't know how they can shoot a person. I can't even shoot birds. Just clay discs."

"Well," Sheilagh said from the far back of the van. "They are pigeons—clay pigeons."

Amanda laughed.

The American ladies were waiting at the train station when I pulled into the adjoining car park. They piled into the van all talking at once.

"Wonderful trip."

"Couldn't have been better."

"We had a table between us so I could spread out my papers and make notes." That was Geraldine.

"Beautiful country. We had great time," Evelyn said.

"We plotted our mystery novel all the way back. I do hope we can extend our trip and return." Norma was enthusiastic.

"I've worked on that," I said. "If you come to my room tonight and bring your credit cards, we can make the arrangements."

"How was your day?" Evelyn turned around and addressed the two couples behind her.

"Very enjoyable," Amanda said.

I deposited everyone at the farm, picked up my Ambleside Farm invoices from my room and walked over to the main house. The two Mrs. Yowlets were working in the kitchen when I arrived.

"Coffee, luv?" Mrs. Yowlet Sr asked.

"Thanks." I appreciated the coffee. She made it the way I was used to in Seattle, strong and very hot.

"How was the butty?" she asked.

Butty? Oh, sandwiches. "Wonderful."

"All is well then?" Aelwen asked me as she took my credit card.

"First of all, thanks for looking after Kala. She really needed the respite."

"No problem. She's a dear."

"My guests have truly enjoyed themselves. This is a great place for them. Allan and Sheilagh, in particular, had a good time."

"They'll be having a big shock, I'm thinkin'," Mrs. Yowlet Sr. said.

"How's that?"

"They are workers the two of them, so that's a good thing as there is nothing but t'work on a farm. They know nowt about farming, really. Nonetheless, where's there's muck, there's brass."

I glanced at Aelwen. I understood that to mean that if they worked, they'd do all right. She was checking my accounts with hers.

"Do you think they will get into trouble with Allan's plans to retire to a farm?" I asked her.

"They are entitled to the chance to try," she said. "We put them in touch with friends of ours who are farming in Wiltshire because that's where they're going to settle. They'll need more experience, and if they can get some guidance, they might avoid big mistakes." Aelwen nodded at me to indicate that we agreed on the total and entered my numbers on her tablet.

"Very dear sometimes, mistakes," Mrs. Yowlet murmured as she kneaded bread, slapping and turning the dough energetically.

"They can be, yes," Aelwen agreed. "Those two don't have much experience. Sheilagh doesn't have any, and Allan had experience as a lad. They'll have to learn."

"He's been working in an office," I said. "Something to do with shipping."

Aelwen handed me my receipt. "A long way from farming. It won't be an easy retirement."

"More like a right hayload of t'work," Mrs. Yowlet said as she divided her dough into quarters and pounded it again.

Farming would be new and very hard and would take a lot of organization. Allan might not have had experience of management, unless he was retiring from importing illicit drugs where he would have had vast experience. Sheilagh would have the experience of a nurse around organization and efficient use of time. She might be a huge help on their farm…if she supported that decision, and they did buy a farm.

I pocketed the receipt and left the Yowlet women to their work.

Mark texted that he wouldn't be back until late. Late, probably meant about midnight.

I let him know we were eating dinner at Uno Momento restaurant in Northallerton, but I didn't expect to see him there.

When we returned to the Ambleside Farm after dinner, I said good night to the two couples and invited the ladies into my cabin.

I started up my computer and pulled up the file I had on possible arrangements for an extension of their holiday. They had all paid the extra fee for the ability to change their flight. We took care of that first. While I was clicking and typing, they talked among themselves.

"I texted Peter," Geraldine said, "and told him to stay in Palm Spring another week. He wasn't all that happy, but he's well-fed, has company because friends live there, and he can golf."

"Maybe he misses you?" Norma said.

"Possibly," Geraldine said. "He can miss me for another week."

"I texted Tony," Norma said. "He is deep into a production of a new line of pottery, and he has a deadline for the art gallery in Santa Fe."

"That exclusive place on Canyon Road?" Evelyn asked.

"The very same. I told him to just put his head down and go for it. I texted my neighbor to go in and stock our fridge. I'll pay her when I get back. Tony forgets to eat if there isn't anything handy."

"What about you, Evelyn?" Geraldine asked. "Did you phone Max?"

Evelyn was quiet for a moment. "No, I texted him."

"What did he say?"

"He said he'd get a ticket and come and join me."

We waited.

"I said, 'No.'"

There was a short silence while we absorbed Evelyn's determination to keep Max at a distance.

"Maybe he could join Peter for some golf."

Evelyn shrugged.

"What about your business?" Norma asked.

"I texted my son to take on any rental deals he wants and sell any houses he'd like to while I was gone. It might be good for him not to have me around to consult with all the time."

Geraldine stared at her. "That's major."

Evelyn said nothing and drew back a little.

"No, really," Geraldine said. "You are so, so…"

"Yes?' Evelyn said with an edge to her voice.

"So conscientious," Geraldine supplied. "Always attending to every detail. It's major that you're letting Leonard unsupervised management scope."

"He's forty-five," Evelyn said.

"And very competent," Norma intervened. "You are right to have faith in him. I'm sure he'll do you proud."

Evelyn looked rigid. She was not happy with the way her friends were analyzing her. This might be another argument in the offing. I interrupted. "Here, look at these." I brought up a couple of B & Bs in Skipton for them to consider.

They picked one and decided whose credit card they would use. I entered it and printed out the receipt for them.

"What about a car?" Evelyn asked.

"Which one of you is under 71?" I asked. I knew none of them were. Their ages were on their passports.

"You mean no one will rent us a car if we are over 71?" Evelyn was indignant.

"Some companies will and some companies won't. Some require a doctor's affidavit before they rent to anyone over 70. Some over 75."

"Think about it," Norma said. "We'd have to drive on the wrong side of the road. *And* we'd have to negotiate those roundabouts."

"Oh." Evelyn was quiet.

"Why don't I find you a car and driver?" Money was not a problem for these ladies.

"Go ahead," Evelyn said.

I did that and they left happy with the prospect of a new adventure. If they didn't write their mystery novel, they would have a lot of fun researching it.

"Are we going back to the same guest hotel in York?" Geraldine asked as they were leaving.

"Yes, is that okay?"

"Marvelous," she said. "I'll look forward to it. They give you chocolate at that place."

Mark arrived just as the ladies were leaving. They smiled at him. Norma raised her eyebrows at me as if to say: Aren't you the lucky one?

I wasn't perfectly sure of that, but I was glad to see him.

"Have you eaten?" I said as he shut the door of the cabin.

"I stopped on the way."

We looked at each other. I was instantly conscious that there might be listening ears to our conversation.

Mark kissed me then whispered in my ear. "They are pretty sure that the man they picked up for questioning was hired to murder Hartley. He was on that local tour from York. He's been suspected of being an enforcer in other cases."

I whispered back directly into his ear. "The one who asked Phillip about the bog?"

"Right. But they have absolutely no evidence to nail him with murder. It's frustrating."

Still whispering, I said. "Yes, I can see that."

He kissed me quickly. I pulled him closer and whispered. "Are you going to be okay about my money?" I had been turning that over in my mind, and I didn't feel we had resolved it.

"I'm working on it. Give me time."

I stopped whispering or talking. I found the idea of being overheard intimidating. We couldn't talk about the case and we couldn't take up our quarrel about money unless we didn't mind being overheard, or we sat in the bathroom with the shower running.

I headed for bed. We might postpone our quarrel so many times it would no longer matter. But it was maddening.

CHAPTER SEVENTEEN

Mark told me he would finish up at the Northallerton police station in the morning and join my tour in York this evening. I had Phillip's ticket for the dinner theatre at the Grays Court Hotel which Mark could use, but he might be late. He'd meet us at the hotel if possible.

After a leisurely start, we arrived about ten and booked in with Mit Sandhu at the same guest house we'd begun the tour. It was wonderful to be back in York. The city exuded a sense of timelessness, as if the Minster, the cobblestone streets, the eclectic crowded buildings of the Shambles jostled together in some kind of harmony and would continue to do so for another several centuries.

"Welcome, back," Mit said to me as I registered the group. "One short this time?"

I stared at him.

"Rooms. You need one less room than you booked originally?"

"That's right".

He passed me over the keys. "That Mr. Saunders, he was trouble. What did you do, dump him on the moors?"

I bit my lip and continued to stare at him. A brief sadness passed over me. Phillip had been aggressive and at times obnoxious when we were here last, but he'd had been alive. "Something like that," I said.

He smiled at the group and offered to carry their suitcases.

I appreciated the offer as did the Tucson ladies. There were no lifts and Mit helped by lugging the suitcases up the many stairs. We dispersed to our rooms and met for lunch at Café Concerto on High Petergate where the Italian style menu gave us varied choices. Everyone settled comfortably around the table.

"I need to buy some clothes," Norma said, "since we are staying another week."

This was the first the couples had heard about it. The ladies explained their interest in staying on to research their mystery novel.

"Not before we've had our murder mystery dinner tonight. I realize this may seem a little tactless," I apologized, "since we have had our own murder which remains unsolved. It's a play, and it was set up before Phillip died. How do you feel about it?"

They glanced at one another. "I don't suppose he's going to mind," Norma said.

Sheilagh half-laughed at that. "I didn't really know him. I don't think anyone did. I would like to continue with the plan."

The rest agreed which was wonderful as, if they'd objected, I didn't know what I would substitute for the mystery dinner tonight.

Amanda wanted to find a toy store and buy for her children. Grady appeared happy to accompany her and to advise and, no doubt, pay for it all.

"Where are the book stores?" Evelyn asked me.

"There are at least twelve bookstores in York," I said and pulled out a list from my rucksack. "Six of them are clustered around the Minster, so you won't have to walk far."

Her eyes lit and she stuffed the list in her purse.

"I'm going to find a stationery shop," Geraldine said." I need pens, paper and a blank book to write in."

"Why don't you buy a e-tablet?" Norma asked. "That way you could transfer the files to your computer so they could be used easily. We could even set up a cloud site and all work on the same manuscript."

Geraldine stared at her. I wasn't sure if she was intrigued or horrified to think Norma would be able to work on her manuscript.

"I might do that when I get back to the States. Right now, I just need paper."

"Signatures on Fossgate is probably what you want," I said. "It's not far."

We agreed to meet at the guest hotel at six and I sent them off to enjoy themselves for the day. I returned to the hotel to finish my paper work. I had to make sure everyone had paid and there were no outstanding accounts. Sometimes a guest puts a bar bill at a hotel on my account, and I discover it after they've left. I checked through all my receipts and found that this group had been scrupulous about paying their own way.

I closed my files and went for a walk to the Minster. I sat on a park bench and listened to the clarion concert which always leaves me relaxed and relatively tranquil. I phoned my nephew Josh and received an update on Gulliver. Josh snapped some pictures and sent them to my mobile. Gulliver did look happy. I wished I could just hug my warm dog for a moment, but I'd see him tomorrow.

Everyone met back at the guest hotel on time. Our dinner was scheduled for seven. The Grays Court Hotel where I had booked the dinner was on Chapter House Street a few blocks away. There was no rain which was a positive for March in York. We headed out full of pleasant expectation.

"The mystery will be set in the 1940s," I said,

"Oh, just when Agatha Christie was in her prime." Evelyn commented a little abstractly as she craned her neck to stare at the Minster. It was, as usual, imposing, grand and elegant.

"Yes, Tommy and Tuppence," Norma said keeping her mind on mysteries of the 1940s. "Modern writers are setting novels in the war period. Jacqueline Winspear is writing about those days."

"But not setting her novels in York," Evelyn pointed out.

"True." I noticed Norma rarely quarreled.

Amanda added her information. "Patricia Highsmith set hers in the 1940s. I don't know if any are set in Yorkshire, though."

The discussion took us to the doors of the Maroon Court Hotel. It was a grand old hotel—very grand, very old. James I was supposed to have stayed here. I thought quickly to my fourth form memorization of the Kings of England and came up with the dates. "James I. Ruled 1603 – 1659."

"That's old," Geraldine agreed.

"The first guest stayed here in 1091."

There was a short silence while they absorbed that impressive fact.

"It's Grade 1 listed," I added.

"That means no one can change it?" she asked.

"Not much," I said. "They can apply to upgrade it with new electrical wires and better plumbing, or they can repair failing structures. They have to make the building look exactly as it did in the past."

"I think that's wonderful," Norma said, "very romantic. No wonder this city is seems steeped in history. The laws require it."

We had climbed the front stairs and passed into the ante room. A smiling young woman met us. "The British Mystery Book Tour?" she asked.

I nodded and presented nine tickets to her, including Phillip's, just in case Mark had time to join us. We followed the hostess through a couple of small sitting rooms with fireplaces, gorgeous Axminster carpets and booklined shelves.

"It's like a manor house from an Agatha Christie novel," Norma whispered to me.

"It is, but airy." The walls were a pale green. Many of the accents were white so, in spite of its age, it seemed light and spacious.

The hostess led us up a couple of stairs, under an arch and into a bright dining room with room for about twenty. A few tables were occupied. Ours was in the far corner, a large round table with a "Reserved" sign on it. We arranged ourselves around the table. A waiter was instantly at my side with menus.

"Could I get a drink for anyone," he asked.

"We will have wine with the meal," I said to the group. "The wine is chosen by the chef and paired with the food, but you can certainly order a predinner drink."

Everyone did. The ladies all chose champagne.

"Just to celebrate our great tour," Geraldine said.

"Yes," Sheilagh said. "Here's to Claire and many thanks for a lovely time."

I was pleased. It is always a relief when the guests are happy. It doesn't always last, and they don't always write good reviews when they go home, but I like to hear it. Considering one of the tour guests was murdered, I was surprised at how much the others had simply disregarded that fact and enjoyed themselves. I couldn't predict the reviews on this tour.

I held up my menu. "We have a set menu with a choice on entrée."

They studied their choices.

"It's five courses," Norma said. "That's a lot."

"We get duck or venison for the entrée," Evelyn said, giving the decision her attention.

When the waiter had taken our orders, he collected the menus and left me with a fist full of brochures. I passed them around. The headline was "Who killed Cynthia? And Why?" The picture was of a young woman dressed in a 1940s' suit slumped over an office desk.

"Ooh. Wonderful. War-time England," Geraldine said.

"Looks like it." Evelyn read the script at the bottom. "Office steno Cynthia Forsyth-Blenkingstoke was found dead at her desk Monday morning by the caretaker of the building."

"Where did she work?" Geraldine asked

"Who hated her?" Norma asked.

"Did she have a secret?" Allan speculated.

It felt a little macabre to bring my guests to a murder mystery dinner so soon after Phillip had died. I was a little uneasy, but I had booked it well in advance, and they group were enjoying it.

"Why don't you ask me?" a voice said from behind me. I turned to see a tall man made up with powder to give pallor to his face. From a distance he would look about fifty. This close, I could see he was much younger, probably in his twenties.

"I am the Honorable Nigel Fatheringham, Minister of Trade and Transport, and Cynthia's employer. We were sorry to hear of her passing. She was a pleasant young woman, if a bit woolly."

"What does 'woolly' mean?" Norma whispered to me.

"Scatterbrained," I translated.

"And I am her sister, Angela." A young woman with dark hair and bright red lipstick came up to our table. All the women at the table, including me, stared at her costume. It was a suit, circa 1940 or even pre-war, with shoulder pads, nipped-in waist and a skirt that ended about mid-calf. She had chunky stacked high heels that were back in fashion today. Her hair style was intriguing with a pompadour piled on top of her head and two clumps of hair on each side of her face. It must be a wig.

"She didn't have any secrets from me," Angela said.

"Watch out you don't get bumped off next, then," Norma advised.

"And I am her boyfriend, Archie. It's 1938. We're engaged. We don't have secrets between us." A young man with improbably red hair, equally improbable freckles and a sad face leaned toward us then turned away repeating as he left, "She didn't have any secrets from me."

They swept away to the next table.

"What's going to happen?" Grady asked.

"As far as I know, the cast will give us a short drama while we have drinks and before dinner is served, then we discuss it throughout dinner. At the coffee stage, they'll add more information."

The waiter brought the drinks, and we settled back to watch the play.

The three actors mounted a small platform at one end of the dining room and staged a quarrel between the employer, the sister and the boyfriend in which we were told that the office was privy to information about troop readiness, supplies, and other preparations for war, and that the murdered steno had been upset for a week before she died.

"Sounds like Tommy and Tuppence.," Evelyn said.

Amanda said. "Yes, it does. Christie involved them in a lot of war-time secret work."

"Christie was writing at the time such activities like spying for the enemy were going on," Geraldine said.

I think my group had discovered the plot before the actors had revealed much of it.

The audience clapped and the waiters came around with the first course which was cured halibut in smoked cream with elderberries. They also brought a tart, light wine. It was a superb pairing. Grady raised his eyebrows and smiled. He appreciated the delicate flavor. I checked on the other guests and realized Evelyn wasn't eating. I stood and walked around to her.

"Not to your taste, Evelyn?"

"Sorry," she said. "I don't want to complain…"

"But you will," Geraldine said.

Evelyn ignored her. "But I don't like the smoke in the cream."

"That is not a problem." Since this was not a restaurant where I could pick up a plate myself, I raised my hand and stopped a nearby waiter.

"Could you remove madam's plate?"

He did so, and I walked toward the kitchen with him. "Can you bring her something small to nibble on?"

"Beef tartare, blue cheese, walnut, pear. It's the next course. I could bring hers early."

"That would do. Thank you." I left him at the kitchen door and turned back toward the tables. On my left was a small room, likely used for intimate parties. At the moment, it continued the actors—and Mark. The actors were eating and listening to Mark.

"You're here," I said surprised to see him. "Want to join us? Unless you have something you ought to be doing?" I know I sounded suspicious, and I was. Why was he talking to the actors? He stood and followed me out of the room speaking to me in a whisper.

"I want them to ask a question and see if there is any reaction in your group."

"In the play, you mean? Like Hamlet? 'The play's the thing wherein I'll catch the conscience of the king.'"

Mark shot a sideways look at me. "Something like that."

I felt a slow tide of heat flush up my body. "Mark, these are my guests. Don't join us in order to examine us. It's disgusting."

He stopped and put his hand on my arm. He didn't raise his voice, but I could tell by his rigid hold on me that he, also, was angry.

"I'm not going to be held back by your scruples when an officer went down. I'll do what it takes to get the creep who did it."

As suddenly as my anger came up, it disappeared. Mark had priorities.

"Do you think it will work?"

He shrugged. "Worth a try."

"What are they going to ask?"

He hesitated then told me. "The boyfriend is going to ask if she had found the files in the filing cabinet that described the distribution system."

"Because that might make the person responsible for Phillip's death think about where he or she might have stashed incriminating files?"

"Yes, and when a person is trying to recollect something, they usually look up and to the right. I'll be watching for that."

"It seems tenuous."

"It *is* tenuous, but I need some kind of direction. Even a tiny lead might help."

Mark walked back to the table with me and joined the group at the spot I'd reserved for Phillip. It was better, in one way, because we weren't constantly reminded by the empty chair that Phillip had been murdered. It was worse, in another, because Mark was a police officer. that in itself was a reminder.

I felt as if Mark put his duty before my needs. I wanted a quiet tour with no police involvement. He was willing to put my guests in an uncomfortable situation to serve his duty. Would I want him to ignore his principles to suit me? I let the thought settle in my mind. No. I didn't think I would.

The waiter brought Evelyn's beef tartare. She thanked him and seemed satisfied. He stopped and asked Mark whether he wanted duck or venison. He served us all with the beef tartare and more wine, a rosé from Portugal. We conversed easily through the venison and duck and the accompanying red wine to the dessert stage. The waiter cleared off all the debris and brought a sweet potato pie with dark chocolate and pecans. There was a collective 'Ooh' in appreciation of the beautiful presentation. Each plate was surrounded with flowers. Edible, I presumed.

"A work of art," Sheilagh said.

While we were eating our dessert, the actors mounted the platform and gave us more instructions.

"Look under your seat for a piece of paper taped to the underside of the chair. You will find more information that will help you determine the solution to the question of who killed the office steno and why. We are now going to give you a few more clues." They resumed their argument about Cynthia's death.

I was a little nervous waiting for the question Mark had planted. That might be why he hadn't wanted to tell me. Perhaps, I was too obviously nervous. I took a couple of deep breaths and sipped some wine. When the question came, it wasn't quite what I expected. The actor said, "She was collecting information. I know she was. She was doing it for the War Office. Something about sending steel to Germany. She was keeping track of where the steel was going. She found the files."

What good would that question do? If Allan, Sheilagh, Grady or Amanda were the head of a drug importing and distribution business, they wouldn't lose their nerve at the question of an actor. Would they look up the way Mark thought they would? I hadn't seen anyone do that, but I couldn't watch everyone at once. I might have missed it. Mark knew the psychology of a killer better than I did. Perhaps Shakespeare was right and a play would reveal a guilty conscience. I doubted it. Anyone who dealt in drugs wouldn't have a conscience.

I smiled my thanks to the waiter who had quietly taken away the empty dessert plates and brought coffee and tea.

When the actors had finished, everyone reached under their seat and extracted their clue. I checked to see if Geraldine was making notes, and sure enough, she was. She wore her reading glasses low on her nose and peered at her notes.

"It seems they are making it simple for us with only two real suspects."

"The boss and the boyfriend?" Amanda asked.

"That's right," Geraldine agreed.

"What about the sister," Grady said. "She might have been the one who was actually selling secrets."

"Getting it from Cynthia, you mean," Evelyn suggested. "Possibly. Let's review the added clues." She nodded at Grady. "You start."

He read from the printed slip he'd extracted from under his chair. "The steno went to the same hairdresser every week."

Amanda read, "The boss traveled to the continent every six weeks to get contacts for his steel sales."

Sheilagh said, "The boyfriend drank at the same tavern every night after work for an hour."

"That's common in Britain," I interspersed.

Allan read from his paper. "The boyfriend had ambitions to be an actor and appeared in amateur productions."

There was a collective, "Ahh" of suspicion.

We all added our clues and, with the addition of a bottle of port, the speculation lasted the half-hour allotted by the actors. Then we voted on it.

We declared the boss the murderer because he was selling steel to the enemy. No one thought the boyfriend's declaration that Cynthia was collecting information to give to the police contributed to his guilt. They did decide he had no real motive and wasn't bright enough to be an enemy agent. The process of elimination left the boss as the guilty party and greed his motivation. We were right. Several tables were also correct, so we shared in the general applause from the diners and the wait staff. We were each given a small box of chocolates, naturally York chocolates, as a prize.

We walked back to the guest hotel in fine spirits. I invited everyone to the snug behind the front desk. I'd ordered brandy and other liquors as a last night treat. We crowded in there and Geraldine sipped her Amaretto and expounded from her notes.

"The boss had a distribution system for his steel. It was the steel that the Germans wanted. Of course, they recruited someone who had steel. That would narrow it down for Scotland Yard. He was too regular. He went to the same place to meet foreign buyer every time and the Cynthia noticed. He couldn't leave his subordinates alone, though, and micromanaged. Looked over their shoulders, according to the evidence, and made sure the steel went to the enemy. The steno suspected he'd been looking through her files. He was so organized; everything was in a file somewhere. Once Scotland Yard had him for the murder of the steno, they checked through his books to find the distribution routes and shut them down. It isn't that hard to figure out a play such as the one we saw. It's a lot harder to figure out an actual murder. Take Phillip's for instance."

Oh no. Don't. I thought. *Please Geraldine leave his murder alone. I'm trying to run a business here. Trying to give everyone a good time. You have no idea how you could harm my tours if you continue to harp on Phillip's murder. No one is going to want to come with me if they might end up murdered. Please, don't talk about it.* She couldn't read my mind and I couldn't stop her.

"While no one is handing us the clues to his murder, there were many left behind," Geraldine said.

"Such as?" Grady asked.

She smiled at him. "Such as only one man was close enough to Phillip to kill him at Ralph's Cross."

"That's depends on what killed him," Allan said.

"True. Long-acting poison could have been introduced into his food earlier, but presuming it was something fast-acting, it had to be that man."

"Evidence would be great," Mark said.

"I'm not concerned with proving anything," Geraldine said, "just figuring it out".

"What else?" Norma said.

"It would be perfectly possible for someone to order that killing. Just text a hit man, or whatever you call them on this side of the pond, to join the tour out of York. I think the man must have been on that tour bus....well, or our tour bus, but I'm not entertaining that idea."

Amanda sipped her Drambuie. She had had more to drink tonight than she usually did. "Why would anyone want to kill Phillip? He was a little eccentric but not dangerous."

Geraldine leaned forward. "We think he was spying."

Grady looked surprised. Amanda interested, Allan skeptical and Sheilagh indulgent. Mark's face showed nothing at all.

Think, Claire. There must be some way to stop this conversation.
"Spying for whom?" Grady said.

"Another chocolate company. Maybe a French one. He was very interested in chocolate and was snooping around the factory. He might even have been the one who killed the guard."

"Chocolate has been important in York since the late 1900s. It's been a staple of the city ever since," I said, hoping to change the direction of the conversation.

Geraldine stopped talking and sat for a moment. "If it's important, it might be worth a lot." She looked at Evelyn and then at Norma.

I hadn't deflected her.

"What if there was something stashed in the chocolates?" Norma asked.

"Such as?" Amanda asked.

"Such as drugs," Geraldine said slowly. "Then the killings would make more sense. Drugs are spread around the world by criminals. Criminals aren't concerned with law or morality. A nice simple scheme."

"It's not so simple to get away with murder these days," Allan said. "Nor would it be easy to hide activities."

"Maybe not. Most people keep things on computer files which can be hacked. And it was in the files where Scotland Yard found the evidence to nail the killer in the play."

"Encrypted these days," Mark said.

"True," Norma agreed, "but I believe in the power of young minds to discover ways of hacking around most problems."

"I agree with Geraldine," Evelyn said. "Today, it would be drugs that would be illegally sold, not steel."

"A criminal would need a distribution system. You could do it, Allan, through your shipping company. Send drugs all over the world, and all over this country just with computer files and directions. You wouldn't even have to see them, just direct other people to pack them and send them off." Geraldine looked at him speculatively.

Allan's eyebrows disappeared into his hair. "Hold on!"

"I'm not saying you are doing that," Geraldine went on, "just that you could."

"I suppose." He looked gobsmacked.

"Sheilagh, could you do it? You have skills."

"You mean management skills as the head of the visiting nurses in my district? I wouldn't have the time."

That might explain the phone call Norma overheard. She might have been giving advice to a nurse. On the one hand, I wanted to distance myself and my tour business from any involvement in murder, and on the other hand, I almost compulsively wanted justice for Jason and Phillip.

"And you." Geraldine turned to Grady.

He smiled at her. "Now what could I possibly do?"

"Oh, I think you could put drugs in all those chocolates you send out, or in the souvenirs."

I thought of the raven stamped on the bottom of the pepper shaker. What if it had nothing to do with a wedding present? What if it indicated that there were drugs in the shaker?

The hairs on the back of my neck prickled. This was not a good idea. Geraldine was far too clever. If Grady or Allan were a drug lord, or even Sheilagh or Amanda, she was putting us all in danger.

"Great detecting, Geraldine," I said trying again to deflect her. "I suppose *I* could be bringing drugs along on my tours."

She laughed. "I don't think so. Not unless your significant other is in on it."

"And that doesn't seem likely," Norma said. "Too much gold in his aura."

Amanda burst out laughing. "Sorry, Norma. I don't think Mark appreciates being told he has a golden aura. I mean he's a bit too..."

"Masculine," Sheilagh said.

"And definitely not an angel," I said.

"You never know," Mark said. "I don't tell her everything."

I wanted to get this conversation off Phillip's death. "How is your mystery novel going, now that you have had a mystery dinner experience?"

"By the time we get the book written and published," Evelyn said, "the world will have turned to something else. Maybe we'll have a mystery around selling illegal drones."

"Or cosmetics? Or diet pills," Norma said.

"Diet pills?" Geraldine asked.

Norma shrugged.

I smiled at her. "Possibly." I did not want any more conversation about Phillip's death or death in general. I made another effort to move the conversation on. "Does everyone have everything they need?"

"Tomorrow is our last day, right?" Allan said.

"We meet for a tour in the morning and everyone disperses after lunch."

Allan stood. "It's been brilliant. Sheilagh and I have had a grand time."

And with that they all moved off to their rooms, except Sheilagh who hung back and walked beside me as we crunched across the graveled car park.

"I wanted to thank you again for opening my eyes to how important this farm is to Allan."

I looked at her, trim, short grey hair, slim almost athletic body, large brown eyes. Altogether, a capable looking woman.

"You'd have worked it out, I'm sure."

She frowned. "We haven't been married very long, just ten years. We both came late to love, and I truly want to support him. The last few years have been difficult. And I love my job, really love it. I'm the head of the visiting nursing service in my area. It's challenging and satisfying. I'm not sure I could give it up."

"Head nurse of a visiting nurse service?"

"I do other things as well, but the home visiting is the most difficult to organize and manage. Many of our patients are elderly and need a lot of care."

"Can you leave it behind when you're on holiday? It sounds like a responsible position."

"I try. There have been a few phone calls, but I try to be discreet. No one wants to hear everyone's work problems when they are on holiday. And I know Phillip annoyed everyone with his constant texting."

"You have been discreet," I said. "I didn't know you were fielding calls."

"There haven't been many. I'll have to learn to let go completely if we retire."

"Perhaps you could work part-time," I said.

"Perhaps," she said. "No one can work forever. And Allan has to do something. He's been so depressed."

She hurried to catch up to Allan, and I headed toward my lodge.

I met Mark as he was on his way out. He kissed me and whispered, "I'm going to put in a few hours at Fawthrop's office. He's left material for me to read."

I whispered in return, "Did you see any reaction at the table when the actor gave your line?"

"Maybe," he said.

I'd hear about it later. I drifted to my room. I wished Geraldine had not said what she had about the possibility of Allan, Sheilagh, or Grady being drug lords. When I thought about what Norma overheard Sheilagh say on the phone, I dismissed it. She wasn't a drug lord planning a hit. She was a manager of nurses planning patient care. Allan and Grady sounded so eminently plausible suspects that I worried they would believe Geraldine had evidence. Or if they were totally innocent, they would be affronted that she had even considered them criminals. Either way it didn't make for a compatible feeling in the group. I hoped she'd stop talking about it.

CHAPTER EIGHTEEN

In spite of the almost overwhelming worry, I was looking forward to our morning's excursion to Castle Howard. I'd only visited it once, and it was an intriguing place. A huge almost fantastic castle, or rather and overstated manor house with a dome in the central section. It should impress my group.

I packed my suitcase, ready for returning home after the Castle Howard tour. It would be a relief to pick up Gulliver and settle back into my own house. First, I had to stay safe and protect my ladies. They had named Alan and Grady as suspects. Speculation about who murdered Phillip could stimulate reaction if the killer was either of them.

The night was dark, but clear. It should be fine weather again for us tomorrow. I didn't expect Mark this early in the evening, but I looked out the window onto the car park in case he had arrived. I saw someone behind the cars, and the interior light blink on as the man opened the door and slipped in. Grady. What was he doing out there? Was he going to the chemists for headache tablets for Amanda? She had drunk more than usual tonight.

No, he hadn't started his car. He was talking on his mobile. The overhead light flicked off. I glanced at my rucksack and, with no tussle with my conscience of any kind, I plugged the bats' ears in and listened.

I heard Mit talking to someone on the phone and the murmur of female voices, probably the American ladies. I walked to the window and faced Grady two floors below me. I heard him clearly.

"Yes. Castle Howard. It's north of York about fifteen miles."

Then silence. Then "Take a bus, join a tour. It worked last time."

My mind sharpened, and I leaned my head on the glass as if that would help me hear more clearly.

"Three old birds, probably walking together. You'll likely only have to kill one. The others will be so shocked, they won't give us any more grief."

Silence again.

Then, "That would do it. Be sure you aren't observed. If the anyone sees you, take care of them. You can't afford to be picked up again."

Silence.

Then. "You can bring in another if you think you need to. I agree, three at once can be difficult. I'll pay for that. Who did you have in mind?"

I could not hear what the other person was saying.

"If the tour guide catches sight of you, get her as well…Oh, about five-foot-nine. A bit skinny, glasses. She wears a rucksack. Name's Claire. You could call her by name and check it is her."

Another silence.

"That's a bit steep. You only have to take a morning. I see. That is a point. All right. I'll double the price. Don't leave any witnesses this time."

I stood there while the silence drummed in my ears. You'd think he was ordering some work done on his car, a detail to be sorted and tidied away. Death was part of business. Grady opened the car door. The light came on, and I saw him pocket his phone. I heard the door slam shut and watched him walk back to the hotel.

I sank down onto the floor.

Grady. Geraldine was right. He looked so respectable. Did Amanda know? I doubted it. She hadn't known him long. She had too tender a conscience to be a partner in this. I couldn't assume that, though. I forced my mind away from speculations and turned it back to the chilling information I now had. Grady had instructed a minion to kill at least one of the trio from Tucson— and me. Tomorrow.

Mark! I had to tell Mark about this. I punched out his number. It rang and rang. Even if he was driving, he should have his mobile on "hands off" speaker. No answer. I texted.

"Urgent. Grady's planning murder. I need you."

There were many things that could go wrong with his mobile. It could be out of charge, under the seat of the vehicle, buried in his luggage or forgotten at the station. As soon as he received this text, he'd call, if he could.

If I was going to find the ladies, I'd better do it before Grady returned to his room. If he had bats' ears, he might not have them on him. I'd be careful. I dialed Evelyn's room.

"Would you three ladies like to join me at the bar for goodbye drink," I said. "On me? It would be a treat to talk to just the three of you."

Evelyn sounded surprised but willing. "That's nice of you. I'll check with the others."

She came back quickly and said, "Sure."

"Meet me in the lobby and we'll go from there." I didn't want Grady to know which pub we were going to—if he was listening.

When we were settled around a corner table at Thomas's of York and I had ordered yet another drink for everyone, I told them what I'd overheard. There was silence when I finished.

"Grady," Geraldine said after a moment. "Imagine. I was right."

"I'm not taking buckets of satisfaction from you being right," Evelyn said.

"This is nasty." Norma screwed up her face. "Why kill us?"

"I think you are too close to working out who is responsible for Phillip's murder." I'd thought about motive.

"Possibly, we're making him nervous. We are a mite too fond of parading our cleverness," Evelyn said. "Thanks for telling us, Claire, but how did you hear him?"

I was not going to tell them I had bats' ears. They were illegal. Rather, it was illegal to use them. Having them with me was a temptation to use. "I was close enough to hear, but he couldn't see me." That was strictly true. I should turn them over to the police soon. It might be easier to just break them apart and put them in the trash.

"What does Mark say?" Geraldine asked. "It would probably be a good idea to have some police input here."

"He's not home yet, I left him a text. When he arrives, I'm going to ask him what we should do. For one thing, he and as many of his officer friends as he can recruit on short notice should be with us. He'll believe me, but his fellow officers might not. I don't have any witnesses to that conversation. Should I cancel the trip to Castle Howard?" I'd hate to do that. I didn't want us to be targets for Grady's minions.

"Hmm. It wouldn't be hard for the hit man to find us in Skipton, would it?" Geraldine said.

That was a chilling thought. The three women were taking a train to Skipton after this tour and would be without any protection there.

"So, either we deal with this guy at Castle Howard tomorrow when we have you and Mark and perhaps more to help us, or we deal with him on our own in Skipton." Evelyn put it with irrefutable logic.

We were all silent, contemplating the choice.

"Do you think Amanda knows?" Norma asked.

We looked at each other and slowly shook our heads.

"Not likely," Evelyn said. "She wouldn't be able to function under that much stress."

We were relying on years of experience in our lives and with the lives of others. It wasn't scientific and a good deal might depend on it being correct.

"Grady does seem convincing," I said.

"Devoted to her, you mean?" Norma said.

"Yes."

"He could be devoted to her and still be a killer." Evelyn, as usual, was rational.

"I hope she never makes him mad," Norma said, a little reflectively.

"About tomorrow," Geraldine said. "What do you suggest?" She turned to me.

I was surprised at how calmly the ladies were taking the news that someone was out to kill them, but I shouldn't have been surprised. They've lived a long time, had to deal with many difficulties, and they were used to working together. That didn't mean they weren't afraid. They just knew how to deal with fear.

I felt helpless. I'd never had to extricate my tourists from a murder plot, and I didn't have a practical plan in my head.

"Tell us about the tour," Evelyn said. "I mean where do we park? Where do we go into the building? When do we come out of the building? Are we with others or do we have a private tour?"

I brightened. "We have a private tour. No one but us is on it, and we're going to be taken all over the house with a guide."

"Can we get a security cop to go with us? "

"I'll ask Mark."

Geraldine pulled out a notebook and a pen.

"So, number one. Claire asks for a security guard to be with us on the tour."

"No one will be armed," I reminded them.

"Of course not."

"The hit man will probably not be armed with a gun," I said, "but he might be with poison."

"Those Russians tried to kill those agents with poison—in Salisbury wasn't it?"

"That's right. Not many guns in Britain. But don't let anyone get close to you. There are knives."

"We have to watch out for anyone getting close to us." Geraldine wrote that down.

"Cars in the parking lot that might aim at us." Norma said. "Cars can be a weapon."

"Good point." I hadn't considered that.

"Something might be thrown at us?" Norma offered.

I felt nauseous. These women were systematically and calmly discussing the ways in which they could be killed.

"If we could get hold of Grady's cell phone, we could countermand his orders." Evelyn proposed.

We stared at her.

"How could we get the mobile?" I was rivetted.

"I bump him," Geraldine said. "He drops his phone. Evelyn, you have the quickest hands. You snatch it and pass it to Claire. Claire you text the hit man and tell him to forget it."

They looked almost complacent, certain they had a workable plan.

"If that doesn't work," Evelyn said. "We will just have to be vigilant."

"I'll talk to Mark and see what protection we can get. We could cancel the tour. Go someplace else."

That did seem sensible. I could take them on a drive to Lincoln. See the cathedral. My brain was buzzing with alternatives when Evelyn spoke.

"No, Claire. That's letting bullies run your life. I expect Grady gets rid of whoever is in his way. We're in his way, so he plans to eliminate us—wherever we are. I don't hold out a lot of hope for those kids of Amanda's once they get to be teenagers. He'll probably find them inconvenient. No, we'll at least thwart him on our murders, and we might catch him. That way he can't murder anyone else."

Geraldine and Norma agreed.

It was a noble thought, but it scared me. These women had far more courage than I did. I thought about Kala and her options. She hadn't wanted to take on the bullies, and I believed she was correct. A vicious gang is not a bully a ten-year-old can face. It was fortuitous that the bully confronting Kala had been badly injured and not in a position to threaten her now. Sad, but definitely fortuitous. Grady was even more vicious than Kala's bully and I didn't want to confront him. He was planning to kill at least one of the Tucson ladies—and me.

"We have a better chance of catching him tomorrow than at some time in the future when we have no idea when he will strike," Evelyn said. Her voice was even. She appeared to be calmly considering options.

"Why are we meeting in the bar," Geraldine asked a we gathered our belonging and headed back to the hotel.

"Because I think Grady has a listening device," I said. "Be careful what you say to each other in your rooms."

They looked at each other. "No wonder he wants to kill us," Geraldine said. "We've been speculating and are pretty sure he is not what he wants us to think he is. We were tabulating evidence, contradictory statements we'd heard, setting it out nicely in a column before we let Mark know. No wonder he wants to get rid of us. We hadn't thought about being overheard."

Mark arrived about ten-thirty. I hustled him back to his car and instructed him to drive to the other side of the Minster where we could park and look at the lights the way countless other courting couples did. I told him what I'd overheard.

He swore vehemently and inventively for about a minute. Some of those words were Welsh and unintelligible to me, but profanity is recognizable in any language. He stared out the window, turned back to me and took a deep breath. "First thing, I call Fawthrop."

"Where is your mobile?"

He searched his pockets. Swore again, and searched under his seat. He found it.

"Is it on ring?"

He shook his head. "I'd turned it off for a meeting." He read my text. "Sorry, Claire. Really sorry." He phoned Fawthrop and repeated what I had told him and asked me for details.

"What time does your tour start there? What time do you expect to arrive?"

I answered those questions and put one of my own.

"Can Fawthrop arrange for a security or a real constable to accompany the tour? That way we can keep everyone safe—at least while we are on the tour."

He put the question to Fawthrop, then answered a question I couldn't hear.

"Yes, I'll be there. I may not be able to keep them all under my eye at all times. I'd appreciate another body."

He finished with his call and turned to me, studying me for a moment.

"I don't like this one bit. How did you get such a *troseddol* on this tour?"

"A *trosehal*?" I attempted that word phonetically.

"A criminal."

"Luck?" I said. "Bad luck?"

"If it didn't matter so much, I'd…." he stopped. There wasn't much he could do if the ladies and I decided to go ahead, but we weren't foolish. If he thought it was too dangerous, we might think up something else.

"You'd what?"

"Get you out of here."

I disregarded that. I wasn't leaving. "We could avoid the hitmen that Grady sent to kill us," I said "by not going to Castle Howard, but he would just rearrange his schedule and get us another day. Isn't it best to try and capture them where we know they are going to be?" That was Evelyn's argument, and it was compelling.

"It is. But I don't like it." He slammed his fist on the steering wheel. I put my hand on his. He turned his up and grasped mine. We sat there, sharing our worries. It was as if we were in a warm, sheltered pool surrounded by a wicked sea. Fanciful, that notion, but reassuring all the same.

I had to face reality, though. I knew there was evil everywhere. "I know I live in a world where people are trying to enjoy themselves and get as much rich experience as they can, and you deal with people who distribute death either by directly killing someone or handing them a pill that will ensure addiction and eventually kill them. I understand we share a world, but we don't live in the same space."

He leaned forward, listening to me.

I continued. "You're comfortable in my world because that is what you aspire to, not just for yourself but for everyone. I'm not comfortable in your world."

He reached over and pulled me into his arms. "May you never get comfortable in it," he murmured into my hair. I wrapped my arms around him and settled against him. I could never be quite as secure in my own world as I had been. Knowing what he dealt with over and over, knowing there were people walking near me, in my social group, appearing respectable while acting despicably, tore away my naivety away and made me face a multi-layered world. If I was going to share Mark's life, I was going to have to remember justice and order were elusive.

He left me at the hotel and said he would spend most of the night arranging the surveillance for the next day, but he *would* join me on the tour.

At breakfast, I announced the last site of the tour to my assembled group.

"Castle Howard is huge." I said, "I've hired a guide for a private tour. It is about a thirty-minute drive, and there's lots to see."

"Then we return here?" Grady asked.

"We do." I made myself look at him and smile. It was hard to do, but our lives might depend on his belief that we were unaware of danger.

"We're all packed," Evelyn said. "We'll leave our suitcases at the front desk and pick them up when we return. We have our train tickets."

"Where are you going?" Grady asked. Yesterday, I would have seen that a polite question. Today, it sounded like an inquiry necessary for his plans. If he missed killing them today, he could follow them and do it later.

"We decided to revisit some sites. We're not ready to go home." Geraldine chimed in. "Absolutely not ready. Peter can golf some more."

They left the table to attend to their luggage.

"Where are they going?" Grady asked me.

"They wanted to arrange their own trip, this time," I said, "so I didn't ask." That was true. I hadn't asked; they'd told me.

Once we were all in the van and we were headed north-east, I activated the mic.

"Castle Howard was designed by a dramatist who had never built anything previously. He was a friend of the 3rd Earl of Carlisle and the castle construction started in 1699. It took over ten years to build and was what the brochure describes as a 'flamboyant baroque design'. The next earl toned it down a little and added a more staid Palladian wing. It sits on 10,000 acres."

"My heavens, a Texas ranch," Norma said.

"Unusual in England," I said.

"I suppose it is owned by the National Trust," Geraldine said. The ladies were doing their best to act normally.

"No, it remains in the hands of the same family and the present earl is George William Beaumont Howard."

"Does he have a son or daughter?"

"I believe the heir is his younger brother, who is fourteen years younger. There have been Howards in the castle for eleven generations."

"Amazing," Norma said. "There are very few families in America, except Native American families, that have been there for eleven generations."

I continued my information session. "I had to choose what aspect of the castle the guide will emphasize, so I chose a brief history, information on the remarkable women including the famous Rosalind who married into the family in 1865, and the last countess, Ela, who was an active, opinionated, and philanthropic woman. As well," I went on before the men could protest if they were going to, "there will be an emphasis of the war work of the family and I'm sure the guide will point out the sometimes-bizarre items some earls brought back from their Grand Tours of the Continent."

"Will we see much of the castle?" Norma asked.

"We will."

"Where will be we going in the castle?" That was Grady. I suppose he wanted to let his minions know how to locate us.

"I'm not sure, Grady. We will get a good tour of the castle…not all of it, of course. The family continues to live there. We won't go into their section, but it's huge."

"And the grounds?" Amanda asked. "I understand there are some remarkable follies and temples."

"I hope we get to them," I said. "We will have to wait and see."

The sign for the Castle appeared just then, and I paid attention to the road, driving onto Malton and, just before the Talbot Hotel, taking a sharp left up the Castle Howard Road. Mark was either ahead of me, setting up security at the castle, or behind, following us. I hadn't seen his car. I thought we'd be safe in the van as Grady wouldn't want to kill himself, or anyone else in front of Amanda. I worried about how to keep the ladies safe while I parked the vehicle.

"We will pull into the 'coaches only' section here. I would like you to stay together, so I can alert the guide and be sure we all get to the right place. This is a three-hour tour with coffee arranged between the inside tour and the outside tour. We will be back in York for lunch and say our goodbyes."

I pulled over, got out and slid open the van door for them. Geraldine gave Evelyn a quick look and strolled up beside Amanda.

"Did I tell you about the wool I found in York, yesterday?" she said.

Amanda turned and gave Geraldine her attention.

Evelyn was walking between Allan and Sheilagh.

Norma stood between two cars, taking pictures of the others. They should be safe for a few moments.

I hurried back after parking the van in its designated spot, keeping an eye out for vehicles that might be aimed at me. Nothing was close. I wanted to get my group into the castle before any of Grady's men could approach them. I herded them in to the ante room where we met our guide, a middle-aged woman dressed in a soft green suit. A badge on her lapel proclaimed her as "Jocelyn". I saw Grady pull out his mobile phone. I expected he was going to message his minions or simply turn off the bell.

Jocelyn started to lead them into another room away from the exit doors. Geraldine stumbled, grabbed Grady's arm and pulled hard. The mobile flew from his hand and hit the ground. Evelyn crouched down. I saw her palm it.

"Not here," she said, looking at the floor. "It must have skittered off in a corner. Allan, can you look for Grady's cell phone? It dropped."

"I *am* sorry," Geraldine said. "Arthritic knees. Very unreliable."

Grady shrugged her off. Amanda held her arm to steady her. Grady moved over toward Allan. Evelyn sidled up to me and slipped the phone into my pocket. She smiled brightly and returned to diligently help search for the disappearing phone.

"I'm sorry," Jocelyn said. "We must move on to the next room. I will have the security people search for the mobile. If found it will be returned to security or me, and we will pass it to you. Please move along. One of the guards, Guido here, will accompany us so you can talk to him at the end of the tour, and he will help you."

"Come on, darling," Amanda said. "You can't use it in here in any case. I know it's important, and we won't go without it."

You'd swear she was talking to a child.

Grady glared at Geraldine who pretended she didn't notice.

I let the group go ahead of me and stayed behind in the ante room. There was another small room off to one side, and I had glimpsed a figure in there. Mark. I passed him Grady's phone.

"Corbett's mobile," I said. "Evelyn filched it. Can you tell his men to cancel the killings?"

Mark's eyes lit. "I can try."

He activated the phone. The screen lit. He touched the message icon and several messages came up. He studied them for a moment.

He typed, "Cancel. Repeat. Cancel. Back off. Go back to York. Contact later. Will pay as if."

"What if there is a code word?"

"I was looking for that and didn't see any, but you never know."

I let out a deep breath. This was nerve-wracking.

"We have an officer with the tour. Did you see him?"

"Guido?"

Mark grinned. "The very one."

"Jocelyn said he was one of their security guards."

"Nope. He's one of Fawthrop's. A detective constable. He probably told her he was a new security guard."

That was a relief. He would have good training. "What happens when we go outside? The group is going to want to go to the Temple."

"I'll join you for coffee. That occurs before they go to the grounds, right?"

I nodded. The inside tour would end at the Café Coffee and my group would get their coffee or tea and pastries before going out to the grounds.

"I'll stay with you outside. At that point, other people from other tours will be milling around. Fawthrop has three men stationed to keep an eye on you. One of them dressed as a groundsman at the temple and two are watching the boathouse. We figured you would go there."

I worried the nail on my thumb. Outside there were a lot more opportunities for assassins. I didn't like taking my tour outside, but I didn't know what else to do. "It might be enough."

"And it looks like those women are looking after themselves," he said with some admiration.

"They're not invincible," I said. "And they are old ladies—smart but not brawny. They could be knocked over."

"We'll do our best. Remember, you're on that hit list."

That was not something I was going to forget.

CHAPTER NINETEEN

Café Coffee was crowded. I managed to snag two tables close to each other while my group joined the line for their tea, coffee and pastries. The Fitzroy Restaurant was quieter, but it wasn't open today. Grady complained to me again about his missing mobile. I promised to check for it.

"You know, Claire. I think Geraldine bumped me on purpose. She wanted my phone."

I stared at him for a second, thinking furiously. "Uh, Grady. Why would an old woman from America be interested in your phone? That sounds highly unlikely."

He smiled with real amusement and I realized how attractive he could be. No wonder Amanda was smitten. His face lit, and he laughed aloud. "I'm paranoid. Sorry. She couldn't have managed to pick it up and hide it. Everyone was looking for it right away. It must have slithered under a cabinet."

"I'll check again with security." I glanced over at the solid-looking officer standing at the exit door. His eyes drifted over Grady and me and moved on to check on others. I was reassured. Guido was alert.

Grady confounded me. I was having trouble processing this genial, reasonable, friendly Grady with the one I'd heard giving instructions to a killer. He didn't match any tourist type, any business man, any friend, or anyone at all I'd ever met.

"Hello, *cariad*," Mark said from behind me.

I turned and smiled with relief. Great. Some personal back up.

"Evans," Grady gestured toward the urns. "I'm just going to get coffee. Can I get you some?"

"Thanks, no," Mark said. "I had some on my way here."

I suppose he was wary of taking any food or drink from Grady. That was sensible.

"Claire?" Grady asked me. I had the same reservations as Mark. "No, thank you. I'll get some later after everyone settles."

I did wait until all were seated fetched myself a very hot and strong expresso. Mark nudged in beside Geraldine.

"This is wonderful, Claire," Amanda said to me. "Truly a great ending to a lovely trip." If she overlooked Phillip's death, she'd had a good time. There was no reason for her to think his death was anything but natural, although she had heard the Tucson ladies' speculations of murder. Perhaps she thought they were romanticizing. It was odd group: Grady, likely the head of a gang, issuing orders to kill at least two of us, the four ladies and me, well aware we were targets, and the other three, including Amanda, were totally oblivious to the dark intent surrounding us. I took a deep breath and concentrated on the tour. In a few hours it would be over.

"There's an hour left on our passes," I said. "What would you like to see? You can't see it all, of course, as the grounds are extensive. What would you like to do?"

Amanda spread out her brochure with the map in the middle pages and studied it for a moment.

"Where would they sell toys? I've yet to get something for my youngest," she said.

"I thought you…" Grady protested.

"Oh. I suppose I should correct that. I've yet to get *everything* I want for Caroline."

"I know the Carriage House sells toys," I said, pointing to its location on the map.

"I'll leave you to it, then," Grady said. "I think I've hit my limit on toy shopping."

Amanda smiled. "We can meet back at the van."

"Good idea." He stroked her arm.

That meant Grady was free to follow us. I didn't like it.

"I see there is a farm shop and a tree nursery and a garden shop," Allan said

I pointed to all three locations on the map.

"This place was occupied by school girls during the war, wasn't it?" Sheilagh asked.

I knew that bit of history. "It was. School girls from Queen Margaret's School in Scarborough were billeted here." One part of my brain operated in tour guide mode, while the other part worked at damping down fear.

"The guide told us they scuttled in and out, saving a lot of paintings and artifacts when the fire took hold. Brave girls," she said.

"I guess there was a lot of bravery at the time," Geraldine said. Since she was talking about the war years in England, I considered that an understatement.

Allan laughed. "That's for sure. I wonder if they farmed the grounds during the war, planted it in food production?"

"They must have planted cabbages," Grady said. "I understand half of England was covered with cabbages during the war."

"We need to see the boathouse and the temple," Geraldine said, peering at her own map.

I hoped Detective Constable Guido was listening to her.

"The Rose Garden will not be impressive at this time of year," I said. "And you probably don't have time to trek through Ray Wood, but the temple and the boathouse would be interesting."

"The temple is a bit of a walk," Mark said. He didn't say the approach was through a wood where snipers could hide, and the boathouse sat at the edge of the lake where snipers could draw near in a boat. It wouldn't be wise to walk to either place. If the men had guns, then the open spaces where they could get a clear shot were dangerous. If no guns were involved, then places where people might come close and brush against us were dangerous.

"The café at the boathouse isn't open yet," I said. "While Castle Howard usually offers Kelly cars, those tractors pulling trains of seats, they aren't operating this week."

"I'd like to see it, anyway," Evelyn said. "If we have to walk, we'll walk. It does look to be quite a distance from the temple to the boathouse. We wouldn't have time to get to both."

"Let's see what I can do," Mark said. He walked over and spoke to the Guido. The officer nodded and spoke into his radio.

"All set," Mark said.

"What did you arrange?" Evelyn cocked her head on the side like a bird, waiting for largess.

"Ten minutes and you will know," Mark said.

When we came outside the café, we saw a golf buggy waiting for us, a big golf buggy that seated six. The ladies were delighted.

"Where did you find this?" Evelyn asked Mark.

"It's the worker's transportation," Mark said. "They are lending it to us."

"Nice of them."

The driver, a young teen, welcomed us and stowed the ladies carefully in the back seats. Mark and I followed and settled in the front.

"Is there room for me," Grady asked?

There wasn't. I was the tour guide. I should offer to get out and let Grady take my place. If I did that, would he would personally dispose of my ladies?

I hesitated and saw our faithful officer, Guido, in a smaller golf buggy behind us.

"Would you mind taking the next one, Grady," I asked.

He glanced at Guido and half-smiled. Perhaps he saw the irony of being carried to the assassin site by someone he thought was a security officer. It was even more ironic for me, knowing Guido was a detective. I felt as if I was participating in two worlds: one as a tour guide in every-day England and one as a mouse pursued by a cat in a deadly video game. I was careful with my words. "We'll stay together."

"Certainly," he said, politely. "See you at the temple."

I wasn't too concerned about our visit to the temple, as it was situated in the open with acres of lawn around it. That made it a difficult place for anyone to creep up on us as well as difficult for anyone to pick out who to shoot on the moving golf buggy. Grady was with Guido and had little chance to attack us from the that buggy. If Mark's direction to Grady's men was effective, they wouldn't be attempting to kill anyone. If that hadn't worked, the boathouse would be a better site for them, as it was surrounded by trees, a perfect hiding spot for hunters.

There were two approaches to the Temple of the Four Winds: one skirted the edge of Ray Wood and the other took a broad pathway over the lawns. Mark leaned over and spoke to the driver. We took the right fork in the road and drove over the lawns. At the temple, I had little energy for appreciating the elaborate columns, the elegant dome and the Romanesque statues because I was scanning the area for killers disguised as wandering tourists. No one looked dangerous. There was a family of two adults and two children of about ten years old exploring the temple. There was a couple, man and woman, who stayed close together. Were they Mark's back-up? Were they Grady's hired killers? I hadn't thought a woman would be a killer, but it was certainly possible. I was flipping through ideas and speculations at warp speed, while at the same time paying attention to where everyone was. I didn't see the groundsman who was supposed to be guarding us. Did Mark work like this all the time?

Grady joined us on the broad steps leading up to the temple. It was an amazing structure, incongruous in the English countryside, but fascinating all the same. It stood on a small rise of land, overlooking the rolling meadows and woods beyond. The woods bothered me. A sniper with a good rifle could pick off the ladies…and me as well. The statistics on gun violence are low in this country, but there are some criminals with guns. I hustled everyone into the building.

It wasn't hard to keep them interested as the inside of this folly was exquisite.

"The floor," Evelyn said in surprise. "It looks like someone went crazy in here."

"The mad mosaic designer," Geraldine agreed.

While the colors, a collection of stone, black, beige with some amber, were harmonious, the shapes were seemingly random with squares, half circles and rectangles laid down without any sense of design that I could see.

"Beautiful view," Norma said heading for a huge glass door.

"Look at it from this angle," I suggested, pulling her to a window where she could look without making a target of herself. She knew there might be killers after her, but she acted as if there was no danger. I hoped she wouldn't decide to wander off today. I felt a sudden stab of fear, imagining Norma meandering in the woods, making herself the perfect target. About twenty harried minutes later, I bundled everyone back onto the carts and Matthew, our driver, drove us to the boathouse with Guido and Grady following. Matthew took us in a straight line around the edge of the property turning a sharp right-handed corner to go along another ridge to the boathouse instead of taking us through Ray Wood. We were surrounded by trees. I didn't think Grady's henchmen would have anticipated us taking this route. Since Grady didn't have a phone, he couldn't tell them.

I relaxed a little in the peaceful setting until we approached the boathouse. Because the café wasn't yet open, there were few tourists. Grady's minions might be one or two of them. They might have decided to stay on the grounds. The message Mark sent could only have reached them after they were already at Castle Howard. It might have lacked a code, the absence of which made them suspicious. They could have decided to watch and wait. They could be any one of the single men I saw sitting on the stairs or leaning on the rail, watching the ducks. They could even be the two men who were near the water's edge. I saw a row boat pulled up onto the grass near the playground. Could they have arrived that way? Could those be the men we had to watch out for? I looked at the men. One of them was vaguely familiar. "Mark, isn't that the bloke who went to Aelwen's? He looks like her photo."

"Photo," Grady said. "You have a photo of that man?"

I scrolled through my photos and brought it up. Guido glanced at it and smiled.

Mark cocked his head—I swear just like my dog when he caught the scent of a pheasant. Guido must have recognized the man in the photo and associated him with something criminal, as he headed toward him. Mark followed Guido. They covered the ground quickly and were on either side of them before they could move.

I heard Guido say, "You're nicked, mate. If you're packing, you're in deep."

Mark had handcuffs on one man and Guido had a firm grip on the other. It was quiet and quick. The men did not resist. Guido spoke into his radio.

We stood there, mesmerized by the scene in front of us.

Then Grady said, "I'm going back to see if Amanda's all right. I don't like this."

I blinked and turned to him. It would be good to for him to leave. One less person to worry about. "That's fine," I said. "I'll see you at the van shortly." I expected he saw the futility of trying to kill anyone today. His hit men had been apprehended. His plans were stymied.

Grady called to Mark, "I'm going to walk back. Check up on Amanda."

Mark stared at him for a second and then nodded.

The ladies and I watched the drama of the arrest from the safety of the deck. The wide deck was empty of anyone but us at now. The rest of the tourists had headed up the path to the Castle. Perhaps like Grady, they didn't like the situation. We stood in the sunshine leaning on the railing and gazing alternately at the beautiful serene lake in front of us and at the activity of the arrest where Guido had found another pair of handcuffs and both assassins not only had their hands handcuffed together but were secured to the bar that kept passengers safely in their seats.

Mark trotted over to me. "Grady went back to the castle."

"Yes. He said he was going to check on Amanda, but I expect he saw the game was up here."

"Right. Guido recognized those two from a previous suspect list as you did from the photo Aelwen sent. Glad I had experienced mates on this."

I smiled at him. We were both relieved.

"The two other officers are here. They're in a rowboat on the water under the deck, just hanging around to keep an eye on you."

"Oh, fancy that? Our own guard?" It was a relief to know we had someone to call on if we needed them, although, the hit men were well away from us.

"I'll have to go back to the castle and turn these two over to the head of security. Guido can't do this alone."

"They'll pay more attention to an inspector, than to a constable." Hierarchy was important in police matters, something like the strict rules of the military.

"Castle Howard security have their own processes and protocols. I'll need to show my credentials to the officer in charge and get him or her moving. I'll be back. Ten minutes?"

I checked my watch. "We can walk. It isn't far."

"Are you sure?"

I checked with the ladies.

"Oh, certainly, if Claire thinks it's no distance."

I assured them it was only a short walk. "The Temple of the Four Winds is some distance, but the boathouse is quite close to the castle."

"All right, then," Mark said and turned back to join Guido and his prisoners. We watched the loaded golf buggy accelerate up the trail and around the curve of the road until it was out of sight. There wasn't a sound. The prisoners were silent, not cursing or complaining, just quiet. Guido and Mark didn't speak and the electric cart made hardly a whisper on the trail. It was eerie. We turned our backs on them.

"It's tranquil here. Look. Is that a sparrow?" Geraldine appeared quite relaxed. I expected we were all thankful that the men had been apprehended so neatly.

I followed her gaze to the small sparrow-sized brown, pale yellow bird.

"That's an aquatic warbler. There are many different kinds of warblers. That one makes a chittering sound followed by a chat chat chat cry—among other sounds, but that's a typical call." I went happily into guide mode. The relief of the arrest made me feel almost light-headed.

"What's that bird song," Evelyn asked, listening to the bell-like notes floating in the air. "It is truly a warbling sound."

"It is a warbling sound but it isn't a warbler. It's a chaffinch."

"This is delightful," Norma said and took a deep breath of the warm air.

I hated to move them but we did have to meet the others. "We'd better start back."

"What a relief to have those two rats arrested. Nice not to die today," Evelyn said.

"I do think you are a trifle premature on your congratulations," a voice said.

We turned to find Grady standing at the stairs. We stared at him. He looked relaxed, but held purpose in his eyes. He was between us and the path to the castle. Behind us was the water. We stood stock still, our eyes riveted on the gun in his hand.

"Claire," Geraldine said. "I thought there were no guns in England."

"Only criminals and police," I said

"Well, that pegs you, Grady," Evelyn said.

He jerked his head. "That's enough. Move back." He motioned with the gun. We obeyed and shuffled back toward the railing. A gun in the hands of someone who was obviously ruthless is compelling. I moved a little away from the others. I caught Evelyn doing the same thing leaving Geraldine and Norma between us, making it more difficult for Grady to cover us all. Where were those two guards Mark left with us? Under the deck? Perfectly useless.

"Could you tell me, please," Norma said with her soft voice. "What you are planning on doing?"

"Not at all," Grady said politely. "You are all going to have a bad accident. So sad. It will be quick because I don't have much time. No one will hear the shot because this gun has a silencer."

I didn't want to look closely at that gun. It was spell-binding, like a weaving snake, and I had to think. I ignored it.

"All of us?" Norma said.

"All of you. You were so busy trying to work out Ferris' murder that you forgot to protect yourself. First rule of life: Look after yourself."

"Ferris?" queried Evelyn with a puzzled tone of voice. Even in this situation, Evelyn wanted the facts.

"The man who called himself Saunders. He was a Scotland Yard detective. Not quite as clever as he imagined he was."

"Oh, I see. A detective. That makes sense." Evelyn spoke as if slotting together the clues she held in her mind and coming up with a sensible solution. "And you figured him out?"

"Of course."

This was not a social occasion. Didn't Evelyn realize how dangerous Grady was? Between the boards on the deck, I caught a glimpse of a boat just below me under the boathouse. Whoever was there was listening. Some help they'd be to us. Were they just waiting to gather evidence and not do anything? Then, over Grady's shoulder, I saw the electric golf buggy drifting down the road in a silent approach. I couldn't see who was in it, but it was likely Mark. We had to keep Grady talking just another five minutes.

"How is your happy marriage going to continue if you kill us all?" I asked him conversationally. "Are you planning on getting Amanda to give you an alibi? And will she? She seems like a principled woman to me. I doubt she'd connive at murder. So, what do you think you can do about that?"

"She won't know about this. She'll back me up. She thinks I'm wonderful. She respects me. You aren't going to tell her anything. You four are not going to upset my marriage. She's sterling, is Amanda, an angel. I won't have you upsetting her."

He saw Amanda as an angel? That was an uncomfortable image to sustain.

"You're afraid we'll tell her the truth about you," I said, his motive finally clear to me. He would see us as a threat. Once Amanda knew about his criminal life, she would lose respect for him.

"You will. A pack of righteous biddies. So confidant you know what's best for everyone. I'm going to eliminate the problem. You won't get a chance to tell her anything. I'm a very good husband and I adore her. She knows that. I'm good to the children. I like children. I even liked your niece. Nice girl. You should be grateful to me. I eliminated her bully."

I stared at him. "You ordered Judith killed? How did you know about her?"

"Kala told me. I get along with children very well. But I didn't do it to just oblige your delightful niece."

He'd ordered the killing of a child. How did his mind work? He was terrifying.

"That girl was supposed to keep a low profile. I want those working for me in schools to blend in. She brought attention to herself with that attack on your niece. She'd never be a good member of my organization."

She'd been a nuisance and he'd ordered her death without any concern that she was just a child. I let the shock of that knowledge roll over me and concentrated on Grady's words.

"She didn't die," I stated that flatly. Everything he ordered did *not* come to pass.

He frowned. "That was careless. I employed young talent for that. On the other hand, he did enough damage for her to realize she'll be disciplined if she doesn't follow orders. I pay attention to details. That's why I'm successful. The rank and file know I watch them."

There was an appalled silence while we processed this.

"What would Amanda say if she knew you'd tried to kill a fourteen-year-old?" I asked.

"I didn't do it myself. I just made the phone call." His voice was almost petulant. He felt no responsibility for what happened. I abandoned that subject.

"But she wouldn't trust you if she knew about your criminal business. She'd be horrified and disappointed."

"That's right. She would. You aren't going to tell her. I won't let that happen." He waved the gun at me, gesturing me to come closer to Norma. I moved only slightly.

"How will you persuade her you didn't kill us?" I had to keep him talking.

"The old biddies will die first. Then, Claire, you'll be lying here, a gun in your hand. Sad. Very sad. Tour guide run amok. Triple deaths and suicide. I can see the headlines."

"No one will believe it," I contradicted him.

"Certainly, they will." He half-smiled. "They've done so before.

I'll have fake psychologist reports, fake doctors' reports. You will have had a history of violence."

That was chilling. He was a gang lord, someone who used murder to solve problems. This was business for him.

"It's not hard to arrange. It only takes minutes."

"What about your alibi?" I was desperately looking for something that would make him pause and consider that his plan was too dangerous for *him*. It was definitely dangerous for me and the ladies.

"I'll convince Allan that I'd been in the rose garden. He's gullible, and I'll see that he repeats that to my wife."

"Poor soul," Geraldine said.

"I treat her very well. Very well." He sounded affronted. "She's happy. I know how to make her happy."

"Not for long," Norma said. "She won't be happy living with a murderer. She won't allow her kids to live with a killer. She's not stupid, in case you hadn't noticed."

"She has no idea about the business side of my life. Nor will she find out."

"She knows a lot about illegal acts," I said. "She works in a law office."

"She won't hear anything. You four will not have any opportunity to tell her. You will not have a chance to poison her against me."

I might as well give the man below me in the boat some information. "Does Amanda know you are running a drug business, killing kids, undermining the government, running a parallel world to law and order?"

He snorted. "You righteous slag! Of course not. She thinks I have a distribution business. And I do. It's just cocaine and…."

"And Fentanyl," I said.

"That too."

"It was Fentanyl that killed Hartley Ferris." I knew why he had died so quickly.

"It was. Very easy to administer. He was dead in seconds. As you will be. I am, as you know, an excellent shot,"

I thought of the report of his prowess at the shooting range. It would be hard to miss at this range, even with a pistol.

He straightened and steadied his pistol hand by bringing up his other hand and supporting it. "Enough chit-chat, ladies."

I had seen Mark and two other uniformed security guards creeping up the stairs as Grady was speaking. What should I do? *Hurry, Mark.*

"You." Grady waved the gun at Geraldine. "You knocked my phone from my hand on purpose."

Geraldine nodded her agreement.

"You get to die first." He smiled.

"Such a privilege," Geraldine said. He raised the gun.

I poised on the balls of my feet, my hands swinging by my sides ready to tackle him. It might be foolhardy, but I couldn't let him kill Geraldine.

Evelyn in one quick movement stood in front of Geraldine. Grady shifted the gun and aimed.

"*You* want to be first to die, old lady?" He smiled. "That is easily arranged."

Evelyn stood straight and waited.

My mind froze. I stood immobile for a second. *You cannot freeze right now, Claire. Do something!*

Mark was at the top of the stairs. A board creaked. Grady glanced over his shoulder.

In that instant, I grabbed a deck chair, swung it high above me and smashed it into Grady's back. When the chair hit him, the gun jerked. Grady must have pulled the trigger reflexively, but without aiming. The bullet missed Mark. Grady whirled back toward me, then took a step toward the railing. I don't know what he thought he was going to do. Dive into the water? Steal a boat? He probably wasn't thinking. Mark had him from behind in seconds. The gun skittered across the deck and dropped into the water.

Mark was breathing hard but held Grady like an iron manacle.

Grady swore, but after a couple of jerking attempts to free himself, screamed and stopped struggling. The hold Mark had on him, must have caused him pain if he moved, or Mark made sure it caused him pain.

"Well done," Norma said, nodding at me. It sounded odd, as if she was praising a child.

"Th...Thank you," I managed.

Except for one quick glance that took in all four, Mark ignored us.

He was swearing steadily at the men below the deck, while jerking on Grady's arm. I heard splashing as the men maneuvered the rowboat to the shore.

From trying to spread ourselves wide on the decking, the ladies from Tucson and I were now trying to get closer, touching each other, a hand on an arm, another on a shoulder, watching as Mark, aided by the two men who had been in the rowboat, shoved and pushed Grady into the golf buggy and handcuffed him to the cross bar.

I heard Mark utter the police caution. "You do not have to say anything. But it may harm your defense if you do not mention when questioned something which you later rely on in court. Anything you do say may be given in evidence."

We huddled together and stared at them. My breathing was fast and I tried to control it with deliberate breathes. Breathe in, breathe out. I did that five times, then I swallowed and turned to check over my ladies.

"Claire," Evelyn said. "That was amazingly quick-witted of you." She sat down heavily on a deck chair.

My heart was racing. "Reflexes," I managed to say. "I had an abusive relationship many years ago. I trained myself to respond quickly." I was glad those days with Adam where I gauged his state of drunkenness in relation to my safety were long in my past but, apparently, the instincts remained. I was out of practice, and I'd almost been too late.

I saw Mark walking quickly toward me. He wasn't running, but he was covering the ground at record speed. Past him, I saw Grady handcuffed to the bar of the golf buggy and forced on his knees with Guido guarding him. The two useless officers were in the back seat.

Mark sped back toward me. His eyes were wide and he was breathing hard when he reached me and pulled me up and into his arms. "*Nghariad.* You're not hurt."

I shook my head. His hands were squeezing my shoulders, my head was crammed against his cheek, but other than that, I was fine. "I didn't see Grady at the castle. I was worried he had stayed behind. I was right."

Without warning, I felt the ground heave and waves of emotion shuddered up my body. Heat flushed through me with overbearing intensity. I couldn't think; all I could do was feel. Mark's arms closed around me and gripped me hard. I gulped air and tried to control the shakes.

"You *are* hurt." I heard the panic in Mark's voice and the anger That steadied me.

"No. Not hurt." I don't think he heard me, because he burst into a torrent of words.

"I shouldn't have left you with those two men of Fawthrop's. That was just mad. I thought they'd protect you. They didn't. Useless gits. I never should have trusted them. I should have stayed with you. I can't lose you. I can't lose you." His hands roamed up and down my back.

I breathed in and out slowly, consciously trying to calm myself. I was almost panting but I was now able to think. I leaned back.

"What was that?" I said.

"What?" I saw tears in his eyes. He blinked, and they disappeared as if they'd never been. He had felt something to cause them. We both had felt something.

"As if the air punched me."

The tension on Mark's face faded and his eyes warmed. "Relief? Joy at being alive?" He leaned in and put his forehead on mine. "Something more?"

I blinked. Maybe something more. I half-turned to see my ladies standing on the deck.

"My tour." They were my responsibility. "You have a prisoner." I was flustered.

I couldn't interpret the look that came over his face. He pulled me in, buried his head on my shoulder and shook. I wrapped my arms around him.

"Take some long, slow breaths, Mark. You'll be fine. I'm fine." I kept repeating that. Because he was losing control, I was gaining some. "I'm whole. In one piece. Right here."

He stopped shaking, pushed me to arms' length, let his eye roam over me as if checking for broken bones, then kissed me with passion, or relief. I had a brief vision of a conquering Viking. I straightened and pulled back.

"Mark! I have tourists."

He snapped his head up and stepped back. "Don't go anywhere." He was calmer, but just stood there, breathing deeply and watching me.

"No, I won't. I'm staying. We'll walk up to the castle. I'll see you there."

"I shouldn't have left you." He was blaming himself again.

"Oh, rubbish, Mark. I shouldn't have stayed down here. We made mistakes. We aren't perfect. We are both in one piece." I felt more myself with every moment.

He said nothing but looked bemused, and headed back to the golf buggy, straightening as he approached it. He'd find his professional mask quickly. I watched, reassuring myself he had recovered.

I was astounded. Mystified. Rattled. First, I was almost drowned in unexpected emotions and then, once Mark knew I was calm, he was overcome. That shook me even more than escaping Grady's gun.

I turned back to my ladies. Evelyn was sitting in her chair, staring at me.

"That man is a fool over you," she said.

"So true," I said. Apparently, I was also affected. Something had changed. There was a huge cauldron of emotions between us that demanded a few hours of peace and solitude to settle. After I had calmed, I would ponder what they meant. Not now. My ladies had had a fright. They might be as upset as I had been. They needed my attention.

"All right, then?" I asked them.

"You were quick," Evelyn said. "You swung that chair like Willie Mays batting a homer." That must be baseball. I studied her. Her L.L. Bean polo shirt was a twisted to one side, one leg of her capri pants was rucked up to the knee. For Evelyn that was being disarranged.

"Very effective," Geraldine said. "Thank you." She walked a little unsteadily until she was standing in front of Evelyn. She looked tidy as usual, light jeans, trainers, light blue shirt fluttering over her hips. Nothing out of place. She ignored the rest of us.

"You were going to take a bullet for me." Geraldine stared at her friend.

Evelyn met her gaze. "I can't believe I did that."

"Why?"

Evelyn glanced away from Geraldine and then back. "I can't imagine."

"Oh, for heaven's sake," Norma cut in with some irritation, "You love her. Just admit it. You love her." She was crying.

Geraldine stared at Evelyn and nodded, as if coming to a profound conclusion. "You do love me."

Evelyn met her eyes. "Well, I…I…suppose so." She sounded reluctant to agree, as if loving was somehow foreign.

"You think you're unsentimental and lack emotion, but you have an incredibly generous heart, a courageous heart. You can't deny that now."

Tears trickled down Evelyn's cheeks. "You're alive. We're all alive."

Geraldine cried and hiccupped. "You're amazing, Evelyn. I love you. And you," she jabbed her finger at Evelyn, "love me."

They sniffed a little, found their tissues and mopped their eyes.

Norma, sniffed and hugged me. "Many thanks, Claire. You're super clever."

I didn't feel clever, I felt lucky. I was crying as well. This was not something I knew how to handle. Luckily, Evelyn did.

"This won't do," Evelyn said. "We'll have to get back and see to the others."

"Poor Amanda," Norma said.

"Better now than when he had corrupted those kids," Evelyn said, finding her usual practical view, "or arranged an accident for them." She rose her feet, and we moved toward the stairs that led down from the deck. That was a far as we wanted to go for now.

We sat on the steps of the boathouse, watching the golf buggy move away from us and toward the castle. We held hands in a kind of chain, not quite huddling together, staying close and getting comfort from each other. My breathing had returned to normal. Evelyn was flushed, but otherwise calm. Geraldine tucked some hair behind her ears, brushed her shirt front and arranged herself back into her usual tidy mode. Norma gazed after the buggy.

I felt sorry for Amanda. She was going to see her rosy future disappear and her secure position drop away. It would feel like Grady, the Grady she'd believed in, had died, and that would be an aching loss. She'd known a Grady no one else had known and experienced him in a way no one else had.

I tried to tell the ladies some of what I was thinking. "I don't think he would have corrupted those kids. I think he saw Amanda and her family as his chance to be respectable and, perhaps, worthy. When he was with her, he was a decent, reliable husband and father—quite different from a drug lord."

"A split personality?" Norma suggested.

"Not exactly. I think he was well aware he was playing roles. He wanted to be loved and respected, and Amanda did that." As far as I knew, Grady genuinely loved her.

"So," Geraldine said, "he was afraid we would tell her—that we would ruin his perfect life?" She dropped my hand and stood, brushing dust from her jeans. We all stood and began the walk back to the castle. We increased our pace, arms swinging and breathing deeply. The birds sang, a chaffinch again and a warbler. I thought about Grady.

"He was so worried we'd tell her about his criminal life that he risked a great deal," I agreed. "It would have made more sense to back off and just let us go back to our homes, but he was afraid we'd warn Amanda. We knew quite a bit about him, after all."

"It wasn't his usual 'hands-off' murder plan," Evelyn agreed, keeping up with me easily. "A bit sloppy,"

"Too focused on protecting his image with Amanda," Geraldine said. "I can see that."

Norma had her own perspective on Grady. "She respected him, looked up to him, admired him. She was kind and generous and Grady responded to that."

"She's gullible as well," Evelyn said.

"At least, he had some real emotion there at the end." Norma would see good in Brutus.

"I wouldn't count on it lasting," Evelyn said. "She's still better off without him."

"Not that she'll see it that way." Norma was sure of her judgement.

We stopped talking and just enjoyed the sunshine, the bird song and being alive.

CHAPTER TWENTY

We followed the golf buggy as fast as we could, but it reached the castle entrance well before us. Sheilagh, Allan, and Amanda were standing near the buggy as Mark and Guido unloaded Grady and marched him up the stairs and through the front door. As soon as he entered the building, Amanda screamed. I shot a glance at Evelyn.

She understood, immediately. "Let's go," she said to Norma and Geraldine. They moved like an experienced drill team and surrounded Amanda. I saw Evelyn give Amanda a tissue, Norma put an arm around her shoulders, and Geraldine take her hand. I had to find out from Guido what to say to Amanda.

"I'll find a room," I said headed up the stairs.

The same castle guide, Jocelyn, was standing at the top. This time she was not smiling. She was talking on her mobile.

I held up a hand, demanding attention. She pulled her phone away from her ear. "I'm sorry," she started to say, and then recognized me.

"We will need a room for the police," I said, "and another for witnesses. Is that possible?"

She looked at her mobile then spoke into it. "Did you hear that?" The answer must have been in the affirmative because she clicked it off without further conversation.

"Follow me."

I passed Mark. "I'm getting you an interview room."

"Thanks," he said briefly, keeping a firm hold on Grady. I did not speak to Grady. The two rooms were side by side, both elegant and both totally incongruous as interview rooms. They had Victoria fireplaces, comfortable sitting room chairs, and a Louis XVI side table with writing paper and pens on it. I pointed my group into one room and beckoned Mark to take over the second. When everyone had been settled into the appropriate rooms. I returned to Jocelyn.

"You can put the room rental on my credit card," I said, again thankful for a healthy bank balance.

"That's not necessary," she said. "We are grateful to you for moving everyone away from the public and out of view and doing it expeditiously. No charge."

I smiled at her. "Thank you."

When I returned to the room, I found an officer on guard at the door. Fawthrop must be here with his officers.

"Sorry, Madam. You cannot go into that room."

I tried for the steely eye my mother had used when insisting I obey. My group was on the other side of the door. I had to get in there.

"I'm a witness, I said. "I arranged for the rooms."

"Identification please."

I produced my driver's license.

He studied it and me and probably checked a mental list of names then allowed me to pass. If there was anything that symbolized the change from a holiday tour to a police investigation, it was that guard at the door—and of course, that attempt to murder us at the boathouse. It was starting to settle into my mind that we had all come close to dying. I didn't want to think about it too much, because I might start to shake again. I was back to the world of tour guiding now, I told myself firmly. *Pay attention to your guests.*

"What's going on?" Allan demanded, as I entered the room.

Amanda looked up. "There must be some mistake. There really must be some mistake."

"Mark and the York police will sort it." I spoke to Amanda with as soothing a voice as possible. I was conscious of my own deception given that "sorting it" successfully meant Grady would be taken into custody. That seemed to satisfy her a little.

"Can we get some coffee?" Evelyn asked from her position as chief comforter at Amanda's side.

"Certainly." I moved to the hall and caught Guido heading for the other interview room.

"Guido," I beckoned.

He stopped. "Yes, Claire?"

"What can I tell my guests about this?"

He was silent for a moment. "You can tell him what you saw, but not what you overheard Mark and I say, or any speculation on what you think may have happened."

"Thank you." I returned to the room. Allan gestured to me. I walked over to speak to Allan and Sheilagh.

"What's going on?" Allan repeated.

"Grady attempted to kill me and the Tucson ladies at the boathouse," I said in a low voice. "Officer Guido and Mark stopped him." *And me,* I added mentally because it was my battering chair that had knocked Grady's aim aside. For once, I'd acted and hadn't just stood there like a wooden dummy, but I didn't want to talk about it with Sheilagh and Allan.

"Shit!" Allan was horrified.

"Why in the world would he do such a thing?" Sheilagh asked.

"We'll probably find out," I said. "But he's being accused of killing Phillip. He admitted to us that he had done so."

"That's barmy," Allan said, looking astounded with wide-open eyes, lowered jaw and the general look of someone who was facing an unbelievable fact. "I thought he was such a good man."

"And devoted to Amanda," Sheilagh said.

"I think he *is* devoted to Amanda. I don't agree he's a good man." Was that speculation? I'd better try to limit what I said.

"Claire," Evelyn demanded. She wanted that coffee. It was a good idea.

"I'll attend to the lunch," I said and moved to the door to confer with the guard. They had changed guards and Guido was again with us.

"Ah," I said to him. "Can I order some lunch for my group here and for those in the other room?"

He thought for a moment, his large, broad, brown face immobile. Then he smiled. "I expect so. Want me to call room service?"

"Please."

We waited only a minute or so for a waiter to scurry up to us.

"Yes?" he asked Guido.

"Madam would like to order room service for these two rooms." He indicated them.

I proffered my credit card. The waiter handed over a tablet containing the menu. I chose some ciabatta sandwiches, a tub of salad for each room, quiches, and sausage rolls, pickles, scones, jam, cakes and pastries, as well as tea and coffee.

"In twenty minutes, Madam."

"Could you serve the coffee and tea immediately to this room?" I asked.

"Certainly."

That would give everyone something to do besides sit in their anxieties. I turned back to the Detective Constable.

"You recognized those two hitmen at the boathouse very quickly, Guido."

"I did. I collared one of them for HBI about a year ago, but couldn't make it stick."

"HBI?"

"Carrying housebreaking tools. York is not as big a city as some, and we tend to know our criminals. Very nice catch today."

I was glad he had a good memory. It had taken me a few seconds to recognize the man who had been to the farm.

Amanda stood as I returned to the room. "You must tell me, Claire. Why have the police taken Grady? What is he accused of? Do I need to call his solicitor?"

I considered her for a moment. Everyone, including Grady, treated Amanda as if she were fragile. But she had been a single mum for years. She must be strong.

"He is accused of attempted murder, Amanda. And yes, I think you should call his solicitor."

"Oh, God!" She looked stunned for a second and then rallied. "The solicitor. I don't have his number."

"Do you have his name?" Sheilagh asked. "We can look him up on the Internet if you have his name."

"Oh, yes. Mr. Crandor. Andrew Crandor."

Geraldine had her mobile in her hand in seconds and typed the name.

The waiter brought in coffee on a cart and left the cart so we could serve ourselves. There was a plate of biscuits as well— shortbread and Welsh cakes.

"Here's the number," Geraldine said.

Amanda typed it into her mobile and hit "call". We listened to her side of the conversation while we helped ourselves to coffee and tea. It was excellent coffee.

"Yes. Mr. Crandor. This is Amanda Atkinson. I am Grady Corbett's wife....Thank you...No. I am calling because Grady has been arrested by the York police and will be detained in York shortly."

I remembered then, that Amanda was a legal assistant. She would know procedures better than I would.

She gave Mr. Crandor directions. "Could you present yourself or your representative at the York police station and apply for bail? ...I would think in an hour or so....Yes. this is my number. I will call you later this afternoon. ...Thank you."

She sat down with a thump. Norma patted her shoulder.

"Coffee or tea?" Geraldine asked her.

"Oh, tea please."

"Sugar?"

"Yes. One."

Geraldine fetched the tea. Evelyn opened her purse and extracted a small bottle of liquor.

"Brandy?" she inquired.

Amanda attempted to smile. "Thank you, just a tad."

Evelyn topped up all the ladies' cups with brandy. She raised the bottle to me.

I shook my head. "Thanks, but no."

Allan and Sheilagh also declined. The four women sipped their brandy-soaked tea and murmured among themselves.

The lunch arrived and with it an officer from the York constabulary.

"Ms. Barclay?" He asked the room at large. "Crossley" his name tag said. Constable, his silver badge declared.

"I'm here," I said "Would you like me to accompany you?"

"If you would, please."

"Just a moment." I picked up a plate and loaded a ham sandwich, pickle and a pastry and took the cup of my coffee, leaving the saucer behind. The interview might last a while, and I was hungry.

The officer eyed my plate with what I interpreted as longing.

"Yours should be delivered soon," I assured him.

"Yes, madam. It has just arrived."

I wasn't ushered into the room Grady and the officers occupied, but into a smaller one across the hall. It made sense to keep the witnesses away from the accused. I sat on an upright chair and put my lunch on the table nearby. Constable Crossley had returned to the room across the hall. Once he was there, Mark and Detective Inspector Fawthrop entered my room.

"Do you want to bring your lunch?" I asked them.

They looked at each other and wheeled around. Once they were back and settled with their sandwiches, quiches, pickles, scones, and pastries as well as their coffee, Mark pulled out his tablet and prepared to take notes. It was only fitting that Fawthrop do this interview. Grady's solicitor would surely object to Mark doing it since his authority in this district could be questioned and his relationship to me could nullify my statement.

"Exactly what happened?" Fawthrop began.

I took a sip of coffee, finished my sandwich and related everything I could remember in the order it had occurred. Mark typed quickly and kept up to my report.

"You heard him admit to killing Hartley Ferris?"

"Not exactly," I said. "I asked him if it was Fentanyl that had killed Hartley Ferris and he said, and these were his words: It was. Very easy to administer. He was dead in seconds. As you will be…"

Neither Mark nor Inspector Fawthrop spoke for a moment. Then Fawthrop complained. "Not exactly an admission. It does tell us he had knowledge of the killing, but it doesn't tell us he did it."

I felt as if I had let them down. "I did know there was someone in a rowboat below the decking, probably listening, and I tried to get him to admit to it."

Fawthrop's eyes widened slightly, but he controlled his face and said, "Please, don't tell anyone else that. That could be construed as entrapment."

"Oh." I was disconcerted. I had thought I was being helpful. There was much I didn't know about the law.

"It does give good evidence for the attempted murder of you and the other ladies. And it collaborates the testimony of the officers who heard it from underneath the deck."

"That's good." At least, I hadn't confounded the case too badly. Parts of my evidence might be useful. I wondered what kind of trouble those two in the rowboat were in for not rescuing us. They had decided to listen instead of acting. I wondered about their competence. I suppose Fawthrop might be questioning it as well.

Fawthrop picked up some papers that were in front of him and stood.

"You, Evans, can take Ms. Barclay back to the witness room and bring," he stared at the papers, "Mrs. Roberts."

Evelyn. She would be a good witness, although she would likely add her opinion to the facts. Fawthrop left, and I stood. Mark stood as well, reached for me and enveloped me in a huge hug.

"Sorry, love. So sorry to put you into danger." I heard that murmured somewhere near my ear. His baritone voice, low and rumbling, sounded like a song, murmuring comfort.

"You couldn't have known there would be danger." I spoke into his shirt.

"Of course, I could. I knew Grady was a killer. I just didn't think he'd try to kill four of you. That seemed inconceivable."

It felt wonderful to be hugged by Mark, as if all was right in the world and no danger could ever reach me here. A delusion, but a reassuring one.

"He was desperate to protect Amanda from finding out about him. He thought we would tell her. He is truly besotted with her."

"And he was used to killing to solve problems," Mark said.

"I suppose so. What an odd man. Desperately in love with Amanda."

"Poor woman."

I thought about her ability to organize Grady's defense. "Some women like a needy man. I think he is, emotionally, very needy."

"Aren't we all?" Mark said.

I looked at him. "Not to the extent of murdering someone to make ourselves feel better. Are you all right now?"

He nodded. "Better. It shook my soul to see how close you came to dying out there. I just fell apart."

"After you hustled Grady out of there."

"True. After that. Still, the reaction was a surprise." Hadn't he realized how much he cared for me? Apparently not. I, also, hadn't known how much he meant to me.

"As Geraldine said to Evelyn, 'You love me.'"

He stared at me for a long moment. "I do at that."

Then he kissed me. Well! That was lovely. A pleasure in the middle of a mess.

"Better get those witnesses," I said, stepping back.

"Yes, Fawthrop awaits." We walked out into the hall. Guido smiled at us.

"Oh, thanks for lunch," Mark said. "That was you, wasn't it? You bought us all lunch?"

"I did." I waited for him to say something critical about my deep pockets.

"Thanks. We all needed it."

I smiled. Perhaps, he was coming to terms with my money. It was like a nettle in our relationship, irritating without being deeply hurtful. It was frustrating as well, since there was nothing I could do about it. He had times when it didn't bother him and times when it did. I'd love it if he had a sudden revelation that my income didn't matter, but it was likely going to be a slow evolution.

Mark took Evelyn into the interview room and, gradually, over the next two hours as slow appears just above everyone was interviewed by Fawthrop.

Grady was taken away in the police car without having a chance to talk to Amanda. She did ask Mark to tell him that she'd called his solicitor.

Back at the guest hotel, Mit had our luggage ready.

"You must have had a wonderful time at the castle," he said. "You were gone quite a while."

"It was truly amazing," Evelyn said, without elaborating.

We all helped Amanda load her luggage and Grady's into her car. The ladies gave advice.

"Get your own lawyer." That was from Evelyn.

"Join a meditation class." That from Norma.

"Keep track of all conversations with all lawyers," Geraldine said.

"Will there be someone with you when you pick up your children," Sheilagh asked.

"My sister will bring them to my house. I'll get the children settled and my sister and I will talk," Amanda reassured her.

"Good. Keep in touch now."

"I will," she said. I doubted that. She'd probably like to put this trip behind her.

We said our goodbyes to Sheilagh and Allan.

"You buy that farm, now," Evelyn said. "I want a Facebook picture of it to post on my site."

"We just might," Sheilagh said, with a faint worry line on her forehead.

I expected they would. It had been a holiday with revelations for them. I don't believe Sheilagh had fully understood how strong Allan's desire for a farm was until she saw him enthusiastically engaged on this trip. I hoped she could work out a way to continue with her own interests while helping Allan farm.

I drove Sheilagh Allan and the Tucson ladies across the river to the train station. The Bristol couple hurried to catch their train. The Tucson ladies had more time. They stood beside the van with their luggage at their side.

"Thanks so much," Evelyn said. "It was an eventful holiday. Couldn't have been more full of mystery."

"It worries me some," I said, "that others may shy away from my British Book Tours when they hear one of my guests died."

"You never know," Geraldine said. "Any publicity is better than none. People might flock to your tours."

I was startled. "I'm not sure I could cope with that. I'm more worried that good people like you won't come."

They looked at each other. "They won't hear it from us," Evelyn said. "We'll put great reviews on your website."

That was kind. I felt my eyes smart with tears. "Thank you."

"It was wonderful. You keep doing it," Geraldine said.

"Thanks for your intrepid support," I said. "You three are like a solid, bracing wall. It's been such a pleasure getting to know you. I admire you all very much."

"You go after that handsome cop," Evelyn said and pressed a hundred pounds into my hand.

"But keep your own assets," Geraldine said. "Thanks for everything. You did your best for us, and I had a wonderful time. I can't wait to write our own mystery." She shook my hand, and I was a hundred pounds richer.

Norma followed suit. "Now you get your psyche back in balance," she said. "You've had far too much responsibility in the last few days."

"I hope you all come back," I said as they turned toward the station. "Have fun in Skipton."

They waved.

I would miss them. They were intelligent, unique and energetic. I was grateful for the fact that they were alive. The trip, although very eventful and at times dangerous for us all, had been a success for the three ladies and Sheliagh and Allan. I hoped they would stay in touch with me.

CHAPTER TWENTY-ONE

I arranged with Mit to park my van in the hotel car park for an hour. I walked from the guest hotel to the Minster and sat on a bench under the trees. The magnificence of the cathedral rose to the sky. It stood for order, justice and, in a way, godliness, a vision of a better world where people were honest and considered how they affected others. The Minster hadn't been aloof from strife. It had endured secular and religious wars, but it *had* endured. Because those spires had stood for centuries, there was a lasting quality to those ideals. When I lived in Canada, I was impressed with the motto for their country: peace, order and good government. They didn't talk about individual rights but of collective order. Was that what our laws were about here? Was that a naïve point of view?

I wandered into the Minster. The choir was practicing for evensong, and I sat near the back wall and listened. I sing in a choir in Aston-on-Tinch. I'd sung in choirs all my life wherever I lived. They gave me solace and peace. This choir was performing something from Handel, very measured and melodious. I had nothing to do right now except listen. The Tucson ladies were away to Skipton. The Whites were on the train to Bristol. Amanda was driving herself home to Kent and into the care of her sister. Mark was, no doubt, up to his ears in paper work at the York police station. Kala was traveling home from her uncle's to a school that was now safe. My dog was secure at Deirdre's and didn't need me at the moment. I had time to just sit. After a while, I stopped thinking and let the music take over my mind. I remained in place after the music died away. I could hear the murmured voice of the conductor advising the choir, melodious even in his criticism, but I couldn't hear the words. It was incredibly tranquil.

It took me almost four hours to drive to Guildford. I deposited my rental car at the company garage and picked up my own van. The silver finish shone with that particular glint of newness that lost luster in a year or so, but was so gratifying to the owner while it endured. When I climbed into the driver's seat, the smell of new leather encompassed me. It was normal, expected and comforting.

I drove to Deirdre's house.

As soon as I crossed the doorway, Gulliver was beside himself with excitement, dancing on his back feet, jumping as high as he could—a whirling, black, white and brown blur with flopping ears. I squatted down and enjoyed his love and attention and gazed into his dark brown eyes. He licked my face and sniffed my hands. I petted him, luxuriating in his warmth and direct love.

"Gulliver," I said, "you are uncomplicated."

He smiled, truly, he smiled and licked my face.

"Hello, intrepid sister. What have you dropped into now?" Deirdre said, her eyes narrowed, her black curls framing a frowning face.

"Not to worry," I said, standing and facing her. "All is copasetic."

The lines of her face smoothed with relief. "I want to hear all about it, but right now, I have to take Josh to football practice."

"Hi, Auntie, Come for the mutt?" Josh popped up behind his mother.

"I have," I said, noting Josh's shorts, club jersey and the black and white ball he carried. "I'll get out of the way. Where's Kala?"

"Cricket practice. Michael took her." Deirdre examined me for a moment and smiled, relief in her eyes. Then she picked up her car keys from the small table near the door.

Kala's life had returned to normal.

"It's a busy time. Thanks for caring for Gulliver." I took Gulliver's leash and the large bag with his food and toys in it.

"He's a dear," Deirdre said. "Any time. Here, I'll hold your ball, Josh. You load Gulliver's crate into Auntie's van."

"Right," he said.

I hugged Josh. "Have fun at football."

He grinned and lifted the crate with ease.

I settled Gulliver inside it with some treats and waved goodbye to Josh and Deidre. Before I pulled out to head home, I texted Mark.

"I am just leaving Guildford. Where are you?" I didn't expect a quick answer. I never knew if he was driving, in an interview, or in a meeting, but he did answer.

"In Alton. Just arrived. Have an hour's paperwork to do. Can you stop here and we can have supper?"

"Where?"

"How about The George?"

"Butts Road?"

"That's the one."

"About nine?"

"Good. See you then."

The roads were clear, so it was only about forty-five minutes before I arrived in Alton. I'd talked to Gulliver the whole way. It was a delight to be reunited with him. I hadn't forgotten how necessary he was to me.

We were about a half-hour early, so I stopped near the Alton Public Gardens, clipped the lead on Gulliver's collar and trotted him onto the grass. With dog treats in one pocket and doggie bags in the other, I ambled along the paths of the park. The daffodils were in full color and the tulips just beginning to bloom. We kept to the paths until we reached the off-leash fenced section where I let Gulliver loose to romp with other dogs. He tore around the enclosure, getting rid of energy, stopped to sniff a black Lab, then hurried back to me. Just before nine, I put him back in the van and drove to The George.

"You can come in with me, Gulliver," I said. "It's dog friendly."

Mark was waiting for me just outside the door. He enfolded me in his arms and gave me a long and passionate kiss. I felt as if we were tapping into that sea of emotion that we'd discovered in our relief of being alive. We'd cared for each other before that but, on that path at Castle Howard, we'd stumbled into a deeper water.

"My goodness," I said a little short of breath.

"*Excuse* me." A sharp female voice demanded access to the pub.

"Sorry," Mark said and moved aside.

I grinned. "Let's be respectable, shall we?"

"Claire, *annwyl*, I'm that relieved you're alive," he said.

I was learning some Welsh words. That one meant darling.

"I am relieved, as well." I had a sharp memory of Grady and his gun, then the normalcy of the pub chased away the image.

We found a table in a corner where Gulliver could tuck in under our feet and be out of the way of the waiters and patrons. Mark fetched each of us a beer and ordered hamburgers from the bar. The noise level was fairly high. A band was setting up in the far corner.

"Are you finished the paperwork?" I asked him.

"Paper work is never finished," Mark said as if pronouncing an axiom. "My superintendent is not happy with me."

"Because you spent time on someone else's case?"

"It was my own time, if you remember. I booked off a holiday. *She* asked me to report to Whelan. She hasn't anything official to complain about, but it doesn't stop her."

I nodded. "Some holiday."

"Yeah." He stared at me for a moment. "You know I had to work. I owed it to Hartley."

I understood that. I hadn't meant to criticize. "Give your conscience a rest, Mark. You were right to pursue those yahoos.

You weren't friends with Hartley, but he worked on the same side of the law. It's you guys against the uglies. You had to work to solve that case. My being in danger was not your plan. It was Grady's. So don't take it on as being your fault."

"Hmmph." He heard me, but I'm not sure he could dismiss his regrets easily.

I gestured to the pub scene. "This is a world of normal, orderly, law-abiding people, for the most part. There seems to be a tide of criminals that live in a parallel world to this one."

"There's another world, for certain," he agreed. "A society that lives under its own laws that include coercion, threats, violence, mutilation, rape, poison, thievery, and any manner of mayhem."

"It's getting worse?" I asked.

"It is. The problem is that the world of crime also contains loyalty, brotherhood, companionship, and sometimes love. It's attractive to many."

The waiter delivered a bowl of water for Gulliver then came back with our hamburgers, complete with chips and sides of coleslaw. We sniffed and dug in with appreciation.

"That's depressing," I said when I had enough food to slow down.

Mark ate his hamburger with great concentration and finally said, "It can be, but sometimes we win. Corbett will not be distributing drugs any time soon. He's a chummy now, arrested and marked. He'll have lost his position as chief boss. Even if he gets out of this, no one in his world will trust him again. He failed. He was caught. They'll look for another leader. Effective leaders aren't easy to find because you need to be brilliant, organized, have good contacts, impeccable background—no criminal record—and have superb management skills. They can't exactly advertise. Gangs have to talk to each other to find that person. We hope they'll choose someone who doesn't have the qualities they need, and so will be inept."

It sounded as if there were hordes of criminals living among us—and more coming. I had a vision of a great flotilla of boats approaching the shores of Britain, something like the Spanish Armada, loaded with drugs, ready to poison the populace. I thought about Mark trying to stem that tide.

"What can stop it?"

"Decriminalizing drugs. That will take the guts out of the gangs. It won't stop crime, but it will help."

We'd talked about this before. I couldn't see that happening soon. There was no political will to change the laws. In fact, many politicians thought more punishment would be effective—in spite of the studies to the contrary.

"What will happen to Grady?"

"He'll probably be out on bail in a week or so. He has Crandor for his defense. Every loophole known to humanity will be explored. Corbett will be under surveillance for some time, though."

"By you?"

"By the National Crime Agency who monitor all drug law infractions. Even if Corbett manages to get off, no one in the drug trade will go near him."

I broke off a little hamburger and slipped it to Gulliver, who took it, licked my hand, sniffed to be sure he hadn't missed any, then settled back down at my feet.

"Will Grady be vindictive toward you?"

"Who knows?"

"What about me? And the Tucson ladies. Will he go after us?"

Mark finished his hamburger and went back to the bar for another glass of beer for each of us.

"I'm thinking about it," he said when I raised my eyebrows, waiting for an answer.

I repeated my question. "The American ladies are in Skipton for another week. Could he get at them?"

"No. He will be in jail at least that long. He isn't in a position to give orders now. He's lost his role as the boss man. Someone else will step in temporarily. The ladies aren't an obstacle to the gang.

Because they aren't in the way and because no one will take orders from Corbett, the ladies should be fine. So should you."

"That's a relief." I didn't like the idea of Grady and another gun hunting me. "Also, if his motivation for killing us was to keep us from telling Amanda, he's lost that motive. She knows. Poor Amanda."

"She organized a solicitor for him and is coming to the station tomorrow with clothes and personal effects for him. She seems to be in a caretaking mode."

"Hmm." I considered Amanda. "I think she will look after him. The Tucson ladies gave her good advice, but I doubt she'll take it. If she didn't stick with Grady, she'd probably pick someone just as flawed. She has a caretaking gene, I think. He might be lucky and settle down respectably with Amanda."

"It's possible." There was doubt in his voice.

I smiled. "How's your superintendent?"

"Crabby."

"Are you back to work tomorrow?"

"Yes. There were a rash of racists crimes in Basingstoke while I was gone. Lots to investigate. I'm pretty sure I know who's behind it. I just have to get the evidence."

There was always something that criminals stirred up. "Do you have to go back to the station tonight?"

"For an hour or so. I'll be home later." By home did he mean my house? That was a change. I could live with that.

"Good."

He smiled at me. "We should have a real holiday someday. One where no one knows us and where the criminals and the law enforcers do their jobs without us."

I felt happy: My love was with me; normal people surrounded us; I'd had a good meal; and my dog was at my feet.

"Where the tour guide creates the illusion of safety and fun with no cares or concerns," I suggested.

"That's right."

"I didn't do such a good job on that for my guests this time."

"No," he agreed. "Not exactly relaxing for them. Where should we go?"

I thought about it. There were many choices. The Outer Hebrides, the Canary Islands, Portugal, Spain, Tuscany. "There is a little island off Greece, Tilos. I have a friend who lives there."

"Sounds perfect." Mark leaned back and sighed. "Blue skies, warm breezes, warm ocean, great food. Let's do it."

We ordered the sticky toffee pudding and made the meal last another half-hour.

I arrived home to a clean house and a note from Rose to tell me she had taken the opportunity while I was away to thoroughly clean out the closets and drawers. The house smelled of the vinegar and the polish she used, a hint of tangy lemon. Every wooden surface glowed and every shiny surface gleamed. It would only take a few hours for Gulliver and me to make it more homely.

I let Gulliver out into the back garden and saw that Peter Brown, my gardener, had planted Swiss chard and lettuce in my raised vegetable beds. My house was in order.

CHAPTER TWENTY-TWO

I had arrived home in time to partake in the annual Tinch River clean-up. For a wonder, Mark had a day off and was coming to help. We were going to pull debris from the shores of the river and separate it for recycling and composting. About fifteen villagers had assembled at Robert's Riverside Veterinary Clinic early on Saturday morning to disperse up and down stream. Our goal was to clean the winter rubbish from the river. The sun emitted some warmth, but everyone expected to get wet and dressed in Wellingtons and waterproof anoraks. I brought rubber gloves, as I didn't know what kind of muck I might encounter. Robert Andrews and his daughter, Sarah, were directing the operation. He'd sent out a notice requesting that we leave our dogs at home. "Too distracting," his note said. "And we'd spend a lot of time dealing with dogs." I supposed people would also divert Robert from organizing the clean-up with veterinary questions about their dogs and requests for exams and diagnoses. Gulliver remained at home with a new chew toy.

Sarah was passing out plastic garbage bags. "Put compost in the green bag, recyclables like bottles and cartons in the blue, and useless junk in the yellow. If you can't lift the full bags, just leave them at the edge of the river. Someone will haul them here to this car park, and lorries will take them away."

"Is it term break, Sarah?" I asked her, as I accepted my bags. Sarah was a serious science student.

"Yes, I have to go back in two weeks for my third term."

"Where's Jay?" Jay Ward was her current boyfriend and fellow student.

"He's coming by later."

"How are you doing at uni?"

"Brilliantly."

I laughed.

Sarah had allowed her father to think she was going to university to learn to be a writer. He'd worried that she wouldn't be able to support herself, and he hadn't seen any signs up to that point that she liked writing. It turned out that she had a strong ambition to be a medical doctor and was quite capable of getting the grades she required to be successful. I expect Robert understood that now.

Sarah was a little shorter than me, trim, athletic and strong. I'd seen her pick up a heavy dog without effort. She had brown eyes, freckles and short, curly hair that was almost frizzy in the moist air. She was appealing, exuding confidence and competence. She'd be a great help on this clean up. Everyone was ready to work. I had only a small part in Robert and Sarah's great plan, but I was looking forward to being out in the fresh air and getting some exercise.

It was good to put Grady Corbett and his drug business behind me and join in the activities of the village. Not that there weren't loves and hates, passions and aversions in the village. I just didn't know about many of them and had no responsibilities for them except the need to maintain a civil discourse. It was relaxing.

"Good morning, Robert," I walked over to talk to him for a moment while everyone picked up their bags from Sarah. "Where is your love?"

Robert and I had dated causally when I first arrived in the village. We both knew we were destined to be friends. I liked his girlfriend. She was good for him.

Robert beamed at me. "Rosemary had to work today. She's setting up a new home nursing program and wanted to meet with all the workers. She had to book the meeting for today."

"I'm sorry to miss her. I don't see much of her."

"We'll have to remedy that. Where's Mark?"

"He wanted to check into the station, but he's coming to help."

"Good to hear." He directed me to the modified tools that were leaning against his clinic wall.

"Help yourself to a rake and take one for Mark as well," he said.

I took the two nearest to me. They had two prongs on the end, obviously meant to catch the debris and pull it ashore. Once I had the rakes, I stood by, ready to be allotted a portion of the riverbank. Robert consulted a sheet of paper and assigned Mark and me upstream from his clinic.

I waited for Mark and watched more people arrive and chat while they picked up their bags and were allotted clean-up territory. It was a community project that Ashton-on-Tinch supported every year in the spring. Mrs. Taylor, Helen, arrived with an urn which she placed on a trestle table outside the door of the veterinary clinic. She unrolled a long flex and plugged it into the outdoor plug point. I saw her go into the clinic with a jug in hand and return with it, then pour water into the urn. She did that three times until she was satisfied that she had the urn full. It would be hot water for tea. She wouldn't be supplying coffee. I was getting used to the social mores of Ashton, and I was drinking more tea. She flicked on a switch then turned to her bags of supplies.

She put out paper cups, just a few. She expected everyone to bring their own insulated thermos or travel mug. After all, the purpose of this event was to eliminate waste, and Styrofoam or even paper cups contributed to waste.

Mary Greenwood arrived with two large bags filled to the brim. She walked over to a stone wall, set the bags down, picked up a rock and banged on the top of the wall. She was informing any resident snakes they must vacate. She waited a moment then spread an oilcloth on top of the wall and proceeded to unload sandwiches and cakes onto the cloth. All volunteers would be fed with the usual overabundance from the cooks and bakers of the village.

Rose waved to me from the other side of the car park. I wasn't surprised to see her here. She was an intrepid worker. I don't suppose my house had been so clean in years. She had her husband Frank with her. I rarely saw him, but he appeared friendly and as quiet as Rose was garrulous. Their two children, ages seven and five, would, no doubt, enjoy playing in the mud. The family headed downstream with their bags.

I roused from my almost meditative state as an onlooker when Mark drove in and parked. He pulled his Wellingtons from the boot of his car and sat on a nearby rock to change. He tossed his trainers into the boot and locked the car. Then he ambled over to me, leaned in to give me a quick kiss while accepting the colored bags I handed him.

"Where are we working?"

"Upstream," I said.

We were the only two on this stretch. We decided to start at the top end of our section, marked by surveyor's bright pink tape. I donned my blue plastic gloves (more plastic. It was going to be years before we were rid of it), tucked the blue bag in one pocket and the yellow in the other and held onto the green one. I wondered if the bags were biodegradable.

I expected most of what we hauled from the river would be compost. I started on a particularly ugly bit of weeds floating near the shore. I saw Mark do the same with an even bigger tangle. When I pulled mine to shore, I realized it wasn't only weeds. In the middle was a small milk carton and a plastic fork. I separated the rubbish into the proper bags and left the bags on the riverbank. This was going to be time consuming.

After an hour, I was tired but had filled my compost bag. There was still room in my recycle and tip bag.

Mark called over to me. "Give me your compost, and I'll take it to the car park. If you give me your thermos as well, I'll get us some tea."

I smiled at him. That meant I could sit and relax for a few moments.

He wasn't long. We sat on a small rise of ground sipping our tea and watching the river slip by.

"Everything okay at the station?" I asked.

"Everything is as usual," Mark said. I noticed the distinction. There must be problems. I suppose it is the nature of police work to face problems every day.

Mark gazed over the river and spoke slowly. "I don't know if I'm going to keep on with that job."

I wanted to ask if he meant the Major Crimes Investigation Team or policing in general, but decided to hold my tongue. The best thing to do with a statement like that was to listen.

"I thought by this time of my life I would have made a difference, solved many cases, brought justice to the world." His voice was sarcastic as if those goals were naive.

"And you don't feel you have?"

"No, not really. I'm a cog in the police machinery. If I wasn't there, other people would just take my place."

"Mark, you just broke up a major drug trafficking gang. *You* did that."

"Me and many others. Even you had a part of that."

We sat in silence for a few moments. I supposed he was at the age when many people re-evaluate their ambitions. Mid-life crisis? Mid-life stress? I had very little knowledge of this. He was doing a worthwhile job, but he didn't feel worthwhile. I'd never had the ambition to make a huge difference in the world; I'd just wanted to be independent and have an interesting life. I didn't feel like a failure, because I hadn't had aspirations. It was as if he'd picked up my thoughts.

"I don't know if my expectations were too high, or I chose the wrong way of trying to accomplish them."

"What's the worst part of the job?" I could help him talk about it. I didn't have any idea of how to advise him. I put my free hand on his thigh, mostly for comfort and to show him that I was listening. He put his much bigger hand over mine.

"The politics. The internal politics. Who pays for what? Who gets the promotion and the rise in pay? Who can't be offended? Who has to be placated? It makes you wonder if it's all just a pissing game, and there isn't any real concern about justice. I feel like a bit of a fool for even expecting it."

No wonder he was questioning his choice of career. It would be depressing to work where no one cared. Did no one care? Was that true?

"Mark, of all the people you work with, how many of them are truly committed to helping the public?"

He stared at me, then spoke slowly. "Most of them."

I smiled. He shrugged, recognizing that he was painting the whole police force with cynicism when he'd just admitted that many were dedicated.

He squeezed my hand, released it, then tossed back the rest of his tea. "Anyway, I don't know what else I'd do."

We seemed to be in accord, listening to each other. Perhaps this was the best time to bring up his attitude to my wealth.

"Mark," I said a little hesitantly. "How are you feeling about my money now?"

He glanced over at me, picked up a stone and lopped it into the river. "Not the way I used to."

"No?" I waited for more explanation.

"It seems I'm getting dragged into the twenty-first century. I looked around and saw quite a few of my colleagues married to lawyers and dentists. They look pretty independent and even happy. Seemed a little foolish to hang onto the old attitudes of old-country Wales when I was living in a different era."

I waited. It was probably different in Wales these days as well.

"So, I guess I could say, I'm getting used to it and it isn't as unpalatable as I thought it would be."

I smiled. That was a big improvement.

We watched the river and were surprised to see a small kayak round the bed. A young man was paddling, two Labradors sat—one on each end.

"That looks precarious," Mark said. "I hope he can swim."

"Probably. He's quite competent. That's Jay Ward. The chocolate Lab is Muggs and the black Lab is Jetty. They're Robert Andrew's dogs."

"And Jay Ward has the dogs because…?"

"Because he's dating Sarah, and Sarah occasionally has her father's dogs."

"Right. In the village, everyone knows everything."

I laughed. I was becoming a villager. We waved at Jay.

"Looks a little dicey, Jay," I called.

"We're sweet," he said abruptly.

Mark gazed after Jay and the dogs as they swung around the bend below us. "He looks like a bad lot. Does Sarah know what she's doing?"

"She does," I affirmed. "He's an accomplished academic at the same university as Sarah and, apparently, has serious ambitions."

Mark shook his head. "Hard to get past the dreadlocks, tattoos and skinny physique."

"I expect he wants people to leave him alone."

A black bird trilled from a nearby willow, its liquid melody floating over the water. Next to the marsh warbler which I love for its aggressive and busy song, the black bird is my favorite musician of the woods.

We returned to our painstaking raking of the debris on the river. In amongst the floating weeds, I found a pen, a waterlogged school lunch bag, four empty Guinness cans, some soda cans, more plastic forks and Styrofoam chip plates. I dutifully separated them and filled my bags. We were almost at the end of our section drawing closer to the pink surveyor's flag that indicated the finish line when I spotted a bundle of clothes. It was caught on a low branch near the shore and hidden by reeds. I hooked into the cloth and slowly pulled it toward me.

"Mark," I called. "This is heavy. Would you give me a hand?" I didn't know what was inside the bundle. It was only clothes. Surely, it was only clothes. I had a vision of a body, a victim of violence or someone who had jumped into the river to escape the pain of life.

Mark walked over and hooked into the bundle with his rake and pulled. It was much easier to move that water-soaked collection of clothes when he helped. As it came nearer to us, I realized it *was* a bundle of clothes. I was almost light-headed with relief. I had to stop seeing violence everywhere.

"I think I'm going to be sick. "

"It's just clothes. Take a deep breath," Mark said.

I did that.

"Can you help me get it in?" He started walking into the water.

I could do that. I pulled on my rake and Mark waded further into the river and guided the bundle to the shore.

"Why would someone throw out old clothes?" I studied them. In spite of the decoration of weeds, I could see that the jacket had once been a good-quality Harris tweed.

"Maybe they were worn when someone committed a crime? I'll take them to the local nick." Mark opened another plastic bag and shoved the sodden mass into it. I wondered which officer at the station would have the pleasure of dealing with that.

"Maybe someone's wife was so fed up with her husband's taste in clothes she flung them out the car window when she was driving over the bridge?"

Mark grinned. "I like your explanation better."

We were getting our bags together to transport to the loading area when we heard shouts and a scream. Mark dropped his bags and ran. I followed.

We came upon a scene that we could have predicted. Jay stood at the water's edge, totally soaked, holding onto the painter from the kayak. Muggs was jumping on Sarah who was also completely wet. Jetty cavorted around the couple. Onlookers laughed and jeered. Jay and Sarah ignored everyone but each other.

"I told you to leave the dogs at home!" Sarah yelled.

"I didn't hear you."

"You don't listen." Sarah was stamping her foot in frustration.

"We were doing fine until you called. When the dogs heard you, they jumped toward you and upturned the kayak. Be reasonable. What did you expect the dogs to do when you called? It's your fault."

"I *told* you to leave the dogs at home."

"They're a couple all right," Mark murmured.

I glanced at him sharply. He didn't talk much about his former marriage, but I picked up hints of what it must have been like. Argumentative, I assumed.

Mrs. Taylor offered advice at the top of her voice. "That Jay shouldn't even be here. A packet of trouble that family."

Mary Greenwood spoke loudly, "Now, Helen. Leave the young people alone. You've been known to raise your voice to that husband of yours."

"That's different," Helen Taylor snapped.

"So you say," Mary said with censure in every syllable.

Robert snagged Jetty's collar as he danced past and held him relatively immobile. Muggs was gloriously free to jump back in the river then back onto the shore, shaking more water on the combatants at the river's edge.

Others were adding their opinions.

"Get some towels and get the young people dry."

"There are some in the clinic."

"I'll get them."

"Someone, catch that dog."

Robert called to Muggs who skidded to a stop in front of him, tongue lolling, eyes sparkling, evidence that he was having a sublime time.

Sarah was angry and almost crying with frustration.

Into this mess stepped my hero. "What's to do?" he said.

I sat down on a nearby log with a thump. 'What's to do?' He sounded like a police officer from Gilbert and Sullivan. I wondered how many times in his life he'd said that. He had been a beat bobby when he first started with the constabulary, walking a district and dealing with domestic complaints and petty thieves. He would have dealt with heated exchanges many times. I watched.

First, he managed to ease Sarah away from Jay until she was standing a good twenty feet distant. He bent his head and listened. He caught Robert's eye and indicated with a nod that he should come and deal with his daughter. Robert did that. Mary Greenwood handed Robert a towel she'd fetched from the clinic. He wrapped it around Sarah and gave her a hug, then helped her wipe the water from her clothes. He wrapped another towel around her and gave her Jetty to look after. That was clever. It would keep her occupied and away from Jay.

Mark went over to Jay. Someone had given him a red towel which he'd slung over his shoulders. He looked like an exotic extra from a Monty Python show. just needing a couple of peacock feathers in his hair to complete the picture. I kept my face straight. No one likes to be reminded they look ridiculous.

"Can I give you a hand with that kayak, mate?" Mark offered.

"Uh. Yeah. Thanks. What about Muggs here?"

"Do you have a leash?"

Jay shook his head.

I slipped over to my car, pulled out my spare leash and handed it to Mark. He snapped it on Muggs and handed it back to me with the dog attached. He waited until Jay dried himself as best he could. Then he helped Jay load the kayak onto Sarah's car.

Jay opened the passenger side door and started to get in.

"Not without a towel on the seat. What are you thinking?" Sarah had held onto her irritable mood.

Jay snorted, pulled the wet towel from his shoulders and flung it over the seat.

The crowd was silent as they watched the car pull away.

"Ah, young love," someone said, and we laughed.

It wasn't funny being young and in love, I realized that. They'd made themselves ridiculous and that must have smarted. Even so, it was a relief to be rid of the quarreling couple.

Mark returned to our clean-up site to collect the full bags and bring them back for collection.

I took my cup over to the trestle table for more hot tea. Muggs trotted happily at my side.

"Nice to have our own police here," Mrs. Taylor said, complacently. "I'm glad your man was here. It would have been a right muck up if he hadn't separated those two."

"They wouldn't have come to blows," I protested. It wasn't a daring rescue. Mark had dealt with it easily.

"You never know with one of the Wards. No good comes from them. And that Sarah has a temper on her."

I turned away and joined Mark. He'd been talking to Robert Andrews and Thomas Greenwood. I handed Mugg's leash to Robert.

"Thanks for dealing with those two," Robert said to Mark. "And the dogs." I could see Jetty in Robert's vehicle.

Mark nodded his acknowledgement.

"Ta for the leash," Robert said to me. "I'll get it back to you."

"Any time," I said. "It's a spare."

I walked with Mark to his car. "Do you have to go to the station?"

"I have a few things to tidy up but I'll be home soon."

"Mark."

He stared at me. "What?"

"When you had the quarrelling couple, the vociferous onlookers and the dogs in front of you, you slipped into the role of peacekeeper easily. I don't think it was even hard for you."

"No. A small problem, really."

"You are incredibly capable of keeping the peace on many levels. The homicide team gives you scope to help people at a much higher level." It worried me that he was thinking of leaving the police force. He was good at his job. I had a vision of him wandering around the world without a purpose. He would not be happy. "Think about it. You can investigate more easily from inside the constabulary than from outside." So much for not giving advice.

He smiled, those warm brown eyes pulling me into him. He caressed my cheek. "Perhaps," he said. "Thanks." He kissed me and left.

I spent a few moments with Robert and Thomas then drove myself home.

I found some special Seattle coffee and made myself a cup. The smell of coffee, the comfort of my home and the warmth of Gulliver who had jumped onto my lap made me feel as if here was a place where I was safe and protected. I loved my village, even when people screamed at each other. I loved having Mark around, keeping the peace. There were Grady Corbetts out there, intent on evil and murder. I recognized that, but my shoulders relaxed. I settled back in my chair with the coffee cup handy. The thick walls of my house seemed to keep the waves of crime and disturbing vibes away from me, as if I was isolated and protected by wood and plaster, brick and flint. I know there are such things as home invasions, fire bombers, burglars and agitated maniacs who could make short work of my physical defenses. But I *felt* safe and that mattered. Perhaps peace and order were obtainable, even if just in this one small corner of the world. It might be a delusion but it was a comforting one, and I was going to enjoy it.

ABOUT THE AUTHOR

© Duke Morse

Emma Dakin lives in Gibsons on the Sunshine Coast of British Columbia where she enjoys the seals, whales, mergansers, eagles and wildlife of the ocean and where she is an enthusiastic, if somewhat amateur, violinist. She has over twenty-five trade published books of mystery and adventure for teens and middle-grade children and non-fiction for teens and adults. Her love of the British countryside and villages and her addiction to cozy mysteries now keep her immersed writing about characters who live and work in those villages. She introduces readers to the problems that disturb that idyllic setting.

CPSIA information can be obtained
at www.ICGtesting.com
Printed in the USA
LVHW032219210921
698373LV00001B/142

9 781603 813877